Lonely Satellite

A NOVEL

Morgan Richter

Copyright © 2013 by Morgan Richter

Published in the United States by Luft Books, New York
www.luftbooks.com

Cover design by Morgan Dodge

ISBN 978-0-9859768-5-9

To Ingrid.
Still the greatest sister in the world.

"See, here's my idea." Laurie looked around and lowered his voice. "I haven't told anyone about this, almost anyone at all, but this is the concept: Let's say there was a nuclear attack back in 1984. Earth laid to waste, cities destroyed, human existence almost eradicated. Right?"

"Sure."

"Okay. So time has passed, almost thirty years, and people have started to rebuild. But things are still crappy, obviously, it's still a struggle to survive. So America has become this totally chaotic post-apocalyptic society." Laurie smiled in triumph. "And I want to design the clothes for that society. But, you know, make them pretty."

Nicola burst out laughing. Laurie looked injured, so she hastened to reassure him. "I'm not making fun of your idea, really. I actually think it's sort of brilliant."

"Really?" Laurie brightened, a plucked and wilting dandelion springing to life in a glass of water.

"Really. God knows I have no idea what people in your post-nuclear society would be wearing, but I'm pretty sure you do. That's great."

—excerpt from BIAS CUT (2012)

CHAPTER ONE

Laurie was almost dead by the time he spotted the field of mushrooms. They shimmered in the distance, gigantic white domes that rose up from the blanket of pale sand to form an enchanted grove in the middle of the poisonous desert. They looked unreal, something from a storybook his mother might have read to him when he was a child.

Sunlight reflected off the sand and threatened to bake him or blind him. The mushrooms were the only shelter from the punishing heat.

He limped in their direction. It was hard to walk now. His ankle looked purple, the swollen flesh bulging out around the strap of his canvas sandal. No chance to rest; the heat from the sand penetrated through the rope soles, and if he lingered in one spot for too long, the bottoms of his feet scorched. He was exhausted and something far beyond thirsty, his cells screaming out for moisture. The magical mushroom grove would have water. They couldn't grow in a desert without some kind of irrigation system, surely.

It'd have to have water, or he'd be dead.

He yanked the hood of his tunic down to his nose and trudged on. Just a little further…

Something blocked his path, something hard to see in the brightness. He groped around in front of his face. His fingers, sausage-swollen and clumsy from the heat, touched a grid. A chain-link fence surrounded the mushrooms. Of course they'd be protected. No one would leave this bounty unguarded, not here.

No use searching for the gate. It'd be locked, and he didn't have the energy to waste on futile efforts. He gripped the fence with both hands and took a deep breath. Forcing down the feeling of nausea that surged up from his stomach at the wave of pain, he wedged his sandal toe between the links to gain a foothold and pulled himself up, moving one hand and then the other. He could do this. He was small and nimble, and under better circumstances, he could shimmy up the fence in a jiffy.

He glanced up and spotted the razor wire for the first time, wrapped in a loose tangled coil around the top of the fence. Silver barbs glinted in the sun, shiny and menacing.

Upon reaching the top, inches from the coil, he clutched the fence with one hand and eased his tunic over his head. This required too much careful maneuvering, and his arm muscles protested at the strain of holding himself in one place. It took the rest of his strength to spread the cloth over the coil.

He swung one leg over. The razors cut through the burlap and dug into his thigh. No big deal. Cuts were okay, just as long as he didn't get stuck here. After some precarious shifting, both of his legs were over. Barbs sliced through his undershirt and gouged his arms and chest.

Climbing down the other side would require too much strength he didn't have. Time for a leap of faith. He closed his eyes and let go.

After a mercifully brief tumble through the air, he hit the ground. His bad ankle collapsed upon impact, and he crumpled into a heap.

His palms burned against the sand. He couldn't stand up, couldn't even try, so he crawled toward the mushrooms, which now lay just a few yards in front of him.

They weren't mushrooms. They were white metal domes. It took him too long to figure out what they really were: satellite dishes, overturned and uprooted, a whole field of them on a wide patch of white cement, here in the middle of the Nevada desert.

Well, that made a hell of a lot more sense than gigantic mushrooms.

He laughed out loud, not much more than a strained rasp through his parched throat. One of the detached dishes was propped up on its side against a thick metal base. The dish cast a short, squat shadow, the only patch of shade he'd seen in hours. He crawled into the shadow and rested his back against the base.

Someone would find him. A field of satellite dishes out in the middle of nowhere, even ones in as bad shape as these, someone had to be keeping an eye on them. He'd probably already been spotted, or he'd be spotted soon, and someone would come to give him water and shelter, and things would turn out all right for him. They always did, somehow.

Laurie closed his eyes.

Male voices. Hands on him, cool fingers pressing against his neck, searching for a pulse. A rough voice, loud, almost angry: "Is she alive?"

"He. He's a boy." The tone was as coolly efficient as the fingers prodding him.

"You sure about that?"

"He's got stubble." The hand on his neck withdrew. "He's probably older than he looks."

"Watch yourself, Frisch. It could be a trap." A note of alarm crept into the first voice. "Hey, the kid's bleeding all over the place."

"He's okay. Strong pulse. Looks like he just scraped himself up on the fence." Laurie felt an arm slip around his shoulders. "Help me get him up. We'll bring him inside."

"No way. Uh-uh. My orders say no one gets in. We dump him outside the fence and make sure he stays out."

"I don't think the pastor would be thrilled if we let someone die on his doorstep. We're bringing him in."

"Your call. But you answer to the pastor if the kid turns out to be trouble. And you can carry him down by yourself."

"Won't be a problem. He can't weigh much. He's so small." The arm around Laurie's shoulders gave him a gentle shake. "Hey, Hey, you. You alive?"

Laurie's eyelids felt heavy and swollen. It was tempting to remain in this lovely, calm, half-awake state. With effort, he dragged himself back to reality.

He could see only a blur at first, two dark shapes crouched in front of him, silhouetted against the white glare of the sand. He blinked, and his vision cleared.

Two men, as he'd thought. One was wide and bulky, with a round ruddy face and a pale crew cut. He wore a black suit jacket with a row of shiny brass buttons down the front and an embroidered insignia over the breast pocket, something that looked like a stylized "Z" with an arrow through it. The insignia was bad news, but Laurie couldn't quite remember why, and all attempts to puzzle it out flew from his mind as his eyes focused on the other man's face.

This man, the one who still clutched Laurie's shoulders, the one the other guy had called Frisch, was probably in his early twenties, about Laurie's own age. He wore a white button-down shirt, which he'd somehow managed to keep clean and crisp in the desert heat. Lots of thick dark hair, high cheekbones, beautiful eyes behind black-framed eyeglasses… Laurie tried to say something, but his parched throat constricted at the attempt.

"What's that?" Frisch asked. He leaned closer. "What did you say?"

Laurie swallowed and tried to speak again. "You're ridiculously handsome, you know," he said. "Even with glasses. You could be a model."

The bulky man in the jacket snorted. Frisch stared at Laurie. "Thanks," he said at last. It came out as a mutter. Beneath the glasses, his cheeks flushed pink.

"You sure you don't just want to dump him outside the fence?" the bulky man asked.

Frisch didn't acknowledge him. To Laurie, he said, "I'm going to help you stand up, okay? We're going to go down a ladder, and it might get a little hairy, so I'll need you to hang on."

Laurie blinked. "Ladder?"

"We're subterranean," Frisch said. "Come on. Grab onto me."

With a little maneuvering, he hauled Laurie upright. He wrapped an arm around Laurie's waist and helped him walk across the cement. It hurt to stand, it hurt to move, and Laurie had no idea where they were going.

Just beyond the cluster of satellite dishes was an open circular steel hatch embedded in the cement. A slim metal ladder led down into darkness. A surge of vertigo hit him.

"I can't climb down that," he said. "My ankle—"

"Just hang onto me," Frisch said. Behind the glasses, the beautiful eyes were soft. "Don't be scared. I won't let you fall."

Laurie hesitated. "I'm getting blood all over your shirt."

"Doesn't matter. Hang on."

In the end, all Laurie could do was cling to his savior's neck as they descended into the narrow hole. After another peek into the darkness below, he couldn't bear looking anymore. He buried his face into Frisch's back and squeezed his eyes shut. Frisch's hair smelled good, like fancy soap. After his trek through the desert, Laurie figured he himself probably smelled pretty rank. Maybe they'd have a decent supply of water here, wherever they were; maybe there'd be a chance to bathe.

About ten feet below the surface, the ladder ended at a concrete platform anchored to the wall, from which a wide metal staircase led down into an open space. Frisch eased Laurie off his back and into a seated position on the platform with surprising gentleness. "He's exhausted," he said to the bulky man. "We'll rest here a moment. Go and tell the pastor I'll need a bed fixed up for him."

"I'm not your errand boy, Frisch," the man said.

Frisch didn't answer, just stared at the man over the plastic frames of his glasses. After a long moment, the man huffed out a sigh and headed down the stairs.

Laurie dared to glance over the side of the platform. The area at the base of the staircase was mostly in shadows, the darkness punctuated by glowing yellow spots. They didn't look like electric lights. Oil lanterns, maybe. He heard voices, unintelligible snippets of conversations that echoed up and bounced around the walls in a cacophony of sound. Smothered over it all was music, a low mournful drone that rose and swelled into a crashing crescendo. He winced.

"The music's awful," he said.

"Don't let the pastor hear you say that," Frisch said. "His wife's the organist."

Laurie didn't have the strength to sit upright, so he leaned against Frisch, his cheek resting against the other man's crisp white shirt. "That guy's dangerous, you know," he said. His eyes closed. He felt himself slipping off somewhere dark and comfortable. "The man in the jacket. You're warm and safe, but he's dangerous."

"Why is he dangerous?" Frisch asked. His tone sounded idle, but Laurie felt his body grow tense.

"Just that he means trouble for me. Not him in particular, but his type. I get into trouble a lot. Which is weird, because I'm really a very good person."

He thought Frisch said something, but he couldn't make it out. A wave of exhaustion overwhelmed him. He closed his eyes and let the funereal drone of the music usher him into another state of consciousness.

CHAPTER TWO

A soft bed, clean sheets, a warm wool blanket tucked around him. Laurie, who'd slept on a rag-stuffed mattress with an omnipresent mildew smell for the past decade, appreciated the contrast.

He opened his eyes. Nothing much to see. He was in a tiny room with gray concrete walls and a bare lit bulb dangling on a chain from the ceiling. The door was open, revealing a narrow corridor beyond it. Apart from the metal-framed twin bed, the only piece of furniture was a folding chair, upon which sat his impossibly handsome savior. Frisch looked up from the paperback book he was reading and frowned at Laurie. He scooted his chair closer to the bed.

"Are you alive enough to talk?" he asked.

Laurie blinked at him. "Oh, sure," he said. He swallowed. Throat still felt thick. "Is there water?"

"Hang on." Frisch picked up a gray plastic bottle from beside his chair and unscrewed the top. He looked ready to put it up to Laurie's lips and help him drink, but Laurie wasn't quite as feeble as that. He took it from him and swilled deeply. The water was glorious and cold.

"Careful. You'll get sick," Frisch said. He took the bottle out of Laurie's grasp.

Laurie looked after it with regret as Frisch replaced it on the floor. "Where am I?"

Frisch ignored the question. "What's your name?"

"I'm Laurie. With an 'au', not an 'o', in case you were wondering."

"Last name?" Keen eyes stared at him from behind those glasses. His eyes were blue, dark blue, rimmed with far too many very black lashes.

"Just Laurie," he said. "I heard that other guy say your name was Frisch?"

A curt nod. "I'm the director of operations here."

"What's your first name?" Laurie asked. "I mean, if you get to call me Laurie, I should be on a first-name basis with you, too, right?"

His lips twitched. Nice lips, a wide curving mouth. He probably had a fantastic smile. Probably didn't smile much, though. A shame. "Jonathan."

"Nice to meet you, Jonathan," Laurie said. "So what is this place, anyway?"

Jonathan didn't answer, just stared at him for a moment. He shifted in his chair, leaned closer to the bed. "What are you doing here, Laurie?"

"Recuperating, I hope," Laurie said. "I'm pretty sure my ankle's broken." Not that he was feeling much pain at the moment. He felt pretty good, actually, sort of drowsy and comfortable. A dull ache in his ankle, a little stinging from the scrapes on his chest, and some overall muscle soreness seemed to be the worst of it.

"You're fine. The facility doctor is busy in the cancer ward, so I iced your ankle and taped it up myself. The swelling's gone down already. You wouldn't have been able to walk if it was broken."

"You might be surprised. I'm tougher than I look," Laurie said.

Jonathan almost smiled. "No offense, but that's a pretty low bar," he said. "You going to answer my question about what you were doing in this area?"

"It's not by design, I assure you. I didn't have any idea this place was here. I mean, lucky for me that it was, of course."

"So you were just wandering in the desert? Taking a stroll?"

Laurie shrugged and didn't answer. Jonathan settled back in his chair. "Why did you say Abbott was dangerous?"

"Hmm?"

"The security guard. Abbott. When we were climbing down into the facility, you told me he was dangerous."

"I said that?" Laurie frowned. "I don't remember. I was pretty out of it, you know. I mean, I was hallucinating gigantic mushrooms. I barely even remember you guys rescuing me." He sighed. "Look, I'm a Benedictine monk. There's a monastery outside Mesquite. That's where I live. Lived."

Jonathan examined him, open skepticism on his face. "So you're a religious type?"

"Sure. Whatever. I mean, it's what I know. I was left at the gates as a babe in swaddling clothes. The brothers took me in and raised me."

"And shot you in the chest?" Jonathan's tone was bland.

Laurie stared at him. "Excuse me?"

"The bullet hole." Jonathan gestured at his chest, which, Laurie noted for the first time, was swaddled in yards of gauze. His torn and bloody undershirt was gone. "You've got an old scar from a bullet wound on your right side. Sort of a funny thing for a monk to have."

"Oh. That. No, when I was eleven, I fell on a steel rod when the brothers were building a new wing to the monastery. It went through my chest and collapsed my lung. Left a perfectly lovely scar."

"Uh-huh. Accident-prone, aren't you?"

"Well, my busted ankle wasn't really an accident, *per se*. I mean, I figured I'd bang myself up somehow. I'm pretty lucky that's the worst of it. I jumped out of a second-story window."

Jonathan raised his eyebrows. "And you did this because...?"

"Seemed like the most logical course of action under the circumstances. A man with an axe was chasing me."

Jonathan opened his mouth, ready to pursue the matter further, but stopped and swiveled his head at a noise behind him.

A man stood in the open doorway. Probably in his forties, clean-shaven, with thick sandy hair swept off his face in a wave. He wore a white linen suit over a collarless butter-yellow shirt, paired with an expression of benevolent concern. He looked immaculate and kindly.

"Ah. I see our lost lamb is awake," the man said. "Maybe he should have time to recover before you ask him too many questions, Jonathan."

"He's fine. Chatty, in fact." Jonathan gestured with his head toward Laurie. "This is Laurie. He says he's a monk, so you two will probably have plenty to talk about, religion-wise."

"Are you the pastor everyone keeps mentioning?" Laurie asked.

The man nodded. "I'm Pastor Kyle. Welcome to the Church of the Scorched Earth."

Laurie glanced around the tiny concrete room. "It's very nice," he said politely.

"This used to be a federal communications facility. It was pressed into use as an emergency shelter right before the bombs fell." Pastor Kyle smiled. "I stayed here as a child with my parents. We came from Las Vegas and sought refuge here, us and almost four hundred others. For weeks and weeks, until the earth stopped burning and the worst of the poison was gone from the air, we lived down here. This place saved our lives."

"And you turned it into a church?"

"Eight years ago. It had lain abandoned for over two decades by that point, and I thought it was appropriate to put it to good use." Pastor Kyle had white teeth and an evenly tanned face. The tan was surprising for someone who apparently lived underground. "We have more than three hundred parishioners staying here at the present. Our living quarters are just about filled to capacity, which is why we had to place you in this rather rustic space, at least temporarily. I assume you'll return to your monastery once you've recovered?"

Laurie shook his head. "No good. It's gone," he said.

Jonathan's brows drew together above the frames of his glasses. "What do you mean, gone?" he asked.

Laurie felt something rattling around inside of him, a flicker of buried terror which, if unearthed, would send him into screaming hysterics. He inhaled. "I mean the whole place is gone. Last I saw it was in flames, but everyone—all the brothers, I mean—was already dead by then."

Jonathan sat up straighter. "Your axe-wielding man?" he asked.

"Men. There were a bunch of them. Some had pipes, or big knives. Not cleavers, I don't think that's the word, but the long curvy kind? You chop open coconuts and stuff with them?"

"Machetes?"

He nodded at Jonathan. "Machetes, that's it. The guy who came after me definitely had an axe, though. He tried to drag me out of my room, and I thought it would be a good idea to jump out the window instead. Which, everything considered, seems to have been a pretty savvy decision."

"You're saying a group of armed men invaded the monastery and slaughtered everyone?" Jonathan asked. Behind him, Pastor Kyle looked pale beneath his tan.

"Yeah. I'm pretty sure I'm the only one who got out. I didn't—I didn't really stay behind to look, but… yeah. It's just me." Laurie's throat was tight. Shaky, very shaky. Damn it.

"Who were these men? Can you describe them?"

"Just some gang. I don't think I'd seen them before in the area. We hadn't run into any trouble with them before, as far as I know." Laurie shook his head. "Does it matter?"

Pastor Kyle patted Laurie on the shoulder. "Of course not. You should get some rest," he said. "You've been through a terrible ordeal, but you're perfectly safe with us."

Jonathan pursed his lips and looked unhappy, like he wanted to ask Laurie more questions, but stayed silent.

"Thanks, Pastor," Laurie said. He leaned back into his pillow and pulled the wool blanket up around him. He watched as Pastor Kyle and Jonathan left the room. Jonathan glanced back at Laurie once, his expression hard to read, before shutting the door behind him with a clang.

As Laurie drifted back into sleep, it occurred to him that there was precisely nowhere in the world he could be perfectly safe. Certainly not here.

CHAPTER THREE

When he awoke, it was to disorientation and a sense of pressing physical needs. He struggled to sit up, his sore limbs protesting at the movement. He shoved aside the blanket and swung his legs out of bed.

It was cool in the room, almost chilly. Funny, considering how close the heat on the surface had come to killing him during his trudge across the desert. He was still shirtless and swaddled in gauze, and his sandals were nowhere to be found. At least they'd left him his pants. Time to go in search of a bathroom.

He felt a muted stab of pain in his ankle when he stood, but it really wasn't bad. He could walk with only mild discomfort, which was a little galling. He'd almost died, damn it. He'd flung himself out a window to avoid a pack of murderers, he'd tromped on foot across the Nevada desert under that merciless sun for several hours, and it seemed anticlimactic to bounce back so quickly.

The door was unlocked, which brought a flash of relief. He didn't seem to be a prisoner here, but all the same, he didn't have a good handle on the situation.

Barefoot, he slipped out of his room and into a grim concrete corridor lit with ceiling-mounted fluorescent bulbs. A shadow at the end of the hallway made him freeze.

A man in a dark suit turned the corner and stopped at the sight of Laurie. He was tall and muscular, with a strong nose and a smooth bald head. Laurie spotted the stylized "Z" embroidered on the breast pocket of his jacket.

Z for Zephyr. He hadn't seen that logo in years, hadn't realized Zephyr was still in business. Could be bad news for him.

The man sauntered toward him. He seemed bemused. "Just where do you think you're going?"

Aware his heartbeat had quickened, Laurie tried to look as mild and agreeable as possible. "In search of a bathroom, mostly," he said. "There's got to be one around here somewhere, right?"

"Back to your quarters, kid. You can't be wandering around."

"My quarters seem to be a closet, and there's definitely no toilet anywhere in it, so unless you can point me in the direction of the facilities, I'm going to have to wander around." Laurie gave the man a nod—friendly, he thought—and tried to move past him.

"No dice. You don't go anywhere unless I say you can." The man grabbed Laurie by his wrist and yanked him to a halt. Laurie stumbled back and yelped in pain.

"Watch it!" he said. "The bandage on my ankle isn't just for decoration, you know."

The man looked down at him and smiled, his lips pulling into a thin line. He was a foot taller than Laurie, easily; Laurie had to tilt his head to meet his stare.

In one swift move, the man slammed him against the wall, one lean forearm pressing against his clavicle. It *hurt*, all of his bruises and cuts and sore muscles simultaneously reminding him of their existence. He let out a small involuntary noise, something between a squawk and a whimper.

"Let go of me," he said. He tried to keep his voice level.

The guard smiled down at him again. He braced his free hand against the wall next to Laurie's head and leaned in closer. "Stop me," he said. "Just try to stop me, princess."

"Mr. Kirby." Both Laurie and the guard swiveled their heads at the noise.

A woman stood in the corridor. Pale-skinned and willowy, with honey-colored hair twisted into a loose braid and coiled around the back of her head. She wore a high-necked peach crepe blouse with billowing sleeves and tiny fabric-covered buttons running down the front, paired with wide-legged white pants and white sandals with cork wedge heels. She was the cleanest, most well-groomed person Laurie had seen in a very long time.

She stepped toward them. "Mr. Kirby, dear, you can release him."

The guard—Kirby, surely—didn't move. "He shouldn't roam around this place unsupervised, ma'am. We don't know anything about him."

"Nonsense." The woman smiled. "Surely you can see he poses little threat to us. I appreciate your caution, but this child is our guest. He's free to explore the facility, if he likes."

"He could be a thief. Or a Red spy, ma'am. We need to—"

"Mr. Kirby." Sharper this time, though she didn't raise her voice. "Let go of him."

After a long, begrudging moment, Kirby lowered his arm and stepped back. Laurie slid away from him, rubbing his bruised sternum and glowering.

"Begging your pardon, ma'am, but you shouldn't be so trusting of strangers," Kirby said. "He's small, but he might not be harmless."

"As I said, he's our guest." She nodded at him once. "That will be all."

Kirby looked ready to argue further. At another sharp glance from her, he relaxed and nodded. "Whatever you say, ma'am."

Laurie watched after him as he strolled off down the corridor. Still shaky, he turned his attention to the woman.

She smiled at him. "Hello, there," she said. "You must be our little lost lamb."

"That's me," he said. "I'm Laurie."

"Very nice to meet you, Laurie. I'm Patricia." She extended a slim hand and shook his gently. Her grip was cool, and her fingernails were dark pink. It'd been years since Laurie had seen a painted nail. "Are you sure you should be up and about? My husband said you were injured."

"Is your husband the pastor?" Made sense. They were a handsome couple, Kyle and Patricia. "Hey, that Zephyr guard was totally going to kick my ass, and I hadn't done anything to deserve it."

"Perhaps you can find it in your heart to forgive him and move on," Patricia said. "The members of our security detail are zealous about their duties, and we're very grateful for it. My husband mentioned the tragedy that befell your monastery. It's due in great part to the diligence of Zephyr that nothing of that sort has ever happened to us. Far better to be overly cautious and risk hurting a few finer feelings than to become complacent."

"Yeah, but I wasn't even…" Laurie stopped, exhaled, shook his head. "Never mind. Look, I'm trying to get a handle on the plumbing situation here. Like, do you *have* plumbing?"

"We do." Another nice smile. Dimples. "We're connected to the water main. We're well equipped here, everything considered. Running water, some of it hot, flush toilets, showers. Let me show you."

"Thanks." Laurie fell into step with her, trying his best not to limp, as she headed down the corridor. "Ah… I don't suppose the hot water extends to baths?" His spirits lifted at the thought. Soaking in hot soapy water, relaxing his exhausted and aching muscles, getting rid of the pervasive stink of his recent trek across the desert…

Patricia's headshake dashed his hopes. "I'm afraid not. There are separate shower areas for men and women in the residence halls on the lower level." She frowned at his bandaged ankle. "You won't want to walk that far. Would you like to use the facilities in our private quarters?"

"Great. Fantastic. That would be very kind." He limped along after her down a series of corridors. "I think you guys totally saved my life by bringing me here, so thank you."

"You're very welcome, Laurie." Patricia patted his bare shoulder with her cool hand. "I'm sure you'll find some way to repay us."

The quarters Patricia shared with her husband consisted of a huge concrete room covered in pale pink paint, the space roughly divided into separate sleeping and sitting areas by a hinged lacquer screen patterned with gold-and-black butterflies. An overstuffed sofa and a matching armchair upholstered in heavy gold jacquard, a glass-topped gold-framed coffee table, a tall brass floor lamp with a pink silk lampshade, a shaggy peach rug covering much of the painted concrete floor. The rug felt soft and plush under Laurie's bare feet.

"When we moved into this suite, it was filled with computers. Huge things, much taller than you or I. Useless to us, of course, and I'm sure they hadn't worked in years. We hauled them out and dumped them in the desert," Patricia said.

A huge oil painting, artless but vivid, took up most of the wall above the sofa. It featured Patricia and Pastor Kyle on what appeared to be their wedding day, both dressed in shining white, both sporting matching white-toothed smiles. They posed on a white sandy beach, framed by the blue-green ocean and tall, graceful palm trees. Laurie stopped in front of it.

"Where was that painted?" he asked.

"In this room," Patricia said. "Kyle and I were married here, in our chapel. I painted the background from memory. I spent the first part of my childhood in Miami."

He examined the painting. Untroubled blue skies, lush palms, clear waters. "How old were you in 1984?"

"Thirteen." Patricia stared at the painting, a small smile playing on her lips. "My family had moved to Las Vegas earlier that year. That's why I was here when the bombs fell."

Patricia ushered Laurie through the bedroom, past the king-sized bed with the pink velvet coverlet and the mountain of satin pillows, and into a very small, very clean bathroom. Sink, toilet, shower stall. Everything he needed.

She gestured toward the shower. "The towels on the rack are clean, and there's soap and a razor, if you'd care to shave. Use anything you like. I should see about finding you some clothes, shouldn't I?"

Laurie glanced down at his bare, battered chest. "Probably, yeah. That'd be great."

She smiled again and withdrew. Left to his own devices, Laurie availed himself of the facilities. He showered—the water wasn't hot, but it was plenty warm, and there was even a full bottle of shampoo. Two kinds of soap. One was pale and creamy and smelled like lilacs, while the other was dense and scratchy and loaded with bits of powdered pumice, designed for decontamination purposes. Laurie considered the latter, then skipped it. They'd kept it on hand at the monastery, too, but nobody used it much. His skin felt delicate and itchy from too much sun exposure, and if he'd picked up any lingering radiation while staggering across the desert, soap probably wouldn't do all that much to get rid of it. He used the creamy bar instead.

None of the scratches on his chest seemed serious, so he shed the gauze wrappings on his torso and ankle and scrubbed every exposed bit of flesh.

When he emerged into the bedroom, swaddled in an oversized towel, he found Patricia standing at a tall metal cabinet that had been converted into a makeshift dresser. She glanced back at him, her lower lip caught between her teeth.

"I'd originally thought you could just wear something of my husband's, but nothing's going to fit you, is it? You're such a tiny thing."

"I know. That was one benefit to living at the monastery. I didn't need to fuss about clothes fitting me any more—all the tunics were equally shapeless and unflattering."

She laughed, though she seemed a little confused. "You've lived there your whole life, haven't you? Kyle told me you were orphaned as a baby?"

"Sure. My whole life," Laurie said. "Ah… you're taller than I am, but other than that, we're probably about the same size, right? Maybe…"

She smiled. "Would you care to raid my wardrobe, Laurie?"

"I'd be delighted," he said.

It took him a long time to thoroughly examine Patricia's clothes, contemplating each garment in turn. Everything was clean and well-tended, made from high-quality fabrics that were soft to the touch. After years of dressing in burlap, it was like visiting paradise. He eventually settled on slim black pants and a silky royal blue shirt—a blouse, really—that wrapped and belted around his waist like a kimono.

Patricia had a full-length mirror. He stared at his reflection for a long, long time.

He looked frail. His nose and forehead were a deep shiny pink, thanks to his unscheduled and unprotected trek across the desert. A damp and disheveled mop of fair hair, pale green eyes that seemed too big for his face, the rest of his features small and elflike.

Patricia came up behind him and met his eyes in the mirror. "The guard who found you, Mr. Abbott, said he thought you were a girl when he first saw you."

"It happens with staggering frequency," Laurie said.

She watched him in the mirror, her expression wistful. "You're so pretty," she said.

"I know. Everything considered, I'm probably wasted as a monk."

She cleared her throat. "Laurie? You really are a monk, aren't you?"

"Oh, sure," he said. "Absolutely."

He bent closer to the mirror, finger-combing his hair into place. He didn't meet Patricia's eyes, but he was pretty sure she was staring at him.

CHAPTER FOUR

Laurie spent the remainder of the day lolling in bed, resting his ankle and recuperating from his ordeal. He was antsy and anxious to learn more about his new surroundings, but at the same time, it was pleasant being here, freshly showered and relaxing on clean sheets. Patricia brought him dinner on a tray, a sandwich made from salty preserved meat spread on two slices of gummy white bread and a sticky bowl of applesauce that tasted dusty and metallic. Wasn't good, wasn't awful. At the monastery, they'd baked their own bread and brewed their own beer, and it was better than this stuff, but there was no sense being snobby. He alternated between napping and staring up at the concrete ceiling, wishing he had some reading material and wondering what was going to happen to him here. Patricia and Pastor Kyle seemed nice enough. Well-intentioned, probably.

The guards, though. The guards could be a problem.

There was someone monitoring him, he knew it. At different times, he spotted feet underneath the crack of his door. Someone kept loitering in the hallway, smack outside his room.

It was probably a good thing, he told himself firmly, good that the church had the Zephyr guards to defend it from the outside world. After the brutal slaughter at the monastery, he should be grateful for their protection.

Still, he'd feel a little more secure if his door had a lock on it.

He kept the overhead light on, even while he napped. Impossible to tell the time of day here under the earth, and there was no clock in his room. Judging by his level of exhaustion, it was probably night now.

The bare bulb went out without warning and plunged the room into darkness. The light from the hallway, which had been radiating under his door, extinguished at the same time. Laurie felt a moment of panic—was this a prelude to some kind of attack?—then relaxed. Way out here in the middle of the desert, the church probably wasn't hooked up to the electrical grid. He sure hadn't seen any power lines during his trudge across the desert. This place was probably powered by generators, which were shut off at night to conserve energy.

It was unnerving, lying in the darkness and feeling helpless and frightened and overwhelmed by recent events. After far too long, he managed to fall asleep.

Morning. Must be morning, because the bulb was now shining overhead, which meant the generators were back on.

He got out of bed. Ankle felt pretty good. He flexed his foot. The swelling had gone down. Still looked a little purple, but he was clearly on the mend.

He pulled on the skinny pants and the kimono blouse. Patricia had delivered his old canvas sandals to him last night along with his dinner tray; they were disreputable, but, as Patricia favored high heels, borrowing shoes from her was out of the question.

If he stayed in his room long enough, someone—Patricia, most likely—would bring him breakfast, probably. But he was feeling antsy and hungry, and anyway, he was curious to learn more about his surroundings. He slipped out of his room as quietly as he could.

Damn it. There was Kirby in the hallway, sitting on a folding chair and eating scrambled eggs piled on toast. At the sight of Laurie, he straightened up and got to his feet. His unbuttoned jacket fell open at the movement, allowing Laurie a glimpse of his holstered gun.

"Good morning. At least I think it's morning. Kind of hard to tell when you're underground, right?" Laurie said, as cheerily as he could manage. "I hope you aren't here just on my account."

"Someone's got to keep an eye on you, princess. Make sure you don't get into any mischief," Kirby said. He swallowed the last bite of his sandwich and licked grease off his fingers, looking Laurie up and down. "Nice outfit."

"Thanks so much. Hey, where can I find breakfast?"

"What'll you do for me if I tell you?" Kirby shifted his position. He leaned a shoulder against the wall, one hand at his waist, propping his jacket open. Making sure Laurie noticed his gun, just in case he'd somehow missed it before.

"Skip it. I'll ask someone else," Laurie said. He moved past Kirby and limped in the direction of Pastor Kyle and Patricia's quarters.

"Just giving you a hard time. Don't be so sensitive." Kirby took hold of Laurie's upper arm and forced him to stop walking. Laurie didn't quite dare jerk his arm away. "That's the wrong direction. Meals are served in the mess hall on the lower level, but there's no breakfast until after morning services, and those are held in the chapel. Straight through the doors at the other end of this corridor, then cross through the reception hall."

Laurie didn't have much interest in attending a church service, but he had less interest in remaining in his room, especially with Kirby hanging around. "Super. Thanks."

He disentangled himself from Kirby and headed in the direction he'd indicated. Kirby fell into step with him.

Laurie glanced at him. "I'm sure I can find it. No chaperone needed."

"I'm responsible for making sure this place is secure. That means keeping a close eye on the riffraff."

"What exactly do you think is so dangerous about me?" Laurie asked.

"Could be anything. Maybe you're a Red spy. Maybe you'll try to murder us all in our sleep."

"That's a little far-fetched, isn't it? What interest would the Soviets have in a church in the middle of nowhere?"

"Commies hate religion. Documented fact." Kirby held open the swinging door at the end of the corridor and ushered Laurie into a gigantic chamber. "You should learn your history."

This must be the reception hall. Dark and cavernous; Laurie could barely see the ceiling overhead. It was lit by torches stuck into sconces built into the cement wall. They glowed and flickered and cast odd shadows. The room was mostly deserted, with just a few security guards, easily identifiable in their black suits, milling about.

Laurie followed Kirby through the hall, trying his best not to limp. "Need me to carry you?" Kirby asked.

"Are Soviet spies even a thing anymore?" Laurie asked. "I mean, do they still exist?"

"Sure they do. This whole country's crawling with them. Just because you don't hear much about them these days doesn't mean they're not here, making their filthy plans, just waiting for us to get complacent before striking again." Kirby considered. "There was that big story in Vegas maybe a decade ago. You remember that lady senator, the one who turned out to be in cahoots with the Reds, the one who got herself killed? They're pretty sure it was a spy who shot her. And that's just what we know about. Who knows what's going on beneath the surface?"

Laurie stared at him for a long, long moment. "You know, I'm not sure you know what you're talking about."

"Like I said, study your history. Nobody likes an intellectual slouch."

"Even if Soviet spies still exist, there's no reason to think they'd be down here. And there's certainly no reason to think I'm one of them."

"No reason to trust you, either. There's a lot funny about you."

There was a staircase along the far wall made of slim strips of steel leading up to a thick concrete platform. He could barely see the skinny metal ladder extending up from it, rising to the surface far above. This was where he'd entered the facility, carried down on Jonathan's back. His memory of that was a little fuzzy, though he remembered Jonathan's hair had smelled pretty good.

All he needed to do was climb up those stairs and that ladder, and he could be out of here. Provided he'd be allowed to go...

"Question for you, Kirby," Laurie said. "If I were to leave this place, would anyone stop me?"

Kirby mulled over the question. "No reason anyone should. Might have to frisk you first, make sure you're not walking off with the good silver. You thinking of leaving?"

"Eventually, sure. It's not like I want to stay here forever," Laurie said.

"I'm betting you wouldn't get far. It's dangerous outside, and that ankle looks like it's still hurting you." Kirby grinned. "Had a girl here a while ago, one of the orphans, dumb little fifteen-year-old kid who decided she was too good for this place. She took off in the middle of the night. Gang caught her just outside the gate, I don't think you want to know what they did to her, but she didn't survive it. Seems unlikely you'd have better luck."

Laurie stared at him, at the sadism plain on his face, the sick smile on his lips. "I'm not a fifteen-year-old girl," he said.

"Maybe not." Kirby winked at him. "Though you could see how someone might get confused, right?"

"Do you get this creepy with everyone, or am I special?"

"Watch it, princess. You might want to be nicer to me, or I can make your stay here pretty unpleasant," Kirby said. "Heard through the grapevine that you're some kind of monk, huh? You take a vow of chastity or anything like that?"

"I can't think of any reason you'd need to know that," Laurie said.

"Aw, don't give me that. I'm sure if you put your pretty little head to it, you could come up with a reason or two." Kirby pointed ahead. "Chapel's this way."

Laurie threw the staircase one last longing look before following Kirby through the chamber.

A set of double doors marked the entrance to the chapel. Unlike most of what he'd seen thus far in the grim, industrial complex, these were made from rich, dark wood, elaborately carved with interlocking images of tangled vines and blossoming flowers. Kirby threw open both doors at once and ushered him inside with a grand flourish. "Here you go. Front pews are for paid members, the back's for the riffraff. In case you're wondering, you fall into that second category. Take a seat and behave yourself." He ruffled Laurie's hair, chuckling as Laurie jerked his head away, then left him alone.

He must be early. The chapel was empty. Laurie slid into the back pew.

The high ceiling was made from hundreds of small glass triangles affixed into geometric patterns to look like faceted diamonds. From somewhere just behind the glass, dozens of tiny white-bright lights shone, making the ceiling sparkle and glitter. The walls were painted a pale blush; the floors were carpeted in pure white. The platform stage at the back of the room looked like it was made from white marble shot through with veins of gold. Upon it stood a huge white electronic organ and an altar draped in yards and yards of gold satin that spilled down onto the floor.

A gigantic painted mural covered the entire wall behind the altar. Laurie recognized Patricia's style, colorful and simplistic, from her wedding portrait. The mural depicted scenes of destruction, mushroom clouds and white-blue flames engulfing and obliterating a city skyline. Towering faceless soldiers in gray uniforms, their smart red caps emblazoned with a yellow hammer-and-sickle insignia, stood in rigid rows before the flames, their faces melting down to bone from the radiant light of the figure in front of them. Pastor Kyle, in his collarless white suit, his arms spread wide, stood bathed in the glow of a golden light from above. Behind him was a paradise, blooming gardens and burbling fountains and flowering trees, around which frolicked a throng of angel-faced children in white robes.

It was the tackiest thing Laurie had ever seen. And he'd *been* to Las Vegas.

The doors to the chapel opened, and three young girls entered, dressed in long pink robes belted with tasseled gold cords. Teenagers, giggly and bubbly. Laurie's spirits brightened at the sight of them, so young and pretty and filled with so much life. They carried white wicker baskets overflowing with blossoms, lilacs and tiger lilies and gladiolas and marigolds. He assumed the flowers were fake, but as the girls drew closer, he could smell their heady perfume.

Upon spotting him, the girls paused. They stared at him for a moment, then one of the girls turned to her companions and murmured something behind a cupped hand. The other girls giggled.

The first girl slid into the pew in front of Laurie and set her basket beside her. She turned to face him, kneeling on the bench. She folded her arms over the wooden back and rested her chin on her hands, then stared up at him with huge brown eyes. "Hi," she said. "Who're you?"

She had frizzy brown hair tied back with a wide stretch of floppy pink lace. Her face was round and very pretty. Her bare arms were curved and fleshy, which was good to see. Meant the food probably wasn't rationed too strictly here. He'd never gone hungry at the monastery, but he'd heard the stories, the orphanages crowded with unwanted children, small kids turned outside to fend for themselves, babies left to starve because there was no food to spare.

"I'm Laurie. I'm staying here now." For the moment, at least. "Who're you?"

The girl giggled and glanced over at her friends, then back to Laurie. "I'm Peach. That's Cara, and the tall one is Melody. We're the altar girls this week."

"Nice to meet you, Peach," Laurie said. "Ah… Am I allowed to be in here?"

"Sure. You're early, though. Services don't start for like another twenty minutes." Peach scrutinized him. "So… I hope you don't think this is a rude question, but are you a member, or an orphan?"

"Neither. I mean, I'm an orphan, sure, but I'm too old for that to mean anything. I'm just a visitor. A refugee, if you will."

She giggled again. "What does that mean?"

"I guess it means I'm staying here until somebody kicks me out," he said.

"They won't kick you out," Peach said. "Pastor Kyle's totally cool about kids living here for free."

Laurie wasn't a kid, but all the same, it seemed like Peach was probably right. From what he'd seen of Pastor Kyle and Patricia, they didn't seem likely to strand him in the desert, homeless and defenseless. He nodded at the flowers. "Are those real?"

"Sure. They get brought in once a week. There's a greenhouse outside Vegas." Peach touched a sprig of lilacs with one finger. "Aren't they pretty? I'd never seen all these kinds of flowers until I came to live here."

Laurie stared at her. "Every week? That's got to be expensive."

Peach brushed this consideration aside with a wave of her hand. "The church has a ton of money. It costs a lot to be a member. I mean, a whole lot, like a lot more than you're thinking right now. We stay for free though, obviously. All the orphans do."

"Peach…" That was the tall one, Melody. "You can flirt later, okay? You have to help us set up."

Peach gave her an irritated glare, then grinned at Laurie. "Speaking of which, I got to earn my keep."

"You guys need any help?" Laurie asked.

She shook her head, frizzy curls flying. "Nope. This is easy. Pastor Kyle's probably going to give you a whole bunch of stuff to do anyway, if he lets you stay here without paying membership fees."

That sounded ominous. He settled back in his pew and watched as Peach and her friends arranged the flowers in gold urns on the altar and passed out hymnals to the arriving parishioners. He was curious to see the members. What kind of people could afford to pay the enormous fees Peach had mentioned? More to the point, what kind of people would be willing to spend that money for the dubious privilege of living here, underground, in this gloomy facility?

Middle-aged people mostly, people who would've already been adults thirty years ago when the bombs fell, though Laurie also saw a few younger couples, some with small children. Not much gray hair, not much wrinkled skin. Wasn't much of a surprise. Thanks to the cancer rates, most people didn't make it too far into old age. All the members were well-groomed and well-dressed. Men wore suits and ties, women wore knee-length dresses. The front pews filled up. Laurie tried to find Jonathan, beautiful Jonathan, but didn't see him.

And these must be the orphans. Teenagers trickled into the back four pews, boys and girls all dressed alike in cheap blue slacks and white short-sleeved button-down shirts. No one talked to Laurie, though he was the clear subject of curious stares and whispers. Didn't faze him much. He hadn't had much contact with teens for a while—he'd been the youngest resident at the monas-

29

tery—but whenever he'd go into town on supply runs with the other brothers, he'd find himself a source of great fascination for strangers. The interest came from all ages and genders, but he was catnip for teen girls in particular.

Pastor Kyle entered the chapel. He wore the same white suit, or one that looked very much like it, which he'd accessorized with a long pink satin scarf. A slim gold chain hung around his neck, glinting in the dazzling light from glittery glass ceiling. He crouched next to Laurie and held out a smooth hand. Manicured nails, neat and shiny. "So nice to see you here, Laurie. I meant to stop by your room last night to brief you on our morning routine, but I see you managed to figure things out by yourself."

Laurie shook his hand. "Peach and her friends got me sorted out. Ah… you have a service every morning?"

"Of course. It's one of the perks of having all my members living on church grounds." Pastor Kyle smiled. His teeth were white and even. Good teeth were a rare thing. Laurie's own were fine— he'd even had braces as a kid, an extravagant luxury available to him because of who his mother had been—but as his wisdom teeth had grown in, they'd pushed his bottom front teeth together, which he found unsightly. It wasn't noticeable unless he smiled, but it bugged him all the same. It was, as near as he could determine, his single major physical defect.

Apart from the bullet scar, of course.

"Surely you had daily services at the monastery?" Pastor Kyle asked.

"Nope. We didn't have much in the way of services at all. No sermons, at least. I mean, we had prayers, religious studies, that kind of thing," Laurie said. "Ah… it's not like I had a chance to stockpile cash while I was there. I don't have any way to pay you to stay here."

"I know. Please don't fret about it. We won't turn you out into the world unprotected, Laurie. There are plenty of ways you'll be able to make yourself useful here."

Laurie didn't like the sound of that. He'd probably be expected to do unpleasant and/or onerous labor to earn his keep. He wasn't built for heavy lifting, he was a disaster in a kitchen, and he loathed housecleaning. "I'm a pretty good scholar. I can read Latin, if that's any help to you," he said hopefully.

"Not at all." A quick smile. "We don't have much use for traditional religious texts here. I prefer a cleaner, purer interpretation of spirituality."

Whatever that meant. Pastor Kyle patted him on the shoulder and made his way down the aisle to the altar.

Patricia, clad in a soft green wrap dress, took her place at the electric organ and plunked out a droning processional. The music reverberated throughout the room, mournful and halting.

The service was inoffensive and perfunctory. Laurie was cheered by the latter and relieved by the former. Under the best of circumstances, church services weren't really his thing, and the possibility he'd stumbled into some dark fanatical sect had been troubling him. Not much in the way of fire-and-brimstone in Pastor Kyle's sermon. No blood was imbibed, no parishioners were flagellated, no pinked-robed teens were sacrificed upon the satin-draped altar. Just a mildly tedious lecture on the dangerous omnipresence of Sin and Lust, another desultory tune picked out on the organ by Patricia, and then everyone rose and filed out of the chapel en route to the dining hall for breakfast. Hungrier than ever, Laurie followed the crowd down a drab flight of concrete stairs to the lower level.

The mess hall had claustrophobically low ceilings lined with banks of flickering fluorescent lights. Laurie took his place in a long line of parishioners and accepted a plastic tray of food from a sulky young orphan in a hairnet. A hefty mound of dehydrated scrambled eggs, two strips of canned bacon, toast with grape jelly, and a paper cup of a watery fluorescent beverage that tasted strongly of chemicals and faintly of oranges. His tray also contained two iodine tablets for protection against radiation exposure, which seemed unnecessary. Most people had stopped taking those years ago—he remembered his mother giving them to him as a kid before taking him to visit blast sites, but that had been over a decade ago.

Tray in hand, he looked around the long communal mess tables. Still no sign of Jonathan. Disappointing.

He spotted Peach's friends, Cara and Melody, still in their pink robes, and headed over to their table. "Can I sit here?"

"Sure, go ahead." Melody scooted over on the bench to give him room.

"Thanks." He squeezed in beside her. "Where's Peach?"

"She skips breakfast. She's trying to lose weight." That was Cara, dark-skinned and petite. "She's probably off visiting the sexy Mr. Frisch." She and Melody exchanged looks.

Laurie perked up. "Jonathan? I didn't see him at the service."

"He never goes. He's Jewish or something," Melody said.

"Why's Peach visiting him? Is it just for the sexiness?" he asked.

"He keeps a bunch of books in his office. He lets us borrow them whenever we want. It gets boring here," Melody said. "But, yeah, it's mostly for the sexiness. You've met him, right? He's *gorgeous*, isn't he?"

"I noticed that about him. What's his deal? What does he do here?"

Melody took a sip of her orange drink. Carefully, so she wouldn't smudge her shiny pink lip gloss. Matched her robe. "He runs the business side, I guess. Handles the money, deals with the outside world, takes care of things. He's only been here a little while. I think he's from New York."

"Philadelphia. That's where he grew up, at least," Cara said. "He was working in Vegas, and Pastor Kyle hired him when he went out there last month during the church's annual membership drive."

Philadelphia. Huh. Laurie almost blurted out that he'd been born in Philadelphia, then stopped himself just in time. Wouldn't mesh well with his "left at the monastery as a babe in swaddling clothes" tale, and if word got back to Jonathan or Pastor Kyle, it could raise awkward questions. "What was he doing in Vegas? Exotic dancer?"

"I wish." Cara giggled. "I think he managed a hotel or something. Pastor Kyle needed to hire someone kind of fast, so he offered him the job on the spot. The guy who had the job here before Mr. Frisch, he stole a whole lot of money from the church and tried to run off in the night. The guards found him trying to hotwire one of their jeeps on the ramp at the south gate, so they shot him."

Laurie stared at her. "You mean they killed him?"

"Sure. What were they going to do? He was stealing from the church. You can't just let that go," Cara said. "It turned out for the best. Mr. Frisch is a whole lot cooler than that guy was anyway. Cuter, too."

He was a little unsettled by her blithe acceptance of homicide within the church. "How did you guys come to live here?" he asked, mostly to move on to another subject. "You're both orphans, right?"

"Yeah. Before this, I was at this gross facility in Indian Springs. As soon as I turned twelve, I got moved here," Melody said.

"We can stay for free until we turn eighteen, as long as we do our chores and don't cause trouble," Cara said. "It's fine. Some of the members look at us like we're trash, and the security guards get bossy and weird sometimes, but Pastor Kyle and his wife are okay."

"Can you leave?" Laurie asked. "If you hated it here and wanted to take off, would anyone stop you?"

"Why would they?" Cara asked. "They don't care if we go. It happens a lot. My old roommate Sammy, she left a couple months ago. Took off in the middle of the night, and I never saw her again. Didn't say goodbye, just split."

If Sammy was the runaway Kirby had mentioned back in the reception hall, apparently Cara hadn't heard the grim coda to her story. Then again, Kirby could have just been trying to spook him. "Was it weird that she didn't say anything to you beforehand?" Laurie asked. "I mean, she definitely left, right? Nothing could've happened to her?"

"Oh, yeah. She took all her stuff, not that she had much. And she really hated it here, she'd skip out of doing her chores, and she got into a lot of fights with the guards. She talked about running away all the time. No surprise to find her gone."

Breakfast wound to a close. The girls finished their meals and rose to their feet, empty trays in hand. "Nice talking to you," Melody told him.

"Same here. Hey, where's Jonathan's office, anyway?" Laurie asked. "I could use some reading material." He didn't want to cramp Peach's style if she was in the middle of angling for some time alone with Jonathan, but it was very, very dull in his tiny, bare room. A book would help pass the time. And Jonathan was far too old for her anyway.

And Laurie really wanted to see him again. There was that.

"You know where the chapel is? Take the hallway to the right of the entrance. Jonathan's office is about halfway down that. His door should be open, if he's in." Cara frowned. "You should probably be a little careful, though. No one's allowed to hang around that area if you don't have business there. That's also where the guards have their quarters. We're supposed to stay out of their way."

"Good advice," Laurie said.

CHAPTER FIVE

Another charmless concrete hallway lined with fluorescent lights. Might be nice if Pastor Kyle spent some of his parishioner's exorbitant membership fees on sprucing up the interior design. Laurie moved as quietly as he could down the corridor in search of Jonathan's office. If the guards were headquartered around here, he'd just as soon avoid drawing their attention.

Six doors, three on each side, all of them closed. Laurie hesitated. He could start knocking, but the guards...

Ah. He heard a voice, high-pitched and excited, though the words were muffled through the heavy door. Peach, probably. Laurie hovered outside and strained to listen.

The girl spoke again, and a man laughed and said something in reply, their exchange unintelligible. Laurie was pretty sure the girl was Peach, and if the man was Jonathan, he sure seemed to be in a jovial mood. Feeling no moral qualms about eavesdropping, Laurie pressed his ear to the door and listened.

No. Peach was crying, and it sounded like she was pleading with someone. There a note of hysteria to her tone that immediately provoked a defensive reaction in him. Without stopping to think, Laurie grabbed the handle and swung the door open.

He found himself in a shabby recreation room. Saggy armchairs made of battered brown vinyl, shabby nylon carpet, a weighty smell of old cigarette smoke. An ancient upright cabinet arcade game stood against the wall, unplugged and dormant, the joystick broken and the view screen cracked, the name on the top barely visible under layers of grime: *Galaga*.

Two men sat at a folding table beside the door, both uniformed guards. Both male, both brawny. Laurie recognized Abbott, the guy with the crew cut who'd been with Jonathan during yesterday's rescue. The detritus of a poker game—playing cards, crumpled bills, half-full glasses of what looked like whiskey—littered the tabletop. The guards looked up from their cards at Laurie's sudden entrance, irritated surprise registering on their faces.

"What's going on?" Laurie asked. Stupidly, because it was obvious what'd been going on.

Peach huddled on a sofa upholstered in threadbare plaid, with Kirby leaning across her. His jacket was off, his shoulder holster and gun resting on the coffee table in front of them. One of his hands was on Peach's bare leg, pushing the hem of her pink robe up her thighs, while the other pressed against her shoulder and pinned her to the sofa.

Her head down, Peach tried to move his hand from her leg and wriggle away from him. With her free hand, she swiped at a trickle of fresh blood from her nose. Her face was red, her frizzy bangs were plastered to her forehead with sweat, and it was obvious she'd been crying.

Kirby glanced at the door. His expression of dark annoyance faded into amusement when he recognized Laurie. He released his hold on Peach and shifted upright.

"Ah, it's my nosy little friend. Might've known you'd find your way here," he said. He nodded at Laurie. "Come in or stay out, but either way, close that damned door."

Laurie remained where he was. "Peach? Is everything okay?"

Peach threw him one frightened look through red-rimmed eyes, her hand still covering her bloody nose. Above her fingers, her left cheek looked swollen and purple.

"Did he hit you?" Laurie asked. He looked at the guards sitting at the folding table, at Kirby, who still regarded him with the same contemplative smile, then back to Peach. "Do you want me to get Pastor Kyle?"

Her eyes widened. She shook her head, quick and fervent.

"She's fine. Everybody's fine. We're having a good time. Aren't we, Peaches?" Kirby asked. He gave Peach an affectionate nudge to her ribs with his elbow. "We're having a party. Come in and join us."

Laurie hesitated. The guards stopped their poker game and watched him. Nobody moved.

"You should probably come with me, Peach," Laurie said. "Come on. We can just walk out of here."

Peach regarded Laurie with the same frightened, uncertain expression, then nodded.

She shifted further away from Kirby, moving slowly and tentatively, like she was trying to avoid provoking a dangerous animal, then rose to her feet. She tugged at her pink robe to straighten it and pushed her sweat-drenched hair out of her eyes. Her hands shook.

When she took a step in the direction of the door, Kirby lazily grabbed her wrist and pulled her back. "Aw, don't go yet, honey," he said. He snaked both arms around her waist and toppled her into his lap. Peach let out a soft cry.

"Shh, honey, everything's fine." Kirby nuzzled his face against her neck and nipped at her throat with his teeth. "I've been in the mood for a ripe, juicy peach."

Laurie stepped into the room. "You need to let go of her," he said, with as much bravado as he could muster.

"Or?" From behind Peach's neck, Kirby raised an amused brow at him.

Good question. He threw a quick glance behind him into the empty corridor. "Or... I'll get everyone I can find in this place to stop you."

"The little fruit's going to be trouble, Kirby," Abbott said.

"No, he's not," Kirby said. He shifted Peach off his lap and stood up. "He's going to be good. Right, Laurie?"

He picked up his holster from the coffee table and drew his gun. Casually, no cares in the world. Laurie froze. Kirby approached him, smiling in a genial manner.

Kirby placed a hand on his shoulder and steered him back against the wall. Too aware of the gun, Laurie didn't resist. Kirby stuck the muzzle under Laurie's jaw and leaned down, close enough that he could count his pores. "You could just disappear, you know," he said, his voice low and intimate. "Think about it. The good pastor would just assume you left on your own. No one knows you here, no one would even think to look for you. Understand me?"

Laurie didn't answer. Kirby grinned down at him. "Take a seat." When Laurie didn't move, Kirby pressed the gun harder against his throat. "Do it."

His face burning with some combination of shame and anger, Laurie sank to the floor, right next to the broken *Galaga* machine. Kirby nudged him with the toe of his loafer. "Keep quiet and enjoy the show."

Kirby turned back to the sofa. "Sorry about the interruption, Peaches. Where were we?"

His back was to Laurie, and for a fleeting second Laurie entertained a satisfying fantasy of attacking from behind, maybe wrestling the gun away from him, somehow gaining the upper hand. He dismissed the thought before he let it fully develop. He was too small, too ineffectual, too outnumbered, and he'd wind up beaten or shot. All he could do was stay where he was and hope things turned out less horribly than the way they seemed to be heading.

Maybe luck was with him. Because all of a sudden there was Jonathan, once more his savior, standing in the open doorway.

"What's going—" Jonathan stopped talking as he took in the situation. He looked at Peach cowering on the sofa, at Laurie on the floor, at Kirby and his gun. His expression darkened. "Put that away," he said to Kirby.

"Stop being such a goddamned busybody, Frisch," Kirby said. "This doesn't concern you."

Without turning his attention away from Kirby, Jonathan spoke: "Hey, Laurie? Go check on Peach."

Laurie rose to his feet. His legs felt shaky, so he grabbed the corner of the arcade game to steady himself. Kirby still had his gun in his hand, but neither he nor either of the other two guards made any movement to stop him, their attention fixed on Jonathan.

He limped over to the sofa, where Peach was now curled up on her side, twisting her entire body away from the action in the room. He crouched beside her. "Peach? I think we can leave now."

She didn't respond. Laurie placed a tentative hand on her shoulder, which she slapped away without looking at him.

"Why don't you two go to my office?" Jonathan said. His voice was soft and calm.

"You don't have any authority here, Frisch," Kirby said. "You're butting into a private matter."

Laurie spoke to Peach again, making an effort to sound as calm and composed as Jonathan. "We're going to go to Jonathan's office, okay?"

Peach didn't move. Laurie was reluctant to touch her again, so he stayed in the same crouched position, his legs trembling from fear and his ankle throbbing from pain, hoping the situation wouldn't explode into sudden violence. Kirby still had that gun…

After a long moment, Peach straightened up. Without looking at Laurie or anyone else in the room, she rose to her feet. Laurie wanted to take her arm and escort her out of this awful place, but he didn't quite dare. Instead, he hovered behind her, feeble and useless, as she stalked to the door.

"This is going to bite you in the ass, Frisch," Kirby said.

Jonathan shook his head. "Don't talk," he said quietly. "You're finished here." He remained where he was, standing in the doorway, shifting to one side to let Laurie and Peach exit while keeping his attention fixed on Kirby. He pulled the door shut behind him and ushered them into his office, which was located straight across the hall.

It was cramped and unremarkable. A metal desk piled high with loose papers and binders, a gray plastic chair on rollers, a bulky filing cabinet taking up far too much of the remaining space. With a final glance across the hall, Jonathan closed his office door and flipped the latch, then pointed to another door on the other side of the room. "My living quarters are through there," he said to Laurie and Peach. "We'll be a little more comfortable."

Jonathan's bedroom was larger and nicer than Laurie's, though not by much. A mattress on a metal bunk bolted into the wall, a ratty corduroy armchair and matching ottoman, a striped rug covering the bare cement floor. The books the girls had seemed so excited about turned out to be two shelves of double-stacked paperbacks, most of them old and decaying, the titles on the battered spines unreadable. Jonathan had his own sink, industrial and too large for the small room, and a dented teakettle on an electric hotplate with a fraying cord. "Have a seat," he told his guests.

Peach sat on the edge of the bunk, her posture unnaturally stiff, still not looking at anyone. Laurie perched on the ottoman. Felt good to give his shaky knees a rest. Jonathan soaked a rag under the faucet and handed it to Peach. "Here," he said.

She took it from him without speaking and dabbed at the smeared blood under her nose. Jonathan picked up a blanket from the foot of his bunk and draped it around her shoulders. "Are you hurt?" he asked. She glanced up at him, then looked back down and shook her head.

"You sure?" Another headshake.

"In any case, you're safe now." Jonathan's tone was brisk but not without compassion. "I'm going to talk to Pastor Kyle about this, and I'm going to make sure Kirby is out of here. Those other guys, too. They won't bother you again."

"You can't tell him," Peach said. "Don't say anything about this. I'll get in trouble."

Jonathan hesitated, then sat on the edge of the bunk, a good distance away from her. "Do you want to tell me what happened?" When she didn't answer, he pressed gently: "Were you coming to see me?"

"You weren't here." She sounded resentful.

"I'm sorry. There was a supply delivery at the south gate that I had to supervise."

"I was just going to leave, but their door was open, and Kirby asked if I wanted to have a drink with them. He's sort of an asshole sometimes—ordering us around, making jokes that aren't really jokes, stuff like that—but he seemed friendly. At least at first," she said. "He got weird and started groping me. When I said I wanted to leave, he hit me. We're not supposed to talk to the guards, or do anything to distract them from their jobs, and we're absolutely not supposed to go into their quarters. If you tell the pastor, I could get kicked out."

"I doubt that will happen. You might get into some trouble, I don't really know. I'll stick up for you if you do. But those guards are going to be in much worse trouble."

She didn't answer, just sat in silence. Her nose had stopped bleeding, and her face looked less flushed. She held the damp rag in her lap with both hands and twisted it into tight knots. Laurie remained on the ottoman, feeling awkward and ineffectual.

After a long while, long enough that the silence had become uncomfortable, she asked, "Can I go now?" Her voice was cold and strained, like it was taking some effort to hold herself together.

"Sure. Of course." Jonathan rose to his feet. "Laurie and I will walk you back to your quarters."

No one was in the hallway, and the door to the guards' recreation room was still closed. Laurie was grateful for that. Peach was silent and prickly during the walk down to the residence level. Jonathan and Laurie left her at the entrance to the corridor where the orphans were quartered and headed back up the stairs.

Jonathan didn't say anything to Laurie until they were back in the reception hall. "What were you doing there?" he asked. There was a faint interrogative note to it.

"Same as Peach. I wanted to see you." Jonathan shot him a startled look. "The word has spread about your lending library. Couldn't find you, but I heard something suspicious going on across the hall and went to investigate. I walked into the middle of the party."

"You okay?"

"I was attacked by some guy with an axe yesterday. By that standard, today's actually going pretty well."

Jonathan almost smiled. "You can find your way back to your room from here, right? I'm going to look for Pastor Kyle."

"Do you want me to come with you? I could tell him what I saw."

"Better not. I might end up snapping at him, so it's best if no one else is around. I've told him before that those Zephyr creeps take far too many liberties with this place," Jonathan said. "You sure you're okay? You were a lot more talkative yesterday, and that was when you were half-dead."

"I'm fine. I guess I'm a little rattled. I'm kind of mad, kind of scared," Laurie said. "Kirby threatened to kill me. Or at least make me disappear, which I assume means the same thing."

"He won't do that."

"He said I could disappear from this place, and everyone would just assume I'd left and no one would look for me. And he's right." His throat felt tight.

"I'd look for you," Jonathan said. "If you disappeared from here, I'd find out what happened to you."

Laurie shot him a quick glance, but Jonathan was staring straight ahead. Jonathan gave him a quick pat on the shoulder—congenial but impersonal—and strode toward another corridor.

The afternoon passed uneventfully. Laurie kept to his room. He half-expected a visit from Pastor Kyle, either to be asked to recount his version of recent events or to receive an update on the situation, but nothing came. He grew hungry, but the idea of venturing out and asking one of the guards in the reception hall when lunch would be served seemed unappealing, so he lay on his bed and stared at the ceiling and tried not to obsess too much about his unknown future.

A soft knock on his door. Laurie hesitated. Aware his heartbeat had increased, he climbed out of bed. "Who is it?"

"It's Jonathan."

He cracked open the door. Jonathan stood in the hallway, dressed in a cobalt sweater and jeans. The sweater matched his eyes. Laurie opened the door wider. "Hi. You want to come in?"

Jonathan shook his head. "Just dropping these off." He passed Laurie a handful of paperback books. "Don't get your hopes up, they're mostly crap. When I started working here, I salvaged them from a heap of stuff they were going to dump in the desert. Must've belonged to someone who was here back when this was a working facility. Someone with lousy reading tastes."

"Hey, cool, thanks." Laurie flipped through the books. Romance novels mostly, lurid covers featuring bosomy women with flowing hair locked in improbable embraces with muscular shirtless men. "Fantastic. How'd the talk with Pastor Kyle go?"

"Could have been better. He frowned a lot and said all the appropriate things, but I got the impression he's not inclined to take the matter too seriously. He's going to talk to Kirby and ban him from going near the orphans, but that doesn't seem like enough. I was hoping he'd boot his ass out of the facility."

"Me too." Laurie was surprised by the intensity of the disappointment that surged through him. "Is Peach in trouble?"

"Not significantly. Pastor Kyle wants Patricia to sit her down for a lecture on the dangers of inflaming the passions of men, which is almost exactly what the poor kid doesn't need right now, but she's not going to be punished."

"I don't think she was doing much inflaming," Laurie said. "I think Kirby was in the mood to mess with someone, and Peach happened to cross his path. On that note, I don't suppose Kirby's banned from going anywhere near me? When I woke up this morning, I found him camped outside my room."

"Yeah?" Jonathan frowned. "Why? Does it have anything to do with what you said earlier about the guards being dangerous?"

"Hmm?" Laurie did his best to look guileless. "Oh. No, I told you, I don't even remember saying that. I think it has more to do with me being really pretty."

"Modest, too."

Laurie waved this away. "Modesty is tedious," he said. "It's a fact that I'm pretty. And it's a fact that Kirby has been acting weird around me because of that. I guess you could call what he's been doing flirting, sort of. But he doesn't mean it in any sort of *fun* way. I think he's trying to make me nervous. Succeeding, too."

"Ah." Jonathan twisted Laurie's doorknob experimentally. "Your door doesn't lock?"

"Nope."

Jonathan cast a speculative glance around the room. "Jam the folding chair underneath the knob tonight. It'll make it harder to open from the outside," he said. "If you left this place, would you have anywhere to go?"

"Not really," Laurie said. "You think I should leave?"

Jonathan shook his head. "Just keep your options open. The Zephyr guards have a lot more clout here than they should. From what I've heard, Pastor Kyle has let them have the run of the place for years, and I don't have any authority over them. If Kirby's got it in for you, I'm not sure how much protection I can provide."

"Got it," Laurie said. It wasn't great news, and he probably shouldn't read too much into Jonathan's words, but something about the suggestion that he'd protect Laurie if he could made him felt better. It was comforting to think he might have an ally in this place.

CHAPTER SIX

Nighttime. It was after dinner—spaghetti in a watery sauce peppered with rubbery cubes of something that might've been sausage—but before the generators were turned off for the evening, and Laurie wanted to see the surface. He entered the reception hall and climbed the stairs leading up toward the hatch.

He should probably check with Pastor Kyle first and make sure it was okay to do this, but he was feeling antsy, and besides, he'd never been much of a fan of asking permission. There were two uniformed Zephyr guards on duty in the hall, one male and one female, who watched him with mild interest but didn't attempt to stop him.

He reached the concrete platform and scaled the slim metal ladder to the surface. His ankle still ached a little, but he could do this, provided he didn't look down. The round metal hatch at the top stood wide open. Probably meant someone was already outside. Maybe guards were stationed up there, keeping a watch for intruders. Maybe he'd run into Kirby.

The night air was cool and dry. It'd probably been blisteringly hot during the day, but the desert temperatures always dropped in the evening, and now it was almost chilly. The air smelled good. More accurately, it didn't smell like anything at all. Inside the facility, there was a faint yet persistent odor of mildew and stale air.

Hard to see much more than blackness in all directions underneath the waning moon and the starlit sky. To his right, far against the horizon, he saw a faint band of golden orange. City lights. Could only be Vegas. He made a note of the direction. No way could he travel that far on foot, but if he was forced to leave in a hurry, it'd be useful to know which way he should head.

He wasn't alone. A tall figure stood amongst the satellite dishes, visible only in silhouette. Pastor Kyle, in his linen suit, turned his head and saw Laurie.

He looked startled, then smiled. "Ah. Laurie. Is everything all right?"

"Sure. I just wanted some fresh air." Laurie walked over to him. The concrete under the dishes was still warm. The heat permeated through the soles of his sandals, the only lingering evidence of a scorching day. "I hope that's okay."

"Certainly. I encourage all members to stand outside for at least a few minutes weekly. The sunlight is good for them." Pastor Kyle regarded him with beatific neutrality. No warmth, no hostility, just a bland and inoffensive kindness. "The majority, however, don't care to come up here. Most have come to the church seeking a sanctuary the outside world failed to bring them. And of course some simply prefer to limit their exposure to the lingering poisons on the surface."

"Thirty years after the fact, I bet there's not much difference between the radiation up here and down there."

"Perhaps not," Pastor Kyle said. "Sometimes, however, the illusion of protection can be a powerful shield in itself."

Laurie nodded. "So they hide beneath the earth and scrub themselves with scratchy soaps and pop iodine pills, hoping the radiation won't find them." He stared up at the sky, black and vast and dotted with bright stars. "You said you had a cancer ward here, right? How many members are in it?"

"Right now? Maybe twenty, twenty-five."

"Out of the, what did you say, three hundred people who live here? That puts it right around the national average, doesn't it?"

"Just about. Perhaps a smidgen lower." Pastor Kyle gave him a small smile. "To most of my flock, however, I think the cancer rates themselves are irrelevant. They feel safer in my church, and that's all that matters."

"Fair enough," Laurie said. "In any case, I like it outside. I was feeling a little claustrophobic. Not that it isn't fine down there," he added. "I mean, seriously, thanks for taking me in. I don't mean to sound ungrateful."

"I'm surprised you're still partial to the outside world after everything that's happened to you. You know first-hand how dangerous it can be up here."

"Sure, but it seems a little dangerous down there, too," he said. At Pastor Kyle's look of confusion, he elaborated. "The security guards. Zephyr. That guy Kirby tried to rape Peach, you know."

"I do. Jonathan told me about that." Pastor Kyle looked grave. "His behavior is, of course, unacceptable, and I told Mr. Kirby that, firmly. But…" He spread his hands to indicate his helplessness. Something glinted on his wrist, a watch with a thick gold band. "The young lady bears some responsibility. These are dangerous men tasked with a dangerous job, and it was foolish of her to put temptation in their path."

"They're adults. They can control themselves. Whatever Peach was doing there, she didn't deserve to get attacked."

"As I said, I disapprove strongly of Mr. Kirby's conduct. Be that as it may, though, the guards are a necessary evil. Without their protection, the church would not survive."

"They seem to be doing a bang-up job of protecting the church from teen girls, at least." Pastor Kyle was beginning to look annoyed, which meant Laurie should try to be a little less mouthy. "We're alone up here. Shouldn't some guards be stationed on the surface? If you're going to get invaded, this is where it'll happen. All you've got to protect you is that flimsy fence, and even I had no trouble climbing over that."

"We have other measures of protection up here. I'm quite sure the guards are watching us right now."

Pastor Kyle pointed toward the fence. Nestled inside the coil of razor wire on top was a clunky black video camera. "Surveillance," he said. "That's how we first spotted you."

He glanced at his watch. Chunky and gold, with a glitter of tiny diamonds around the casing. "Ah. It's almost time."

"For?"

"Watch the stars. Right there, directly above us. This is what I came up here to see. It took me months to uncover the patterns written in the skies." He pointed at the sky, black and vast, broken only by that white sliver of a moon and fiery pinpoints of starlight.

Laurie craned his neck back and stared up at the stars. Pastor Kyle remained still, chin jutting skyward. He could've been a marble statue, the illusion broken only by the faint breeze that ruffled his hair and flapped at the hem of his linen jacket.

Minutes passed. Laurie was ready to give up and go back inside when Pastor Kyle raised a finger and pointed. "There."

Something white and bright tumbled through the sky and fell toward the horizon in a graceful shining arc. After traveling for a few seconds, it disappeared. "A shooting star?" Laurie asked.

"A satellite." Pastor Kyle smiled at him. "Probably a very old one. My pet theory is that it was originally controlled by this facility, years ago. A communications satellite, most likely, judging by how close its orbit brings it to the earth."

He motioned toward the satellite dishes. "It belongs here, I feel certain of it. If we can learn how to reestablish contact with it, imagine what we could do."

"Communications? Like telephones?" Laurie asked.

"Yes, sometimes, but in this case I mean television. Satellite television." Pastor Kyle gazed at the sky again. "You're too young to remember this, but there was a time when every home had a TV."

"I know. Even after the bombs and stuff, people still had televisions. I mean, we never did, not at the monastery, but I know about it. A lot of people still have them, don't they?"

"Not to the extent I mean. Not anywhere near. In the years just before the bombs fell, we experienced a golden age of television, channels beamed into homes around the world through satellites. Imagine the possibilities." Pastor Kyle smiled. His face grew fuzzy with the haze of nostalgia. People who were old enough to remember the world before 1984 tended to get that look a lot. "There were channels that would only show motion pictures, or sporting events, or programs for children. There was even an entire television network devoted to broadcasting church services, can you imagine such a thing?"

Ah. "Is that what you want? To contact that satellite and create a network for the church?"

"You're very quick, Laurie," Pastor Kyle said. He seemed approving. "I want to recapture that time. Men of God reaching a massive audience of believers, tens of thousands of viewers at a time, uniting the world through their words of faith. There was a special name for these men: Televangelists. Television evangelists."

"Catchy," Laurie said.

"They were treated like movie stars, these men. And they broadcast their sermons from dazzling churches, ones that glittered with crystal and gold, and they wore sumptuous clothes and drove luxurious cars, because God rewarded their piety with wealth and fame."

Laurie didn't have anything against either wealth or fame—come to think of it, he could handle a healthy dose of each—but it seemed like maybe those things shouldn't be the primary goal of a pastor. Still, he couldn't begrudge Pastor Kyle his fantasy.

Pastor Kyle seemed lost in thought. "I believe it's possible to achieve my dream, but there's still so much groundwork that must be laid first. You, Laurie, might be able to help me with this."

Startled, Laurie frowned at him. "With the satellite, you mean? I don't know anything about that sort of thing."

"I don't imagine you do. That's not quite what I meant," Pastor Kyle said. "Eight years ago, when Patricia and I decided to convert this facility into my church, we were perhaps a bit overenthusiastic in our renovations. There was so much debris—computers, equipment, files—that we had no earthly use for, and we needed all that room to adequately house our parishioners, so we loaded it into our trucks and drove it out through the south gate and dumped it in the desert. In hindsight, though, all that might come in very handy, if we were to attempt to make contact with the satellite. Which is where you come in, Laurie."

"You want me to dig through piles of crap in the desert looking for, what, satellite instruction manuals?"

"It's more complicated than that, I'm afraid. Six months ago, our trash heap disappeared. Scavengers must have carried it off, no doubt to make a profit off whatever they could."

Laurie mulled this over. "This was a federal facility, right? So that means government equipment, government files. Probably not the kind of stuff anyone could sell out in the open without getting into a lot of trouble."

"My thoughts have been running much along those lines," Pastor Kyle said. "If our scavengers knew what they were doing—and I have reason to believe they did, or they surely wouldn't have taken such pains to cart away our entire heap—they'd need a contact in the black market to broker the sale."

"Which probably means Las Vegas," Laurie said. "So how do I factor into this?"

"I think—forgive me if this is in any way offensive—you're the sort of person who might know the sort of person who might know something of this matter. It has become increasingly apparent you might be something other than what you seem."

In the dim light, Pastor Kyle's face looked calm and composed. He kept his eyes turned upward to the night sky. Laurie hesitated, then cleared his throat. "Oh?"

"Patricia and Jonathan have each mentioned that there are elements of your personal history they find somewhat... inconsistent. And Mr. Kirby, I've found, has unerring instincts when it comes to the seamier side of human nature. He confided to me that he has some suspicions about your character."

Laurie almost laughed. "I'll bet he did. Between you and me, I have some suspicions about his character, too," he said. "He told me he suspected me of being a Soviet spy, which I most certainly am not, so maybe you shouldn't rely on his crackerjack instincts quite so much."

"Then let me be a little clearer." There was a new note to Pastor Kyle's tone, something slinky and cunning creeping in underneath the usual mild bonhomie. "You're a monk with a bullet scar and a handful of pretty tales that don't add up. At best, you're a liar; at worst, you're a danger. I've weighed the risks and allowed you to stay here because you may prove useful. This would be a splendid opportunity to show me that I made the right decision."

Laurie opened his mouth to protest, saw something in Pastor Kyle's face, reconsidered. "I see." He stared out over the horizon, the golden glow of Las Vegas too far away. "I might know a guy," he said at last.

"Somehow I felt certain you would." Pastor Kyle smiled again, the shrewdness retreating and the bland kindness returning. "Let's go back inside, shall we? We have plans to make."

He clapped a hand on Laurie's shoulder and gestured toward the open hatch. Laurie hesitated, then followed him. Even though the air had grown chilly, even though Patricia's borrowed blouse wasn't providing much protection against the night breeze, he found himself reluctant to enter that dark hatch, to climb down that narrow metal ladder, to descend into the facility once again. Everything considered, it was better on the surface.

Pastor Kyle led him to a dark, low-ceilinged room with two rows of long countertops positioned in front of a bank of television monitors. The monitors had seen better days; two were broken and all were dark, save one, which showed a grainy black-and-white image of the satellite dishes framed by the vast expanse of the desert.

There were two people in the room. A security guard sat at the front counter in a high-backed chair in front of the monitors. She was fortyish, tough and lean, the part of her neck visible above the collar of her Zephyr jacket covered by a stylized tattoo of a snake that looked like a lightning bolt with a forked tongue. Her long black hair was pulled away from her face and winched into a tight bun.

Jonathan was there, too. He leaned back against the counter, deep in conversation with the guard. His sleeves were pushed up, his arms crossed casually over his chest, and he was grinning. Laurie had never seen him look this carefree. He felt a prickly, irrational resentment toward this guard, whoever she was, for getting him to relax like this.

"Jonathan. I didn't expect to see you here," Pastor Kyle said. He seemed displeased. "Maybe you shouldn't distract Miss Rosado from her surveillance."

"We were just talking business," Jonathan said. He straightened up, cold and purposeful once more. "Is everything okay on the surface?"

"Of course. I was just showing Laurie our satellite," Pastor Kyle said. "Laurie, I'd like you to meet Miss Rosado. She maintains the work schedules of the Zephyr guards assigned to this facility."

"I do a hell of a lot more than that. And it's just Rosado. No-body calls me 'Miss.' Nobody should, anyway." She nodded once at Laurie, her expression severe. "Frisch was just talking about you."

"Oh?"

"You're about as he described," she said. She flicked a glance over him. The corner of her mouth quirked up, then the grim expression returned.

"Laurie believes he might be able to help us track down the missing files and equipment," Pastor Kyle said.

"Don't get your hopes too high," Laurie said. "I said I might know someone who could help. Only there's no way to contact him, other than finding him in person. He's in Las Vegas."

"We can arrange that. We have a pair of trucks we use when-ever we go into the city, and the Zephyr guards have their own vehicles," Pastor Kyle said. "Is your friend reliable?"

"He's not really a friend. He's a monk. Former monk, I guess. He was kicked out a year or two ago for his overly-entrepreneurial spirit, which the other brothers deemed insufficiently spiritual, but I always got along okay with him. The last I heard, he was working out of one of the casinos. I don't know much about his situation, but he's probably pretty well-connected. If anyone in Vegas has been trying to sell your missing files, there's a good chance he'd know about it."

"Well. That sounds promising." Pastor Kyle smiled. "Our next order of business, then, is to get you to Las Vegas to meet with your friend." He turned to Rosado. "Laurie will need protection. I trust you'll be able to spare a guard for a day or two?"

"No. That's definitely not going to work," Laurie said. "No of-fense, but your guards are way too rape-happy to make good traveling companions."

A shadowy flicker of irritation passed over Pastor Kyle's face, ruffling that implacable benevolence again. It was gone almost as soon as it appeared. "It was one incident, Laurie, involving one rogue guard, and it's not likely to happen again. You'd be quite safe in their care. Certainly safer than you'd be on your own."

Laurie shook his head. "Absolutely not."

Rosado shot him a look of sympathy. "I'll send you with Casey," she said. "She's tough enough to keep you out of trouble, and I guarantee she won't have much interest in raping you or anyone else. How does that sound?"

"Nope. If you want me to go, I'll go by myself. I'm not traveling with anyone from Zephyr, period."

"You will if you want to keep staying here," Pastor Kyle said. His mouth pressed into a thin line, and for the first time he seemed dangerous. "I will not send you off on your own with one of our vehicles. I've been generous with my hospitality thus far, but unless you start offering some value in return, that courtesy will be revoked."

Laurie was ready to retort that he was fine with being booted out into the desert, then thought better of it. "I'll go with Jonathan," he said at last. "I trust him."

Jonathan, who'd been following the discussion with a look of ever-increasing dissatisfaction, raised his brows.

"Out of the question," Pastor Kyle said. "Jonathan has important duties here. I can't spare him."

"I'll take him," Jonathan said. "It's a short trip. We can go on my bike."

"Ah... bike?" Laurie asked.

"Motorcycle. Not a bicycle. It'll be fine."

Riding on the back of a motorcycle through the heart of the desert sounded like a bad idea, but the alternatives sounded worse. "Okay. Sure, I guess."

Pastor Kyle shook his head. "I need you here, Jonathan."

"An overnight trip. That's all," Jonathan said. "If we leave tomorrow, I'll probably make it back in time to supervise the food delivery on Monday morning."

"The road is too dangerous for the two of you on your own. This is a brutal area. You'll need protection."

"I got here on my own just fine without any protection. So did Laurie, for that matter, and he was on foot. We'll be careful."

Pastor Kyle glowered. After a moment, he made a noise of irked resignation. "I suppose it's all right. You'll be responsible for making certain nothing goes amiss, Jonathan. That means keeping a close eye on our young friend here."

"Of course." Jonathan looked at Laurie. "Tomorrow night, okay? As soon as the sun starts to go down, we'll set out. It'd be idiocy to travel in the heat of the day."

"That'd work. Sure." The idea of leaving the gloomy underground facility was both thrilling and a little frightening.

Laurie looked at Pastor Kyle, who still seemed annoyed, and then at Jonathan, at that grim expression on that beautiful face, and hoped this wasn't a terrible mistake.

CHAPTER SEVEN

They left by the south gate, exiting through a concrete drive-way that began at the far back of the facility and rose up a long narrow tunnel to the surface. The gate itself was made of thick panels of rusty metal; one of the Zephyr guards unlocked it from the inside and rolled it open before bolting it shut behind them. They emerged out the side of a low hill, Jonathan pushing his motorcycle, Laurie trailing behind him. Laurie saw the fence-enclosed field of satellite dishes several hundred yards away across the sand.

They traveled light. Still in his borrowed clothes, Laurie didn't have anything to pack; Jonathan carried a canvas shoulder bag that was too small to hold much more than a clean shirt.

It was dusk now, and the air was still plenty warm. Made sense, not traveling during the heat of the day, but nights were scarier in the desert. Laurie stared out over the empty expanse of darkening sand and shivered.

Jonathan frowned. "You okay with this?"

"Yeah. Should be fine, right?" Laurie examined the motorcycle. It was smaller than he'd thought it'd be. "It'll be a bit cramped with both of us on it, won't it?"

"You don't take up much space." Jonathan shot a quick glance about the horizon and lowered his voice, even though there was nobody around to overhear them. "Do you think your friend in

Vegas can find what the pastor's looking for? You really do have a friend in Vegas, right?"

"He exists, sure. Whether he'll be able to help us, I have no idea. He's pretty resourceful, but this sounds like a fool's errand."

"Agreed. This whole satellite business, it's ridiculous. Even if that satellite could originally communicate with the facility, and that's a pretty big if right there, it has to be more than thirty years old. I don't know how long satellites last, but it's probably long dead. And even if we could reestablish contact with it, that's still a long ways from getting it to broadcast a television signal."

"Oh. Yeah. I guess it didn't seem too likely this would work."

"You sound disappointed. Don't tell me Pastor Kyle managed to sell you on his televangelism dream."

Laurie rolled his eyes. "I don't care about that. I just think it'd be nice to be on television. I like the idea of being able to reach a lot of people at once."

"Hmm." Jonathan stared at the horizon. "Should we get going? Sooner we get there, sooner we get this over with."

"All right. So I just hang on to you? Around your waist?" Laurie asked. "Do you have a helmet?"

"Don't sweat it. I'm good at this," Jonathan said. He straddled the bike. Mere inches of available seat space existed behind him. "You've been to Vegas before?"

"Sure, but it was a long time ago. I don't remember much about it. I was..."

"What?"

Laurie shook his head. "Nothing. I was a lot younger at the time, that's all." He climbed on behind Jonathan. Wrapped his arms around his waist, felt the softness of Jonathan's shirt beneath his arms, breathed in the scent of good soap. "I'm ready."

The words were cut off by the sudden roar of the motor, heart-stopping in volume, as Jonathan kicked the machine into life. And then they were off, zipping down the road leading away from the facility entrance. The road was unpaved and in terrible shape. Every jolt and wobble convinced Laurie the bike would fly out of control and spill onto its side. Jonathan was as good of a driver as he'd claimed, though, and they flew along without incident.

After several nerve-shredding minutes of this, they reached the state highway. There were a few large potholes, which Jonathan did his best to avoid, but apart from that, the journey became much smoother and less traumatizing. They were the only vehicle around as far as Laurie could see. He clung to Jonathan and tried to view the situation as a madcap adventure.

The night grew cold and dark. Particles of dirt kicked up by the bike's wheels whipped at his skin in little pinpricks of pain. He buried his face into Jonathan's back and kept his eyes shut. The roar of the bike merged with his heartbeat, the engine powering his vital systems, making him feel alive and terrified and thrilled all at once.

Las Vegas. A golden glow on a black horizon that intensified as they approached it, until the dark night was bathed in radiant light. Laurie lifted his head and gawked openly. He'd been born in a city, and something in his soul rekindled and expanded at the sight of buildings. Not too many of them, and none were very tall, but since most of his last decade had been defined by wide, empty spaces, this felt... not quite like home, but like the beginning of something important. He'd been in a holding pattern for far too long, and while it wasn't quite time for him to fly, he could feel the grip of years of inertia beginning to ease.

Downtown, Fremont Street. Glittering lights, dazzling and colorful, each successive casino desperate to draw passersby into their illuminated interiors. Huge lit signs emblazoned with foot-high letters spelled out promises of girls and cash and sex and cocktails and lobster and more sex, glowing and pulsating with the magical words that would draw visitors inside to spend their money.

Jonathan stopped at a light. He swiveled his head around to talk to Laurie. "Well? Where do we find your friend?" he shouted over the roar of the bike.

Laurie's ears burned from the noise. He couldn't hear anything clearly, but he picked up the gist of Jonathan's words. "He works at the Saint-Tropez. I don't know exactly where it is."

Jonathan bobbed his head. "I know it. It's by the convention center," he shouted.

They continued down Fremont. There was some traffic here, yellow taxis mostly, plus some cars that looked in decent shape, better than the battered old trucks Laurie used to see on the dusty roads around the monastery. A stretch limousine slid past them, black and boxy, windows tinted the color of dark smoke. The lights of the casinos reflected off the polished exterior in a glittering display of distorted patterns, sleek and enticing.

The Saint-Tropez was easy to spot. It was a tall, blocky building of chrome and glass and concrete, the casino's name emblazoned in huge letters at the top, illuminated by a gajillion individual light bulbs. Matching twin rows of palm trees framed either side of the entrance. There was a valet stand out front, with two red-jacketed young men standing in attendance, but Jonathan ignored them and zipped into a mostly-empty public lot across the street.

Jonathan parked his bike. Laurie eased himself off of it. His thighs felt numb, and his neck hurt from keeping his head pressed into Jonathan's back for so long. Felt funny to be on solid ground, felt funny not to be hurtling through the desert at crazed speeds. "Should we find your friend?" Jonathan asked.

"I guess. That's what we're here for, right?" Laurie threw a longing glance down Fremont. Pretty lights and fancy food and beautiful people leading decadent, lavish lifestyles. Must be nice.

They crossed the street. Jonathan headed for the entrance to the Saint-Tropez; Laurie paused, hesitating on the sidewalk. Jonathan stopped and glanced back at him. "Laurie?"

"That's the convention center, right?" Laurie said. He gestured at the building beside the casino. It was a huge triangular structure, placed at an angle a dozen yards back from the sidewalk. Two high towers rose up from the back of the triangle. The exterior was paneled with panes of blue-green glass, many of them smashed, plywood boards haphazardly affixed over the worst of the damage. The doors had been removed from their hinges, leaving a dark gap at the open entrance. "I didn't realize it had closed."

"I don't think it ever opened," Jonathan said. "They sunk a lot of money into building it and never got it up and running."

Laurie shook his head. "It opened, I remember. The towers in back, they had hotel rooms there. I stayed there once."

He thought Jonathan said something, but he wasn't listening. He headed down the long walkway to the entrance. The sidewalk was cracked and overgrown with clumps of brown weeds. Broken glass crunched under his sandals.

Jonathan took his arm. "What are you doing?" he asked.

"I want to check it out," Laurie said. He slipped out of Jonathan's grip. "You can stay here. I'll just be a minute."

"It's not safe. There are probably people squatting there, and they probably don't want to be disturbed."

Laurie ignored him and continued down the sidewalk. Jonathan hesitated, then followed him. Laurie climbed the low cement steps and ventured through the open doorway.

This would've been the lobby. Laurie tried to match up the reality to his memories. No electricity, but the shattered windows let enough light in for him to get a good look. High ceilings, three levels of glass-walled balconies running along the perimeter of a wide open space. It'd been stripped of the furniture, the fixtures, the carpeting; Laurie walked across exposed floorboards.

It smelled rank in here, like unwashed bodies and old garbage. Jonathan was right, people were living here, dozens of them huddling against the walls inside makeshift cardboard shelters. A few faces turned in his direction. Laurie glimpsed unkempt hair and dull eyes.

Jonathan was right behind him. He rested a hand on his shoulder. "Laurie, this isn't safe."

"I know. I just wanted to see it. We can go now," Laurie said. He turned and followed Jonathan out.

"What was that about?" Jonathan asked when they were back on the sidewalk.

"Nostalgia. Like I said, I stayed there once," Laurie said. "Should we look for my friend?"

They approached the entrance to the Saint-Tropez. A doorman in a long red coat with gold braid at the shoulders and a matching gold-trimmed cap held open the door for them. "Have a happy and successful evening, gentlemen," he said.

Laurie was going to answer him, but then his attention was captured by the interior of the casino. Bells and chimes and the nonstop clatter of coins spilling into metal drawers, lights and movement everywhere. A thick green carpet, a black-walled interior lit by banks of gaudy multicolored slot machines. The clientele was largely male and largely middle-aged, everyone in flashy suits and gold chains. Leggy women in plunging one-piece gold bathing suits and gold sandals with teetering heels bore trays loaded with martini glasses and champagne flutes. Cigar smoke hung in the room like a low gray cloud.

Jonathan twisted his mouth in what seemed like distaste. "Where do we find your friend?"

"I don't know. I guess we look around for him."

"You think there's going to be any problem?" Jonathan asked.

"What? Finding him? We can always just ask someone." Laurie almost collided into one of the tray-bearing women. She winked at him and sashayed on her way.

"I mean in general. We're going to be asking about certain unlawful activities, and while it might look fun here, it can get dangerous. You know that, right?"

"Oh, sure, I know. But Dominick's okay." Laurie made his way through the crowd, Jonathan following. He craned his neck to look past the slot machines to the table games, which were held in a back section of the casino behind a wine-colored velvet rope. Ah, there. A head of close-cropped white hair, a deeply-tanned rodent-like face. "There's Dom. Let's go over and say hello."

Dominick was engaged in a conversation with a stocky man in a red velvet suit and a voluptuous woman in a backless turquoise-sequined cocktail gown. The couple looked unhappy and agitated; Dominick radiated nothing but laid-back good humor. He patted the man on the shoulder, then leaned closer and spoke earnestly to him.

Dom was short and lean. A white tuxedo to match his tidy white hair, his face appearing almost orange above his white satin bow tie. When he looked up from the couple, his eyes caught Laurie's. He nodded once at him, then continued his conversation.

"He sees us. Just wait a minute," Laurie said to Jonathan.

Jonathan exhaled. His expression was composed, even relaxed, but his posture seemed a little rigid.

"You're not worried about anything, are you?" Laurie asked.

Jonathan scowled. "It's fine." He darted a look over his shoulder at a sudden burst of raucous laughter from a group of men surrounding a nearby slot machine. "This just isn't my kind of place."

"I'm not sure it's mine either, frankly, but it's kind of neat being here, isn't it? I mean, this is the sort of thing I don't see every day."

"Yeah, but I did see this sort of thing every day. I used to work here, just down Fremont at Le Tigre. Haven't missed it. There's something a little poisonous about this city." Jonathan gestured with his chin toward Dominick. "I think he wants us to go over there."

Dom had apparently soothed over whatever conflict the couple had brought to his attention. Now alone, he beamed at Laurie and walked toward him, arms spread wide. "Holy hell, Laurie, it's good to see you! What are you doing here?" Laurie found himself caught up in Dom's wiry embrace. Dom released him, then clasped Laurie's small hand between both of his and pumped his arm. "You look great! You finally broke free of the brothers, huh?"

Dom would have to be told about the slaughter at the monastery, but the news could hold for the moment. "Something like that," Laurie said. "Dom, this is Jonathan. Jonathan, meet Dom."

A quick look up and down, a lightning-fast assessment of Jonathan, a flicker of uncertainty on Dom's face that vanished before it had time to settle. "Nice to meet you. Any friend of the kid gets automatic points with me." He stuck out his hand. There was an almost-imperceptible hesitation before Jonathan shook it.

"It's a surprise seeing you here, but it's not exactly the shock of the year you left that place. Hell, I remember when you first arrived at the monastery, back when you were just a little squirt. What were you, ten, eleven?"

"I can barely remember," Laurie said. He didn't dare look over at Jonathan.

"Even then you were a sophisticated little thing. I wouldn't have been surprised if you'd run off and headed for the nearest big city the second you were healed up enough to split."

"Healed up from getting shot, you mean?" Jonathan's tone was dry. Laurie felt his face grow warm. He assumed his most nonchalant expression.

"He told you about that? Yeah, he was still pretty weak when he showed up on our doorstep. Even then, though, he had a hell of a mouth on him. Drove us all crazy, the way he expected us to wait on him hand and foot." Dom winked at Laurie. "Good times. Hey, really, it's great to see you. You just taking in the sights, or…?"

"We're here to see you. Not entirely a social call."

"Figured as much. I'm on the clock. Give me the quick version."

"I've been staying at this place in the desert. Subterranean church, maybe a hundred miles northeast of here, not far from the monastery. The Church of the Scorched Earth," Laurie said.

"Jazzy name," Dominick said.

"It's located in an old government facility, and they threw away a bunch of equipment and files and stuff when they moved in, and six months ago someone scavenged it, but now they're looking to get it back. They wanted me to see if anyone in Vegas was selling it. They're trying to get in touch with the seller."

"What type of equipment?" Dominick's eyes were sharp and beady. They glittered with a sudden focus.

"Couldn't tell you. It was a communications facility, so it would be stuff about satellites. Computers, probably. I don't know much more than that."

"Huh," Dominick said. "I'm working the floor until four. I can put out some feelers while I'm here, then meet you in the lounge for a late dinner or early breakfast or whatever and compare notes. You guys cool with hanging out until then?"

According to the ornate golden clock dangling from the ceiling, it was just after nine, which meant they'd be hanging out for a while. Couldn't be helped. "Sure, no problem."

"You staying anywhere?"

Laurie shook his head. "We just arrived."

"I got some pull at the desk. You want a room, I can hook you up. On the house."

A hotel room. Laurie loved hotel rooms. He *missed* hotel rooms. "Really? That'd be fantastic." He didn't dare look at Jonathan, so he had no idea what he thought of the idea, but he didn't care. He wanted a hotel room, damn it, and they were going to have one, and Jonathan had no say in the matter.

"Come with me." Dominick bustled them through the casino and into the attached hotel. He guided them across the lobby, all glass and gold and big velvet sofas and huge leafy potted palms, and led them to the front counter. After a few words with the poodle-haired woman in a gold tuxedo vest behind the desk, he handed Laurie a key on a bronze numbered tag. "Here you go. Twelfth floor. You're all set. See you guys at four, right?"

"Thanks, Dom," Laurie said. Next to him, Jonathan was silent and, Laurie suspected, disapproving.

They stepped into a chunky bronze elevator that smelled of perfume and cigar smoke, the green velvet carpeting worn down to threads, and rose swiftly up to their floor. They had a single room, not a suite, and while Laurie knew he had no grounds to be snobby—hey, free room!—it still disappointed him, just a little. It was pretty, though. Same green velvet carpet as in the elevator, a black velvet sofa, a black marble dining table trimmed in gold. A king-sized bed with a wildly patterned black-and-gold jacquard comforter and a reassuring stack of pillows arranged in front of the leather-wrapped headboard. Laurie slipped off his sandals and padded barefoot across the room, the luxurious feel of velvet unfamiliar to his feet.

He proceeded to the heavy green drapes and yanked them open to reveal a panoramic view of the city, the low desert hills on the horizon and the glittering lights in the foreground. Only this small stretch of downtown was lit up, just the casinos and hotels and maybe a few fancy restaurants; beyond them, he saw the spectral outlines of dark office buildings, apartment complexes, homes. Off the power grid, probably; they probably turned off their generators at night to conserve energy, much like Pastor Kyle's church did.

Jonathan stood at his shoulder. "Nice view," he said.

"Yeah." Laurie stared in silence for a moment. "You ever wonder what it should look like?"

"Hmm?"

"If the bombs hadn't fallen, I mean. We've lost about thirty years of advancement. Ever stop to think where we should be, progress-wise, if that hadn't happened?"

"Not particularly. It did happen. Before either of us were born, it happened."

"Yeah, I know. But…" Laurie gestured at the skyline. "This city, these buildings, there's not much new here, you know? Some of it was rebuilt, sure, but not enough. Everything kind of stopped in 1984, and it hasn't really started up again. By now, that skyline should be bigger, shinier, sparklier."

"I think it's got enough sparkle for my taste as it is," Jonathan said. "Nice of your friend to spot us the room."

"He's a good guy. Or he might not be *good*, exactly, but he's always been nice to me."

Jonathan flopped down on the sofa. More reluctantly, Laurie tore his attention from the skyline and sat beside him. Jonathan threw him a sidelong look, and Laurie knew, just knew, what he was going to ask. "Should we discuss it?"

"What do you mean?"

"How you're a rotten little liar." Jonathan sounded amused. "You told me you'd been at the monastery since you were a baby. And you insisted that wasn't a bullet wound."

"I didn't think my past was any of your business. Still don't," Laurie said. "I do lie sometimes, I freely admit that, but it's not out of malice or anything. It's more like taking a conversational short-cut. I don't like talking about things that bore me."

"So you're not going to tell me how you got shot?"

"Hadn't planned on it. I'll just point out that I was eleven at the time, and I didn't deserve it."

Jonathan stared at him for a long while. It was hard to read his expression. He nodded. "Okay," he said. "So how do we pass the time before we meet Dominick?"

"You can do whatever you want. I'm staying right here." Laurie tilted his neck over the back of the sofa and stared up at the ceiling. A large brown circle of water damage spread out from the corner, and the plaster was cracked around the dangling bronze pendant lamp. "Do we have a bathtub here? Did you see if we did?"

He got to his feet and peeked inside the bathroom. Green marble floors and countertops, glossy black porcelain fixtures. A gigantic marble tub was built into the bathroom floor, so big it had stairs leading down into it, so big it could fit a small party inside it. Laurie let out a happy sigh at the sight. "Hooray. We do. I'm going to spend the next hour or so using up all the hot water in this entire building, and there's nothing you can do to stop me."

"Knock yourself out," Jonathan said.

A cluster of free toiletries in tiny bottles rested in a basket on the rim of the tub, shampoo and bubble bath and pale ovals of soap that smelled like flower gardens. He filled the tub, gratified by the rush of hot water that roared through the taps, then dumped in the bubble bath, shed his clothes, and stepped in.

Glorious. Heaven. Easily the greatest thing that had happened to him in recent history, this bath. Laurie shampooed and soaped every inch of himself, then soaked in the scented water, adding more hot water as soon as it started to cool down. When he felt he'd exploited the tub to its fullest, he dried himself off on a fluffy towel with the Saint-Tropez name embroidered in gold, then swaddled himself in an enormous green velour bathrobe that hung on a hook on the back of the bathroom door. He could get used to this lifestyle very easily.

When he finally padded back out into the room, clean and pink and wrinkly, he found the dining table covered with a white linen cloth. Jonathan lifted metal domes from several platters of food. He grinned at Laurie.

"Your friend sent us dinner. On the house," he said. He raised the final dome with a flourish. A grilled steak lay on the porcelain platter beneath it, a real steak, accompanied by a mound of mashed potatoes, whipped and creamy and piped out into stiff flower shapes. Laurie looked at the other platters. A rack of lamb, the bone tips swaddled in ruffled paper booties. Gigantic pink shrimp on skewers, a slab of chocolate cake topped with vanilla ice cream. A bottle of champagne in a silver bucket. Laurie's eyes widened.

"Is that champagne? *Real* champagne?" He plopped down at the table and reached for it. Fancy bottle, indecipherable French writing scrawled across the black label. "How do you open it? You just pop the cork, right?"

He fumbled to tear off the foil and remove the wire cage surrounding the cork. He yanked at the cork in vain. "It's not coming. Do we need a corkscrew or something?"

"Here." Jonathan took the bottle from him. He wrapped a linen napkin around the neck and eased the cork out with a soft pop. Laurie was a little disappointed it didn't sail across the room. Jonathan poured it out into two graceful cut-glass flutes and passed one to Laurie. "There you go. You might not like it. First time drinking it, it can be kind of rough on the palate."

"I'll like it. I know I'll like it." Laurie raised his glass in the air. "Cheers."

"To the generosity of your friend," Jonathan said. He clinked his glass against Laurie's. Laurie let it roll across his taste buds. Sour taste, almost bitter, almost harsh, and yet so sophisticated and glamorous that none of that mattered.

They dug into the food. Damn. Laurie could get used to this. He wolfed down everything in sight, drained his glass, poured himself more. Jonathan, who was eating with gusto but more restraint, nodded at the bucket. "You might want to be careful with that. You don't weigh much, it'll go straight to your head."

"I certainly hope so." Laurie giggled. "Come on, you can't say you're not having a good time." He leaned across the table and topped off Jonathan's glass with more champagne.

They ate and drank in silence. Laurie felt happy, warm and secure and full of a glowing, all-encompassing love for everything around him.

"Are you planning on going out tonight?" Jonathan asked. "Hit the town, play the slots, find romance with one of those leggy women in bathing suits?"

Laurie upended the bottle over his glass. A few paltry drops trickled out. A terrible shame. "I should think it'd be obvious leggy women aren't a big draw for me."

Jonathan's lips twitched. "Well, yeah, but I didn't want to make assumptions." He sipped at his champagne while examining Laurie. "Are you and Dominick…?"

Laurie wrinkled his nose. "Ew. No way."

"I thought that might be why he arranged all this for us. Seems like a pretty nice perk for just an acquaintance."

"As I said before, he likes me. Many people do. I'm very likeable, you know. But he's not my type. Too old, for starters."

"How old are you, anyway? You're so small, and you act like just a kid sometimes, but then other times you almost seem like an adult."

"I'm old. I'm, like, really old. I'm twenty-four." Laurie settled back in his chair and regarded him. "What about you? Planning on going out tonight? Going in search of those leggy women?"

It sounded like more of a taunt than he'd intended, but Jonathan didn't take the bait. "I'm going to get some sleep. You might want to do the same. We've still got several hours before meeting your friend." He hesitated, looking around the room. "I can take the couch."

"Don't be stupid. The bed is huge, and as you've pointed out before, I don't take up much space." Laurie got to his feet. The room tilted a bit, but he'd be damned if he'd let Jonathan have the satisfaction of knowing he was right to warn him about drinking too much, so he took pains to walk very, very carefully, no wobbling or stumbling.

There was a behemoth of a television, a gigantic clunky cube that took up most of the top of the dresser, and he was curious to see if it worked. He sat on the edge of the bed and twisted a broken dial. The television surged into life in a snowstorm of static and incoherent noise. The static resolved itself into a fuzzy picture; Laurie fiddled and fussed with the twin antennae until the image became clear. "I haven't watched television since I was a kid. We didn't have one in the monastery," he said.

"It's going to be the same crap you remember from your childhood. And by that I mean literally the same crap," Jonathan said. "I don't think any networks have been in operation for the past decade. Nothing big, in any case."

Laurie glanced up from his careful antennae ministrations. "None? Why?"

"Federal restoration money kept the networks afloat for a while, but that's all been cut off. Nobody has the funds necessary to run a full-fledged network, so TV has been a dead zone. Repeats of old shows, maybe some local reports, that kind of stuff. You haven't missed much." Jonathan grinned. "Are you still awake? You're leaning. You look like you're about to topple onto your side."

Laurie struggled to sit upright. "Champagne might be hitting me, just a little," he said with great dignity.

"Imagine that." Jonathan pulled off his shoes. "You sure you don't mind sharing the bed?"

"Not a bit." Laurie stared at the television screen. It was broadcasting some sitcom he sort of remembered, something about an army medical team during some war he'd never studied in school. Vietnam? He didn't think that was quite it.

Jonathan neatly folded the blankets and sheets back. Still fully clothed, he slid beneath the covers. "Good night, Laurie." He reached over and switched off the bedside lamp.

Laurie flipped the dial around to other channels and found only static. He turned off the TV. He felt drunk and warm and happy. Still wrapped in the soft, velvety folds of the bathrobe, he climbed into the other side of the bed and pulled the covers up around his neck. Nice to be here, with Jonathan.

He fell asleep.

CHAPTER EIGHT

Jonathan shook him awake at three-thirty. A trip down in the elevator, a confused trek around the casino floor, and finally they found the lounge. Dark and small. No sign of Dominick, so they nestled into a corner booth to wait. The booth was red leather with brass tacks along the top and sides; someone had gouged the leather across the back, and it'd been patched together with a great deal of white glue. A topless woman in a gold sequined miniskirt sang a torch song on a stage next to the bar.

A waitress approached. Same gold sequined skirt, same lack of a shirt, though she wore a sparkly gold bowtie at her throat to add what Laurie assumed was a professional touch. "Drinks, gentlemen?"

Laurie felt moderately awful from the champagne, thick and slow-witted. He shook his head. "Two coffees. Strong as you've got it," Jonathan said to the waitress.

She smiled and retreated to the bar. Jonathan leaned across the table. "I did warn you about drinking too much."

"Nobody likes a know-it-all," Laurie said. "I don't see Dom."

"We're early. Have patience."

The waitress plopped two mugs of coffee on the table, along with the check. Jonathan drew a wad of cash out of his canvas shoulder bag and paid her.

The coffee was black and bitter, almost sticky with congealed oils. Laurie winced and emptied a small stack of tiny paper envelopes of sugar into his mug. Didn't improve it. Jonathan sipped his without comment; Laurie tried to drink his, then decided it'd do his fragile stomach more harm than good and pushed it away.

"If you're going to throw up, at least give me ample notice, okay?" Jonathan said.

"I won't. I'm fine," Laurie said in his most injured tone. "The coffee's just really, really awful."

"It certainly is. Either drink it or don't; it won't kill you. You complain a lot, don't you?"

Laurie ignored him. He stared at the singer on the stage. "She's not very good, is she?"

"Not especially. But I doubt you could do any better."

"You never know," Laurie said. "I might have hidden talents."

"I'm sure you do." Jonathan looked bemused. "But I'm not sure singing is one of them."

While Laurie was trying to decide whether he'd just been insulted, three men in expensive suits approached their table. Big. Broad shoulders. Very broad. Kind of scary. Without changing his expression, Jonathan sat up a little straighter. "Something we can help you with?" he asked.

The middle guy stepped closer. He was the smallest of the three, which probably meant he was in charge. Short and barrel-chested, in a green plaid suit with a pale lavender shirt beneath it. "Him," he said. He pointed at Laurie and addressed Jonathan. "I'll give you two hundred for him. Right now, no hassle."

"Why?" Jonathan asked. He seemed composed.

"Kid looks like him, I can find a use. Two hundred in cash, and he leaves with me."

Laurie watched this with a faint sense of unreality. He should probably be scared, but it was impossible to summon up more than a mild curiosity to see how this turned out.

"Not interested," Jonathan said. "Get lost."

The man looked over Laurie once more, then shrugged. "Your loss," he said. He turned to leave, gesturing with his head for his entourage to follow him. The men moved on.

Jonathan watched them until they left the lounge. "So that was creepy. You okay?"

Laurie frowned. "Two hundred seems kind of low, right?"

"Huh?"

"Two hundred. I mean, I don't know the going rates around here, but if you were going to buy me, you'd expect to pay a lot more than that, wouldn't you?"

"I wouldn't buy you, Laurie."

"No, I know, but if you wanted to, I'd probably be really expensive, right?"

Jonathan stared at him. "You have the weirdest priorities," he said. "And you're welcome."

"Oh. Right. Sorry. Thanks for getting rid of them." Laurie stared at the door, still frowning. "Though it didn't seem like he was too invested in me. He didn't even try to haggle."

"Don't sound so disappointed. I could've haggled right back, you know. Aren't you at least a little concerned about that? I could've sold you off to him and pocketed the cash, then told Pastor Kyle you'd ditched me. Didn't that even cross your mind?"

"No, because you wouldn't do that. You're not that kind of person. Obviously."

"Well, no, I'm not, but there's no way you can be sure of that. You've only known me a couple days. You shouldn't be so trusting."

"I don't trust everyone. But I like you. You wouldn't do anything to hurt me." Laurie nodded toward the door. "Dom's here."

Dominick, looking as crisp and composed as he had several hours ago, crossed over to their table and slid into the booth. "Hey, how's it going?" he asked. To the hovering topless waitress, he said without looking, "Whiskey, neat."

"Bitch of a night," he said to Laurie and Jonathan. "Whole lot of problems on the floor."

"What do you do here, exactly?" Jonathan asked.

"I solve problems," Dominick said. His tone didn't invite discussion on the topic. "So how's the room? How's everything going?"

"The room's fantastic. Thanks for the dinner," Laurie said. "Hey, some guy just tried to buy me."

"Yeah? Not surprising. You've always been a real pretty kid," Dominick said. Jonathan stirred in his seat, but said nothing. "You sent him on his way?"

"Jonathan did," Laurie said.

Dom nodded at Jonathan, then shifted his attention back to Laurie. "You haven't told me what you're up to these days. Why'd you leave the monastery?"

"Not by choice." Laurie frowned. "A group of guys, some gang, they stormed the place. I got out, but I don't think anyone else did."

"No shit, huh? Everyone got killed?" Dominick raised his eyebrows. "Damn, that's rough."

"Yeah." Laurie tried not to think about it. As long as he could distract his brain, he was okay. "But I made it across the desert to that church I mentioned—it's this whole big compound or something, I don't know, it's all underground—and that's where I met Jonathan."

"Yeah? You a churchgoing man, Jonathan?" Dom's gaze flickered over Jonathan.

"Not really," Jonathan said.

"What do you do there, anyway?" Dom asked.

"Director of operations. I've been handling the business end of things."

"Ah." Dominick stared at Jonathan, a long, searching stare. The waitress brought his whiskey; Dominick took a long pull from it, then turned his attention back to Laurie. "I made some discreet inquiries about the junk you're looking for, and yeah, it surfaced here. Few months ago, this gentleman of my acquaintance was trying to fence some stuff that sounds about like what you're after. Gigantic old computers, not functional, but maybe good for parts. He said his source was a little cagey about where it came from, but it looked like government issue."

Laurie and Jonathan exchanged glances. "Did he ever sell the stuff?" Laurie asked.

"Uh-huh. No takers around here, but he sent out feelers beyond Vegas. A buyer in California eventually surfaced, bought the whole shebang, carted it all back to Pasadena."

"Pasadena," Jonathan said.

Dom nodded. "Caltech. You know, the school, right? My guy wasn't too keen to give me the name of the buyer, but I convinced him you wouldn't cause problems, Laurie. He said it was a Japanese guy, said he was kind of sketchy. Name of Izumi."

"How was he sketchy?" Laurie asked.

A headshake. "Didn't say. Just that the whole thing was a little weird, but hell, he was a paying customer, and one who lived all the way on the coast, so it's not likely their paths would cross again. He took the money, and that was that."

Pasadena. Caltech. That'd be a dead end; Pastor Kyle wouldn't expect him to go that far in pursuit of the missing files and equipment. "Okay. Thanks for looking into that, Dom. I appreciate it."

"For you, kid, I'm happy to go to some trouble," Dominick said. "You should know, I asked a few questions about that church of yours while I was at it. Church of the Scorched Earth, that place has a real bad name around here."

Jonathan sat upright. "What have you heard?" he asked.

"I'm talking to Laurie. Not you," Dominick said. "You work there, you probably can't convince me this is anything you don't already know."

"I've worked there all of six weeks. There's a whole lot about that place that I don't know, and the more I find out, the faster I can start fixing things." Dominick seemed unconvinced. Jonathan leaned across the table. "Look, up until recently, I worked just down the street at Le Tigre. Night manager in the hotel for the past three years. Ask your contacts, they'd probably know about me, and they'd know I'm clean." He sat back in the booth. "So what have you heard?"

Dominick stared at him, then exhaled. He turned to Laurie. "This church. They got a supply of kids there? Teenagers, I mean, maybe ones who don't have anyone looking after their best interests, ones who don't have anywhere else to go?"

"Sure, yeah," Laurie said. "Orphans stay there for free, as long as they do chores."

"They do a whole lot more than that." Another glance at Jonathan. "The former director of the church, I guess that'd be the guy who used to have your job, he used to do a lot of purchasing in this area. Nice clothes, flowers, furniture, all sorts of expensive things for the church. Sometimes he'd pay in cash, sometimes he'd pay in trade."

"The orphans," Jonathan said. His voice sounded flat.

"The orphans, yeah. Teens are in short supply around here, at least ones that aren't all used up, and there's a big demand. You have a girl, and if she's cute enough and clean enough, you can find someone willing to pay for her. Boys, too."

Laurie's eyes widened. "That's horrible," he said. "The church was doing that? That has to be illegal."

"Well, yeah, of course it is. But dial back the revulsion a notch. Near as I can tell, no one was coerced. Those orphans, if you talk to them, I bet you'll find some who think going to Las Vegas and earning some nice money in the hotels sounds a lot more appealing than scrubbing toilets in some crappy underground church," Dominick said. "But it's a lousy situation all around, not going to lie."

Jonathan stared at Dominick. "That sort of thing won't happen with me in charge."

"Yeah? How much are you in charge? You're not much more than a kid yourself, and no offense, but you don't seem like much of a force to be reckoned with," Dominick said. "Look, it's not like your church is doing anything that other places aren't doing, and I'm not going to feel too personally invested in the fates of a bunch of kids I don't know. Laurie, though, I know Laurie pretty well, and that church of yours isn't someplace he should be."

Laurie's brain seemed to be moving too slowly, still processing what Dominick had said. The girls, Cara and Melody, they'd talked about the kids who'd left the church...

It took him a second to realize Dominick was addressing him. "So you want to stay here? I got a nice place, I can take care of you, maybe find you work in the casino. No obligations."

Laurie's first instinct was to refuse, but Jonathan started talking before he could express this. "That's not a bad idea, actually," he said. He turned to Laurie. "You know it's not safe for you in the church with Kirby around. If Dominick can protect you, that'll solve your problem."

"But I can't stay here," Laurie said. "I have to go back with you. I mean, the satellite..."

"You're still thinking about that?" Jonathan asked. "The satellite's a pipe dream. You know that."

"No, I know, but..." Laurie turned to Dominick. "Dom, thanks, that's a totally great offer, and I appreciate it, but I can't. I need to go back to the church with Jonathan."

Dominick stared at him for a long, hard moment. "Don't make stupid life decisions just because you've got a crush, kid."

To Laurie's eternal gratitude, Jonathan stayed silent at that. "I'm sure I don't know what you're talking about," Laurie said. "It's nice that you're concerned about me, but I'm fine on my own."

Dominick huffed out a sigh and leaned back in the booth. He gulped down the last swallow of his whiskey. "Suit yourself. You got to live your own life, I suppose." He nodded at Jonathan. "Just make sure that guy takes good care of you. You require a lot of supervision, you know."

Laurie spoke before Jonathan could jump in to explain that it wasn't his job to take care of him. "I know. I do. I'm awful that way."

"Okay, then." Dom smiled and seemed to relax. "Hey, I'd stay and get caught up, but I've been on my feet all evening and I got to crash. Change your mind, you can find me here most nights." He got to his feet.

"One more thing, Dom. What do you know about Zephyr?" Laurie asked.

Dominick paused. He wrinkled his brow. "Zephyr? The security guys?"

"Yeah. They're crawling all over the church. Just wondering if you know anything. Anything bad, I mean. They're creepy."

"They're okay, far as I know. I mean, they've been around for years. You run into them all over the place in town, they've got their main offices here. A lot of the casinos have standing contracts with them instead of hiring their own security people. They seem to attract a lot of power-mad dickheads, but you can say the same about any security service. They're not *evil*."

Laurie nodded. "Okay. Thanks."

Dom clapped him on the shoulder in affection. "Good seeing you, Laurie. I'm glad no one killed you."

"Me, too." A nod to Jonathan, and then Dominick was gone.

Jonathan turned to Laurie. "You know, I don't like any of this."

"The orphans? Yeah, me either. You think Pastor Kyle knew about that?"

"I'm not sure it matters. It's his church. If he didn't know, he should've. Let's get back and see what he has to say. I'd like to get out of Vegas sooner rather than later."

Laurie was inclined to agree. He loved their hotel room—the bathtub especially—but was sort of on the fence about the rest of the city. He trailed Jonathan out of the cocktail lounge, out through the casino, out to the parking lot where the motorcycle was parked. It was still dark out, no hint of sunrise yet.

On the back of the bike again, which was still terrifying, flying down dark streets. Getting out of the city was a little hairy, as all of the lights beyond the immediate downtown area were black. Jonathan steered as if by instinct, navigating the streets like a bat moving around a pitch-dark cave.

The sun came up as they made it out of the city limits, the first beams of red fire peering above the low hills of the desert. Laurie was glad to see it.

They sped along a barren stretch of the highway. An old gas station, the pumps removed and the windows missing, a burned-out shell of a car in the middle of a field, not much in the way of anything else, nothing living or vibrant. Just outside of Vegas, a flatbed truck passed them on the road, its open back stacked high with crates. Jonathan pointed after it, and Laurie took his meaning: The truck was heading toward the church, delivering food and supplies.

It was daylight when the bike broke down. Laurie first became aware of a reduction in speed and noise, the omnipresent roar lowering to a dull rush and then fading away altogether as they rolled to a gradual stop on the shoulder. "Shit," Jonathan said.

"What is it? Are you out of gas?" Laurie asked. His ears still roared from the noise, and he suspected he was inadvertently shouting, because Jonathan flinched away. He crawled off the back of the seat.

"This happens sometimes. Condensed air gets in the tank, and it messes up the works for a while. Only thing to do is wait it out." Jonathan got off the bike and walked it further onto the shoulder.

He crouched down and unscrewed the top of the gas tank. Laurie heard a small moist pop. Jonathan wrinkled his nose in irritation. "Yeah. We'll have to let it cool down. Lucky thing it's not hot out yet."

"We're not too far from the church, are we? Maybe somebody will come by and give us a ride."

"Believe me, we're not going to want a ride from anyone who comes by here." Jonathan looked frustrated and cranky. Laurie knew how he felt. "That delivery truck that passed us, it'll have to come back this way on the return trip, but that won't be for a couple of hours. We'll be long gone by then."

Laurie stretched his arms above his head, then bent and touched his toes. His back hurt from hunching forward and grabbing Jonathan's waist. He looked down the highway. Nothing coming in either direction.

Wait. A low buzz in the air, a pack of gigantic hornets coming from a great distance, honing in for the kill. Motorcycles.

"Hey, Jonathan? I think someone might be coming," he said. Mouth felt a little dry, heartbeat increased its rhythm.

Jonathan faced the noise, alert. He nodded. "I hear it."

"Should we hide?" Laurie asked. "It might be nothing, but..."

Jonathan was searching the horizon before he even finished the sentence. He pointed off the road at a ramshackle structure a few hundred yards away. Looked like a shed, ruined and long-abandoned. "Head there. Run. Fast as you can. I'll be right behind you."

Laurie ran, spurred into action by the supercharged spike of fear coursing through him. Bikes, several bikes, coming this way.

Didn't mean it was the gang that had slaughtered everyone at his monastery, but it could be, and he didn't want to hang around to see if his fears were justified.

The shed turned out to be a small house, partially burned, one wall entirely crumbled away. Laurie hopped up through the ruined entryway, charred floorboards sagging and cracking under his slight weight, then turned to see Jonathan close behind him. "Did you see them?"

"Yeah. Keep moving. There's five of them. They saw us." Jonathan grabbed Laurie by the arm. "Come on."

He half-dragged Laurie toward the back of the house. A small, bare bedroom, a gutted kitchen, a shell of a bathroom. "We'll pull up the floorboards and hide underneath. It's our only option."

Laurie shook his head. "Better idea. Here." He pulled Jonathan into the bedroom. A large jagged hole revealed a narrow gap between the bedroom and bathroom walls. It started a couple feet off the ground and wasn't much more than a foot wide, with remnants of long disused electrical wiring dangling down from it.

He stepped into the gap. Tight. Very tight. He slid into the space between the walls, angling his body to take up as little room as possible.

"In here. There's room for both of us," he said. He spoke low and fast. "Come on."

He squeezed back as far as he could into the space, trying not to choke on the dust that kicked up and filled his lungs. Jonathan joined him in the narrow gap. Much maneuvering, much shifting, and then they were both wedged inside the wall, hidden from sight.

Laurie grabbed Jonathan's hand and yanked him closer, drawing him as deep into the cramped space as possible, until they were pressed up against each other, no room to move, barely room to breathe. He wrapped his arms around Jonathan's waist and locked his hands around his own wrists. No way to escape. If they were discovered, they'd be dead. He stayed as still as he could, gripping Jonathan until his arm muscles twitched.

Footsteps on the decaying floorboards, the sound of large men with heavy boots. "Damn it all. Where'd they go?"

A male voice, harsh and angry, and Laurie had to resist the compulsion to shudder. Jonathan's hands gripped his shoulders, his chin resting on the top of his head. He felt firm and warm and comforting.

"They went in here. Nowhere else they could run." Another male voice.

"You get a good look?"

"Girl and a boy. Didn't get much of a look at the girl. We catch up to them, I'll get a better look and let you know what I think of her."

A laugh. Laurie didn't breathe. He kept still, very still. He and Jonathan were statues, or they were dead already, corpses waiting to be discovered in the dirty walls of a burned-out shell of a house in this wreck of a land.

"Yeah, well, there's nobody here." Sounds of scuffling. Walls kicked in frustration, loose floorboards tossed aside. "Maybe they ran out the back."

"Check under the house. There's a crawlspace." Heavy boots stomping, kicking through the floor, broken boards ripped up by hand. "Hello? Little rabbits, anyone down there?"

"We lost them. They went out the back, they're gone."

"Nowhere to go. They try to run across the desert, easy thing to hunt them down."

More noises, more booted feet on the floorboards. Retreating voices, a lengthy silence, and then the roar of their motorcycles again. Jonathan started to pull away almost as soon as the engines started, but Laurie held him in place. "Not yet. Wait," he said, his words garbled against Jonathan's chest.

Jonathan just patted his shoulders in response. A full minute passed, then another, and then Jonathan pulled gently out of his grip. "It's safe now, Laurie," he said.

It was harder to get out, because they'd wedged themselves in as deep as they could go, and Jonathan had no room in which to turn. He slid backwards, inch by inch, until he reached the gap in the wall. He stepped back into the bedroom, then reached in to guide Laurie out.

Laurie's knees buckled upon standing on the floorboards. He couldn't stop trembling, and it was hard to breathe. Every time he'd try to inhale, his breath would get caught midway to his lungs. Felt like his heart might burst from lack of oxygen.

"Breathe, Laurie. Deep breaths. They're gone. You're okay," Jonathan said. He rubbed Laurie's shoulders. "You did great. They didn't know we were here."

Laurie nodded. The panic receded a little, just another visitor at the gathering instead of the guest of honor. "They could come back, though."

"We'll be gone before they do. We're going to be fine." Jonathan's calm voice helped stabilize Laurie's shot nerves even further. He could probably stand on his own now, even without Jonathan holding him upright, but it felt better to have his support. "Were they the same guys who destroyed your monastery?"

"I have no idea. I didn't see them." An overwhelming wave of exhaustion crashed over Laurie, almost knocking him to the floor. "It doesn't matter. It's not like they were better or worse than the other gang."

"Okay." Still that same calm tone. "We're going to head back for my bike, okay? Keep next to me. We should have plenty of warning in case they circle back, but we're going to do this fast, all right?"

"Sure." It was hard, very hard, to leave the dubious protection of the ruined house. The desert seemed too wide open and terrifying in its bleakness. They didn't run, just walked quickly toward the road. Laurie had to resist the urge to cling to Jonathan again. He still felt light-headed with fear, unstable, like his head weighed more than the rest of his body, like he could topple to the ground at any minute.

"Crap." Jonathan spotted it first. The motorcycle, their only transportation back to the church, was now a tangled ruin of metal beside the road.

"Will it start?" Laurie asked, and then regretted it. It was twisted and crushed, mangled beyond repair, the back tire completely detached. Maybe someone could fix it, but it'd require time and tools, neither of which they had.

Jonathan shook his head. The sun inched up the horizon. Not blisteringly hot yet, but warming up.

"We're going to have to walk to the church," he said. Matter-of-fact, his tone brisk and neutral. "We're probably still twenty miles away. Could be less. It's doable."

"Is it?" Laurie asked. "We're going to enter the heat of the day, and we don't have any water, and if we walk on the road that gang might find us." His voice sounded a little high and squeaky.

"What are the options?" Jonathan asked. "You walked almost that much a couple days ago on a twisted ankle, and you survived. We'll manage."

"I almost died, though," Laurie said. "I don't think I can do it again."

"Tough luck. You're going to have to. Come on." Jonathan started walking along the shoulder. Laurie hesitated.

"Are we going to take your bike? Maybe it can be repaired."

"Leave it. It can't help us, and it'll just slow us down." Jonathan kept walking. He seemed certain of the direction. That was good news, at least, as Laurie had gotten himself hopelessly turned around during their recent brush with terror, and now he had no idea which way led to the church and which led back to Las Vegas.

Laurie fell into step with him, because of course Jonathan was right and there was nothing else to do, but he felt a sinking hopelessness encompass him. They were too exposed here. They'd die of heat stroke, or dehydration, or they'd be slaughtered by the motorcyclists or by any other roving pack of miscreants that happened to come along.

Jonathan's expression was soft. "We're going to be fine, Laurie," he said. "The delivery truck will come back this way soon enough, and if we have a little bit of luck, we'll flag it down and talk them into taking us back to the church."

He smiled to himself. "Besides, didn't you tell me you were tougher than you looked?"

"I don't think I am, though," Laurie said. "I don't even think I want to be. I like clean sheets and nice hotel rooms and champagne."

"Don't we all?" A genuine smile this time, a flash of nice teeth. "But even still, you seem to handle yourself okay under rough circumstances. You're more of a survivor than you let on."

Almost without thinking, Laurie's hand crept to the long-healed bullet wound on his right side. He fell silent and walked alongside Jonathan.

They trudged on. The sun rose and rose, shining in the sky like a lethal orange fireball. Laurie's throat grew dry. His sandaled feet hurt. This was too much like his exodus from the monastery, and unlike Jonathan, he had no faith he'd be lucky enough to survive it twice.

CHAPTER NINE

They'd been walking for about an hour by Laurie's estimation when they saw the vehicle. His ankle, which he'd thought was fully healed, had begun to throb along the way, a dull pain that grew more pressing the further they trudged. He was thirsty and exhausted; his mouth felt fuzzy and sour, his tongue thick and clumsy.

Jonathan still seemed dewy-fresh and filled with vigor, which was irksome. He strode along easily, hands in his pants pockets. He didn't talk much, just glanced at Laurie at frequent intervals, as though making sure he was still alive.

He straightened up at the sight of the vehicle on the horizon and tapped Laurie on the arm. "There," he said.

It wasn't much more than a dark dot heading in the direction of the church. Laurie felt a flash of fear. "Should we hide?" he asked.

Jonathan shook his head. "It's not a motorcycle. We could try to hitch a ride," he said. He sounded nonchalant. The set of his jaw was a little tense, maybe, the visible cords in his neck the only outer sign of tension.

This was the only vehicle to come down this road since they'd been stranded. Friend or foe, the driver was their best chance for survival.

It was a jeep. Charcoal gray body, no doors or windows or roof. Two occupants in the front seat, both in mirrored aviator sunglasses. As they drew nearer, Jonathan waved his arms above his head.

It worked. The jeep pulled over to the shoulder and stopped a few yards ahead of them. Laurie followed Jonathan over to the passenger side.

There was a yellow Zephyr logo painted on the side of the hood. Both the driver and his passenger wore button-down shirts with the sleeves rolled up. Laurie spotted their dark Zephyr jackets folded up on the tiny backseat. Both were men, both in their early forties.

Jonathan held both hands up in the air as he approached, making it clear he was harmless. "Thanks for stopping," he said. "Are you guys heading to the Church of the Scorched Earth?"

"That's right." The man in the passenger seat smiled at them. Dark hair, attractive features. He was movie-star handsome almost, with straight teeth and a cleft chin. Laurie stared at his face for a long time. "That where you boys are heading?"

"We ran into some trouble a few miles back. We were on our way back from Vegas and had a bad encounter with some gang. They smashed my bike," Jonathan said. "I work at the church, I'm the director of operations, and if you're heading in that direction, we could really use a lift."

"You must be the new guy. I don't think we've met yet." The man smiled again. Firm jaw, clean-shaven. Laurie wished he could see his eyes behind his sunglasses, because he had the sick, sinking feeling he knew who this was. "Fisher? Something like that?"

"Frisch. Jonathan Frisch."

"Nice to meet you, Frisch. I'm Ferris. Western division chief." He gestured with his head at the driver. "This is Cowell, he works in my office. This is good timing, actually. We were driving over to speak to you anyway, and it's just as good to hear the full story from you before we arrive at the church."

"Full story?" Jonathan asked.

"You know Rosado? My deputy liaison? She radioed the office day before yesterday, said you'd talked to her about some trouble with my men. Said the pastor and his wife were disinclined to do much about it, but you were feeling sufficiently steamed that she thought we should look into it."

"Great, yeah, absolutely," Jonathan said. "That's great that Rosado contacted you. Yeah, we've had behavioral problems with some of the guards, and nobody seems to be taking it seriously."

"Hop in the back," Ferris said. "You can fill me in on the way to the church." He nodded at Laurie. "Who's this?"

Jonathan climbed into the backseat, scooting over to give Laurie room beside him. "This is Laurie, he's been staying at the church. He's been sort of in the middle of all the trouble, so he might be able to help you out."

"Laurie…" Ferris stared at him through the mirrored glasses. Laurie felt his knees lock. If Ferris recognized him…

Ferris smiled. Seemed relaxed and genuine. "You don't look like trouble, Laurie."

If he climbed in the jeep, he'd be trapped. Every fiber of his being wanted to balk, but what choice did he have? He'd die in the desert on his own.

Then again, he'd die if Ferris recognized him. He was pretty sure of that.

All options stank. He climbed in beside Jonathan. His palm left a sticky, sweaty print against the vinyl seat. He was soaked with perspiration, the back of Patricia's blouse plastered to his skin. The sweat seemed to chill him, incongruous on this hellishly hot day.

He nodded at both men, ducking his head. "Nice to meet you both. Thanks for the lift."

"Lived at the church long, Laurie?" Ferris asked. He smiled. It seemed like an idle question. Friendly, just making conversation.

"No, sir. I was at a monastery outside Mesquite before this. Lived there since I was a baby." Jonathan would know that was a lie, but surely he wouldn't call him out on it right now. "It was raided by a gang a few days ago, so I took sanctuary with the church."

"Right. We heard a report about that." Ferris shook his head. "A damn mess. Total massacre. You're lucky you got out of there alive."

The mirrored gaze was still fixed on him. Laurie willed himself to keep calm. There was a panic attack here somewhere, still pent up from when it had built inside him while they were being menaced by the gang, and it might explode out of him if he wasn't very, very careful.

If he slipped out of the jeep now, before they got moving, and booked it as fast as he could across the desert, how far would he get before someone caught him? Not far enough. No chance of escape that way. There was nothing to indicate Ferris had recognized him. It had been a long, long time since their paths had crossed. It was smarter to wait it out.

They drove along. The driver, Cowell, had brown curly hair and a nice grin, and his very innocuousness made Laurie feel better. Maybe he'd be okay.

Jonathan leaned into the front seat to talk to Ferris. "Good thing you came along when you did. I didn't care much for the idea of walking the rest of the way."

"Glad to help you boys," Ferris said. Laurie could see his face reflected in the rearview mirror, and even though he couldn't see his eyes through the glasses, he knew Ferris was still staring at him.

Damn it all. He recognized him. What could he do? The best, smartest course of action was to stay calm until they reached the church, and then plan an escape from there. No. Laurie couldn't do that, couldn't face the thought of going back into that dark underground facility in the company of someone who, sooner or later, would try to kill him.

Jonathan's canvas bag was on the seat beside him. He had some cash in it, though Laurie didn't know how much. Maybe enough to pay someone to take him back to Vegas, if he could get away from Ferris now, if he could flag down a driver and hitch a ride to safety.

They turned off the highway onto the unpaved road leading to the facility. He saw a cloud of dust on the horizon. That would be the delivery truck, returning from the church at last.

The truck drew closer. The road was too narrow to accommodate both vehicles. Cowell slowed the jeep to a crawl and edged closer to the shoulder, the driver of the truck did the same, and Laurie snatched up Jonathan's bag and vaulted out of the jeep in a fast, coordinated burst of movement that surprised even himself. His feet skidded on gravel when he hit the ground, but he stayed upright. As the truck slowly edged past the jeep, he jumped up toward the open back.

For a glorious moment, he had it. One foot landed on the back bumper, one hand grabbed the side of the truck. As Laurie started to haul himself up, the driver put on a sudden burst of speed. Laurie tumbled back.

He landed on the dirt road with enough force to knock the wind out of him. Dust kicked up around him, blinding him and filling his nose and lungs. Some primal, adrenaline-fueled instinct kicked in—*get the hell out of here, move, go*—and he was up and running. He blitzed across the sand at a flat-out sprint, angling back up toward the highway. If he was really, really lucky, maybe he'd make it there before the truck. Maybe he could flag down the driver, maybe he could hitch a ride to safety.

"Hey!" Shouts, commotion, sounds of pursuit. Laurie didn't look behind him. This was a futile enterprise, and he knew it, but running felt better than tamely waiting for Ferris to kill him.

He moved fast, but the attempt was doomed. He got a few hundred yards across the sand before someone slammed into him from behind and tackled him to the ground. Ferris pinned him down and wrestled his arms behind him in a modified headlock.

"Did that make you feel better, Laurie?" Ferris asked. He shifted his grasp to hold Laurie's wrists together in one hand, kneeling on Laurie's back to keep him in place while he knotted a plastic cord around his wrists.

"Let go of me. I don't know what you're—" Laurie squawked in pain as Ferris yanked up on his bound wrists. Felt like his arms were coming out of their sockets.

"Shut up," Ferris said. Calm, no anger to it. "You know who I am, I know who you are. Shut up and listen. You're a sneak thief, and I'm arresting you. That's the story. Tell me you understand."

"Why should I—" Laurie cried out again at another yank on his arms. Ferris leaned forward and hissed in his ear.

"Because if you say anything else, it'll cause problems. I'll have to shoot Frisch, you know that, right? Right here and now, I'll kill him. I'll probably have to kill Cowell while I'm at it, and that'd be a damned shame, because he's a decent guy and one of my best employees. So just shut up and go along with this. Got it?"

Laurie didn't have time to answer, because now Cowell and Jonathan had caught up to them. "Ferris? What's going on?" Cowell asked.

Ferris hauled Laurie to his feet by his bound hands. "It's under control, Sandy. I've been fielding reports on Laurie here for the past few months. Kid's been doing a lot of pickpocketing in the casinos, been working Fremont pretty heavily. Small stuff, more of a lingering nuisance than anything." He held onto Laurie by his shirt collar and nodded at Jonathan. "The bag is yours, right?"

Laurie was a little afraid to look at Jonathan, afraid he'd see betrayal or anger on that beautiful face, but there was no discernable emotion there at all. Jonathan was composed, almost blank, which was maybe worse than anger. "Yes, it is. Thank you." He bent down and picked up the canvas bag Laurie dropped when Ferris tackled him.

Cowell's brow wrinkled. "I don't remember any reports about this."

"Didn't file any. Ted at the Castello asked me to keep an eye out for this kid, just as a professional courtesy." Ferris gave Laurie a small shake. "Just a punk, that's all. We'll take him with us and leave him for the Vegas cops to deal with. I'm sure they've got quite a paper trail on little Laurent Sparks."

It'd been over a decade since anyone had referred to Laurie by his full name, and the sound of it was a jolt, an electric current running through him. He should say something, right now. Ferris wouldn't dare retaliate. Shooting Jonathan and Cowell would be too risky, would cause far too many problems for him down the road.

No. Ferris might dare. He might very well dare, and then Jonathan would be dead, and it'd be Laurie's fault. He kept his mouth shut.

"Under the circumstances, we're going to postpone our trip to the church," Ferris said to Jonathan. "You can walk the rest of the way, can't you?"

Jonathan still seemed too composed. Maybe a little disappointed, as though his private suspicions about Laurie had been confirmed, even though he'd hoped they'd be unwarranted. "It's still a couple of miles down the road," he said. "You can drop me at the gate, can't you? Wouldn't take you that much out of the way, and it'll save me some wear and tear."

Ferris considered, then gestured with his head toward the jeep. "Yeah, fine. Come on."

Laurie found himself marched across the sand, Ferris keeping a firm grip on his collar. When they reached the jeep, Ferris snaked his arm around Laurie's waist, hoisted him up, and dumped him into the backseat. He turned to Jonathan. "Sit up front. I'll stay in back to make sure he doesn't make another break for it."

"Sure." Jonathan jumped into the passenger side. Before Cowell could climb in, he slid across the seat, slipped behind the wheel, and turned the key in the ignition, too quickly and seamlessly for anyone to process what he was doing.

"Hey!" Cowell grabbed at the steering wheel, but Jonathan shifted the gear stick, and the jeep surged forward. Ferris tried to grab the side, missed his grip, and stumbled backwards.

Jonathan turned the wheel with both hands and took a hard right off the unpaved road. The jeep skidded across the sand. The wheels spun and kicked up a hurricane of dust. Laurie started to sit upright, then ducked at the sound of a gunshot from somewhere behind them.

"Stay down, Laurie." Jonathan still sounded calm. He curled his torso over the steering wheel, keeping as low as possible. They sped across the sand in the direction of the highway. Laurie glanced behind and saw Ferris, gun out, chasing them on foot for several meters before giving it up as a lost cause.

Jonathan drove the jeep the same way he drove his motorcycle, fast but not reckless. They bounded over sand, the wheels only rarely seeming to touch the ground. In the backseat, Laurie bounced around so much he thought he might fly out the open side. He flailed his tied hands behind him and caught hold of one end of a seatbelt. He clung to it, a life preserver in a squall, and anchored himself in place.

Jonathan kept his eyes straight ahead, weaving and bobbing around dips and bumps in the sand. Laurie craned his neck to look behind again and saw only the desert. And then the jeep bounced up a small incline to the highway, and then they were flying effortlessly along the paved road, and Laurie could finally let himself think that maybe, just maybe, they might actually be getting away with this.

CHAPTER TEN

They'd zipped down the highway for several minutes before Jonathan pulled over and stopped. "How're we doing, Laurie?" he asked.

Laurie leaned forward, hands still bound, to talk to him. "We should keep going," he said. "Ferris and the other guy, it won't take them long to walk to the church, and they'll take one of the Zephyr vehicles and come after us. We should move."

"We will. We can afford a couple of minutes. Turn around and let me untie your hands." Jonathan leaned into the backseat and examined the plastic cord binding Laurie's wrists together. He popped open the glove compartment, rooted around, and produced a pocketknife. "Aha. This should do it." A few seconds of sawing, and Laurie was free.

Laurie climbed into the passenger seat. He rubbed at his chafed wrists. "Thanks," he said. "Let's keep going."

Jonathan put the jeep in gear again. They continued down the road.

"We should go faster than this," Laurie said.

"No backseat driving, please. This is plenty fast enough. We've had a good head start. You know, now might be a good time to reassure me that I didn't just ruin my life for nothing back there."

Laurie was quiet. "Thanks for the rescue," he finally said.

"I can't go back to the church, obviously, and I'm pretty sure I'm a wanted criminal now. I just committed a carjacking."

"I'm sorry."

"I don't need you to be sorry. It was my decision. But I could use some answers." He shot a glance over at Laurie. "You're not a pickpocket."

"No."

"And that guy Ferris is why you've been so scared of the Zephyr guards, right?"

"Right." Laurie stared at the open road, at the barren landscape, the sun scorching the wide expanses of sand. "He killed my mom."

If he just kept staring at the road, he could get through this. "He shot her in front of me. I was just a kid, and he shot me too."

"Why'd he do that, Laurie?" Jonathan's knuckles on the steering wheel were white. His beautiful face still looked composed. "Who was your mom?"

"Margaret Sparks. Do you know who that was?"

Jonathan shook his head. "The name sounds familiar."

"You're from Philadelphia, right? Me, too. That's where I grew up. My mom was a senator for Pennsylvania before I was born, back when the bombs fell. She did a lot of work right at the start trying to get the country up and running, like helping businesses rebuild and reopen, stuff like that. So around the time she had me, six years after the bombings, she was appointed Secretary of Redevelopment."

Jonathan was nodding. "Maggie Sparks, yeah, I remember this. She was the one who was shot, right? Didn't she turn out to be...?"

"She wasn't a Soviet spy. And she wasn't assassinated by the Soviets, either. It was that guy Ferris, he was part of our security detail while we were in Las Vegas. We were there for the opening of the new convention center, that was one of the projects she'd overseen, and he walked into our hotel room and shot her. And then he shot me."

Jonathan stared at him for so long Laurie wanted to tell him to turn his attention back to the road. "Why did he do that?"

"I don't know who he was working for. She had a lot of enemies, I know that much. She wasn't a communist or anything, she was just trying to make sure the government helped everyone, make sure the hospitals were up and running and the schools reopened and everybody had food and someplace to stay. That's all she was doing, and I know some people thought it was wrong or suspicious or something—which, by the way, I totally don't get—and so one of her enemies probably hired Ferris to kill her. All those stories about the Soviets, that was just to cover for it."

"Wait. I don't get it either. Why would anyone kill her for that?"

"Don't know. I've thought about it a lot, and I bet it's the money. It costs a lot of money to rebuild stuff."

"And that money would have to come from taxes," Jonathan said.

Laurie nodded. "Right, yeah. And I think a lot of the people who managed to keep their money even after everything was destroyed hated the idea of giving it to the government."

"Linking your mom's efforts to the Soviets would be a pretty good way to turn public opinion against the whole idea of rebuilding. Seems to have worked, if that's the case. As near as I can tell, most redevelopment plans have been stalled for years," Jonathan said. "How'd you end up at the monastery?"

"I was in the hospital for a long time, and I thought Ferris or somebody else might come after me again, so I just left. I walked out, walked as far as I could, and somehow I found myself at the monastery. They were nice to me there, and I didn't know if anyone was still looking for me, so I stayed where I was and kept quiet."

"Ferris was going to kill you back there, wasn't he?"

"I think so. Or maybe he was going to bring me to whoever gave him the order to kill my mom. They'd probably want proof he'd found me," Laurie said.

"Now that he knows you're alive, he's going to keep looking for you. And he's probably going to let whoever hired him know you're still out there."

"I know." Laurie exhaled. "What are we going to do?"

"Damned if I know. Let's head back to Vegas, okay? Dominick seems to have some resources at his disposal. He might be able to keep you safe."

Laurie was quiet. When he spoke, his voice was small. "Can we go to Los Angeles instead? It's not that much further. I mean, it is, but we can make it. Can we do that?"

"Why?"

"The satellite. Caltech, right? Pasadena? That's where Dominick said the guy who bought the satellite equipment was from. Izumi. We could go there."

Jonathan stared at him. "Yeah, but again, why? You can't go back to the church, you know. Contacting the satellite was a long shot before this, and it's impossible now."

"I know I can't go back. I don't *want* to go back. But if I had some way to access a satellite and get on television, I could tell people about my mom."

"And then once people knew about it, you might be safe from Ferris and whoever hired him to kill your mom? Is that what you're thinking?"

"Not really. I guess that's a nice side benefit, though. Mostly I want people to stop believing my mom was some kind of awful person. She did so much good for everyone, right when they needed her, and now everyone thinks she was a traitor. I want people to know who the bad guys really are."

"Yeah, but even you don't know who they are." The scenery whizzed by. "Los Angeles might be safer for you than Las Vegas. I can take you into the city, at least."

"Thanks, Jonathan," Laurie said. "When we get there, what will you do?"

"I don't know. Mexico, maybe. From California, it might be easy enough to slip across the border. I hear it's healthier there anyway. Fewer blast sites, lower cancer rates," Jonathan said. "It might not be a bad idea for you to come, too. As soon as you go on television—hell, as soon as you start making a fuss about wanting to go on television—it'll be harder for you to keep a low profile."

Laurie nodded but said nothing. Lost in his own thoughts, he stared ahead at the unending vista of sand and dirt and low hills.

For all the horror of the past day, he sort of enjoyed his road trip with Jonathan, at least after he was able to reassure himself no one was hot on their trail. As soon as they reached the California border, they stopped by the side of the road to assess their situation.

The back of the jeep held rudimentary supplies: a tool kit, a box of meal bars, a few cans of water, a plastic blanket. Jonathan grunted in satisfaction. "Not much, but it's a good sight better than nothing, right?"

"Sure." Laurie stretched his legs, waved his arms around, tried to return life to his limbs. "We've also got their jackets. Those might come in handy." He reached into the backseat and picked one up. A leather billfold fell out of the inside pocket. He flipped through it. A Nevada driver's license in the name of Mark Ferris, his Zephyr identification badge, a gun permit, some loose bills. "Hey, look at this."

Jonathan glanced over at it. "Keep the cash and bury the rest by the road. It's trouble if anyone links us to him. Smarter not to have that in our possession."

"The ID could be useful, though, right? Like the uniform jackets. Maybe at some point we'll need to impersonate security guards."

"I'm not sure either of us could pass for authority figures." Jonathan took the wallet from him and stashed it in the glove compartment. "Still, it makes sense, I guess. Ready to keep moving? We're going to need gas soon, but there should be a station before we're empty."

"Or we could break down somewhere in the middle of the Mojave. When Ferris finds us, our bones will be picked clean by vultures."

"Optimistic, aren't you?" Jonathan said. "Buck up. We're not doing all that poorly, everything considered." He climbed into the driver's seat. "Shall we?"

They bounced and jostled along. They saw a gas station, finally, just outside of Barstow. Peeling white paint over rusted corrugated metal, an oval metal sign on a tall pole. Almost half the letters had fallen off of the sign, and now it enigmatically proclaimed "OCO." Jonathan pulled up to the single pump out front.

The windows were shuttered. A rusted-out shell of a pickup truck that probably hadn't been driven in decades was parked at the side of the building. "I don't think it's open," Laurie said.

"It's open, probably."

"It looks so run-down."

"Does it? I mean, I guess it does, but most gas stations look like this. At least the ones out here do. Probably ones in other places too."

"I haven't been to a gas station in years. Not since being at the monastery, and not many times before that."

"Your mom didn't drive?" Jonathan slid out of his seat. With another worried glance at the station, Laurie followed suit.

"We had a driver. He'd make sure the car was filled with gas before picking us up."

Jonathan pushed open the glass door to the station. Frowning, Laurie followed him inside. A young black woman with crimped hair and delicate features manned the register. She nodded in reply to Jonathan's greeting, her face registering only humorless exhaustion, and accepted several folded bills from him. She picked up a handgun from a shelf beneath the register and stuffed it down the front of her jeans, then came around the counter and went outside to pump their gas herself. Before long, they were filled up and on their way again.

Jonathan turned to Laurie. "You're quiet. What are you thinking about?"

"I don't know. Just how everything's so ugly around here. Things should be better."

"Could be worse, though," Jonathan said. "What brought this on?"

Laurie shook his head. "That lady in the gas station, I guess. I mean, she just seemed so unhappy. It's got to be bleak and scary, working out here in the middle of nowhere, hoping nobody comes by and kills you."

"She seemed like she could take care of herself."

"Yeah, I know. It's just…" He shook his head. "Never mind."

Jonathan smiled. "You're tired. Why don't you try to sleep for a bit? We're still a ways outside of the city."

Laurie didn't feel like sleeping. He felt like explaining his point again to Jonathan until he understood, but his brain felt cluttered and uncertain, and he wasn't altogether sure he himself knew what he was trying to say. He settled back into his seat and closed his eyes. Eventually, he relaxed enough to drift off into a serene, meditative state.

"We're here," Jonathan said, the sound of his voice rousing Laurie back into consciousness. He gestured at the scenery with his chin. "Los Angeles, I mean."

"Really?" They were still surrounded by the same low sprawl, mostly desert areas interspersed with some higher hills. The road was wider, and there were a few more cars, and more buildings dotted the landscape—a diner, a motel, a gas station—but it didn't look like much.

"The outskirts, at least. It's going to look like this for a while. The city's spread out over a big space," Jonathan said. "You've never been here? Not even with your mom?"

"If I have, I was too young to remember. We mostly stayed on the east coast. I spent most of my time as a kid with my mom in Washington and Pennsylvania."

Jonathan smiled. "Born in Philadelphia, right? I grew up there. Under other circumstances, we might've met earlier."

"How'd you end up in Las Vegas? It seems like a weird career path for you."

"No big mystery to it. My parents ran out of money, same as everyone's parents, and college wasn't an option. I had to do something with my life, so I headed west. I lived around here for a while, working wherever I could, and then I got a line on the hotel job in Vegas. I turned out to be pretty good at administrative work," Jonathan said. "Moot point now, since that career seems to be pretty effectively derailed."

"You'll be better off in the long run," Laurie said. "You were made for bigger and better things."

"I appreciate your confidence in me," Jonathan said dryly.

The scenery rolled past. More and more signs of civilization—more houses, more restaurants, more businesses. A range of hills loomed before them; Jonathan lifted one hand from the steering wheel to point in their direction. "Pasadena is on the other side, I think, though I couldn't tell you exactly where. We'll have to ask someone for directions."

"Are you going to go with me?" Laurie asked.

"To Caltech? Sure," Jonathan said. "You know we're not likely to find what you're looking for, right?"

"I know," Laurie said. "It's just... I don't know what else to do."

They crossed over the hills. Laurie expected to see a panoramic vista, tall buildings like New York or at least signs of a populated downtown area like Las Vegas, but there wasn't much worth seeing. Los Angeles was a vast grid of low, flat buildings interspersed with wider barren areas, all of it punctuated by the occasional tall palm tree, some rising higher than the buildings. The trees were impressive, Laurie had to admit, graceful and spectral, like the guardians of the city.

"This is it? I thought L.A. was a bigger deal than this. I thought it was a real city."

"It is a real city. Just not one with much in the way of skyscrapers or anything. Downtown was a blast site, and they never rebuilt it. Earthquakes, you know, so they have to be careful about building anything up too high. And nobody has the money to be careful these days, so…" Jonathan nodded at the horizon. "Low and flat is the way to go."

"It's ugly, isn't it?"

"It's not a bad place. I spent almost a year here, and I liked it. There's not that edge of desperation that you see in the east, maybe because the weather stays decent all year. Nobody's in much danger of freezing to death, even if they're living on the streets."

Jonathan took an exit that led into the old downtown area, which consisted of a cluster of low buildings at the base of a hill. Looked like warehouses mostly, slapped up quickly and cheaply in recent years, sheet metal and plywood and white paint. Many of the signs were in Spanish. Laurie saw a few people on the sidewalks, bronzed men in plaid work shirts and heavy boots, their wide-brimmed straw hats shielding their faces from the late-afternoon sun.

"Industrial area," Jonathan said. "Sweatshops. Textile manufacturing, I think, clothes and such." He parked at the curb. "Come on. We'll grab food somewhere and get directions."

"Any particular reason we're stopping here?"

"Blast site. Anonymity. It's still perceived as hazardous, so nobody goes here unless they've got a purpose. If Ferris traces us to Los Angeles, this won't be high on his list of places to search, and even if he comes here, probably nobody's going to be interested in speaking to him. And the food's great. You know any Spanish, incidentally?"

"Some French. And I'm fluent in Latin, if that helps."

"I can't picture any circumstances anywhere where that would help." Jonathan slid out of the jeep. He frowned at the Zephyr logo painted on the side. "It'd be nice to cover that up. When we get a chance, we should get some paint."

Jonathan led Laurie to an open-air market in an old parking lot, a sprawl of tents and makeshift stalls set up on the crumbling pavement. Laurie's stomach grumbled. It smelled good, like sausages and toasted corn and grilled onions. He hadn't eaten anything other than a meal bar from the stash in the back of the jeep, which he'd consumed outside Barstow. It tasted like fish and dust, and Laurie spent the next several miles trying to get the taste out of his mouth. Jonathan took charge, approaching one of the stalls and speaking to the woman occupying it in what sounded like functional Spanish.

The woman was small, not even as tall as Laurie, and her face was creased with lines. Her head was draped with a striped wool shawl, even though it was a warm day. She seemed incurious about her customers, regarding them with neither friendliness nor hostility. She spoke at length in Spanish; Jonathan nodded slowly and handed her a couple of bills from his shoulder bag.

"I ordered us food. Have a seat." Jonathan gestured toward a battered cluster of picnic tables. Laurie sat gingerly. The bench wobbled and tilted to the side under his slight weight. "She gave me directions to Caltech, but she's pretty sure the campus closed years ago."

"We can check it out, at least. See if anyone's there, see if they know that Izumi guy." Laurie squinted up at the sun. Low and hot and bright in the sky, only slightly more merciful than the one in the Nevada desert. "Do people really like sitting out in the sun like this? I'm frying."

"Not everyone is a delicate blossom like you," Jonathan said.

A young girl approached their table with two trays of food. She plunked them down and scurried off before either could thank her. The trays held an indistinguishable mess of cooked beans and rice, plus chunks of some kind of brown meat splashed with a red sauce and wrapped in toasted corn tortillas. "What is this?"

"Not sure. I couldn't understand what she told me. Tacos of some kind. Just eat," Jonathan said. He picked up one of the tortillas and stuffed it into his mouth. He nodded vigorously while chewing. "It's good. Try it."

Laurie hesitantly lifted the edge of a tortilla. He sniffed it. Smelled good. He took a careful nibble, then chewed.

Ambrosia. Rich and meaty, with a charred taste that exploded in his mouth. Spicier than he'd anticipated; his tongue burned. The beans were salty and greasy and delicious.

Jonathan watched him, amused, as Laurie devoured everything on his tray, ravaging his way through what had seemed like a very substantial pile of food. "Slow down. You're going to make yourself sick."

"If I do, it'll be worth it," Laurie said. "This stuff's awesome."

Amazing how much better he felt after a good meal, with all kinds of meaty, beany vitamins coursing through his veins. He felt invigorated, less sick and scared than he'd been during most of their flight from the desert. Here, in the middle of Los Angeles, it seemed impossible Ferris would track them down. In fact, it almost seemed like things were going to be okay.

CHAPTER ELEVEN

As the woman at the stall had warned them, Caltech was a ruin. Laurie had expected that, but he wasn't prepared for the extent of the damage.

Destroyed buildings, the windows smashed out, gigantic holes punched in the walls. Statues overturned, yards torn up, gardens ripped apart, mounds of trash strewn across dead lawns. School desks and podiums and chalk boards and books in festering piles. The last bit of Laurie's optimism faded as he walked across the campus.

"This is awful," he said.

"You want to leave?" Jonathan asked.

"Not yet. Let's see if we can find someone to ask about this Izumi guy." Laurie led Jonathan across a courtyard, navigating around broken cobblestones, looking for a friendly face and seeing only decay.

A flicker at the broken window of a building, a pervasive sense of being watched. "Hey, Jonathan? I think people might be living in the buildings."

"I'm sure they are. Should we go in and ask someone about Izumi?"

"I guess." Laurie frowned. "I don't like scary situations. I don't like confrontations and violence."

"Most people don't. I don't. But sometimes it's unavoidable," Jonathan said. "Probably nothing violent will happen. Most of the people staying here will keep hidden from strangers. And if we see someone, maybe they can tell us where to find Izumi. It'll be fine."

The words were barely out of his mouth when a brick sailed through the air toward his head. Jonathan ducked, then grabbed Laurie's elbow and dragged him behind the relative protection of a low, crumbling wall. Another brick struck the top of the wall, sending a small shower of chips down on their heads.

Laurie peeked over the wall. He spotted a flurry of motion, which resolved itself into a small urchin with unkempt hair and baggy red shorts rooting around the lawn. He grabbed more loose bricks before dashing back into the protection of a bristly thicket of dead shrubs. He was shirtless and shoeless, his bare feet and legs covered with dirt and scratches. When he saw Laurie, he angled one scrawny arm back and hurled a brick at him with as much force as he could muster, his features twisted in determined anger. It hit the wall and crumbled away into bits.

Armed or not, he was maybe six at the oldest, and Laurie had a firm rule against being bullied by toddlers. He stood up. "Hey, quit it!" he yelled at the kid.

Jonathan grabbed onto his shirt hem and tried to pull him back down. "Stay low, you idiot."

"It's only a little kid," Laurie said.

The kid winched his face up in fury. Asian features, twigs and leaves caught in his tangled hair. "Go away! You're not allowed to be here!" he shouted.

"We're looking for someone named Izumi. You know him?"

"What you want with Izzy?" the kid asked. His eyes fixed on Laurie, he raised his final brick near his ear, ready to hurl it if provoked.

"You know him?" Laurie asked again.

The kid nodded. "He's the boss. Me and my friends, we make sure no one bothers him who's not supposed to bother him, get it?"

Laurie boosted himself onto the wall and sat cross-legged on top of it. Behind him he heard Jonathan make some noise of frustration, which he ignored. "Great. Because we've got business with your boss. *Important* business," he said.

"Make an appointment." The kid grinned. He was missing two of his lower front teeth. Laurie revised his assessment. The kid was small for his age, probably from malnourishment, but there was a shrewd maturity behind the near-feral animosity. Could be eight, maybe even ten. "I'm his social secretary."

Jonathan finally rose to his feet. "Okay, can we make an appointment to see him?"

The kid looked from Jonathan to Laurie, his expression wild and wary. "You got money? I take bribes," he said.

"No," Jonathan said firmly. "No money. *Absolutely* no money."

"We've got food," Laurie said. He gestured toward Jonathan's canvas bag, where he'd stashed their food rations before leaving the jeep. "We've got these fish bars. Jonathan, toss him one of those."

His eyes fixed on the kid, Jonathan opened his bag and produced one of the meal bars. He held it up, making sure the kid could see it wasn't some kind of weapon, and tossed it over to him.

The kid dropped his brick and dove for it. He ripped open the wrapper and sniffed it. "Hell, yeah, mackerel!" he said. He tore into it, small sharp teeth biting into the leathery mess with evident relish. "How many you got?"

"We can give you two," Jonathan said.

"We've got like a dozen. We can give you all of them," Laurie said. At Jonathan's incredulous stare, he shrugged. "What? I don't want to eat them. They're disgusting."

Jonathan opened his mouth to argue, then shook his head. He reached inside his bag and produced two handfuls of the bars. "This is what we've got. You take us to Izumi, and we'll give you all of these. Okay?"

The kid considered, then gestured for them to follow him. "Deal. You guys come with me, okay?"

He led them through the campus, cutting straight across lawns and long-dead flower beds, until they reached a once-stately building, white stone with pillars and a marble fountain in front. The fountain was smashed, one half of it dissolved into rubble; the pillars were cracked around the base. The double doors were missing, and the dark entrance looked like a gaping mouth, open in a silent wail of unheard despair. Laurie and Jonathan followed the kid up the cracked stone steps and through the mouth.

They found themselves in an open atrium, two levels, a balcony running around the length of the second floor. Dozens of bookcases, some toppled over, shelves empty or broken. Looked like a library, though there wasn't a single book in the place. Plenty of debris, though, food wrappers and empty cans, a smell of rotting vegetables and body odor. Laurie's nostrils twitched, and he had to resist the urge to step back outside.

"Hey, Izzy!" the kid yelled up at the balcony. "Izzy, there's people!"

"If you wanted to enroll, you're maybe a decade too late." A voice from the second level made them whip their heads up. Almost unconsciously, Jonathan moved in front of Laurie.

A man. Asian, forty or so. Shaved head, long black trench coat over jeans. He waved down at them. "The university's been closed for years. If you were looking for books, I might've been able to hook you up, but I sold off the entire collection a month ago."

Laurie craned his head back to look up at him. "Are you Izumi?" he asked.

"Who're you? Philip, who are they?" the man asked.

"Don't know. They said they had business with you." The kid nodded at Jonathan. "I'll take my payment now, thank you."

Jonathan handed over the meal bars to the kid. The kid bundled them up in his scrawny arms, clutching them to his chest, then scampered off without another glance at them.

"Hang on. I'll come down," the man said. He descended a center staircase until he reached their level. He had a pleasant face under scraggly black whiskers. He smelled a little ripe, like his long coat hadn't been laundered in months.

"You two look okay. Wrong for this neighborhood, but okay," the man said. "I'm Izumi. That'd be Doctor Izumi, technically, but everyone calls me Izzy. Or at least they used to call me that, back when I was a student. Got my doctorate here in 2001, just before the cutbacks and closures." He nodded at them. "How'd you get past Philip?"

"Bribed him with fish bars," Laurie said.

"That sounds about right. My bodyguard," Izumi said. He gave them a wan grin. "So, who're you?"

"I'm Laurie and that's Jonathan. We just came from Nevada," Laurie said.

Izumi nodded. "Nevada, okay. Why do you want to see me?"

"We heard you bought a bunch of stuff a few months back from someone in Las Vegas. Government stuff. Old computers and files and equipment."

Another nod. "I buy stuff, I do. I bought stuff in Vegas, yes."

He seemed a little distracted, or vague, like part of him was somewhere else even while keeping up his end of the conversation, but there appeared to be nothing dangerous about him. "We'd like to see the stuff. We might want to buy some of it back," Laurie said.

Izumi snapped into focus at that. He stared at Laurie as though seeing him for the first time. "You're Laurie," he said.

"Yes. I'm Laurie."

"You can't buy it back. But I can show it to you, Laurie," he said. He gestured with his head. "Come with me."

Laurie and Jonathan exchanged glances, then trailed him out of the building. They headed across the courtyard again. No sign of Philip or anyone else, but it was tough to shake the feeling of being watched.

Another building, this one newer, blocky and bare. Concrete walls covered in graffiti, no windows. Izumi led them down a flight of stairs into the basement.

At the base of the stairs was a heavy door made of reinforced steel. Izumi produced a bunch of keys that hung from a length of twine around his neck and unlocked it. He flipped on the lights.

"This is my laboratory," Izumi said. "All the very best scientists have laboratories, you know."

Even given Izumi's apparent harmlessness, Laurie was primed for something awful, dissected human organs in apothecary jars or something similarly icky. Instead he found a large, clean room. The walls were aggressively white; the room smelled of fresh paint. Steel countertops, glossy white tile floors.

Three mainframe computers took up much of the back wall. Huge, blocky, taller than Laurie. The metal fronts were covered with rows of colorful plastic buttons; at the tops, gigantic tape drives spun in endless circles. Laurie stared at them, at the logo in the upper right corner: IBM.

"Here they are. Meet my children." Izumi pointed at each computer in turn. "Kogane, Shirogane, Kurogane."

"Are these the computers you bought in Las Vegas?"

Izumi nodded. "These are them."

Jonathan walked up to the nearest computer. Izumi watched him carefully, as though afraid he'd harm it. "What do they do?"

"They do everything. They can solve everything."

Jonathan leaned forward and examined the tape drive. It took Laurie a second before he figured it out: The wheels on all three drives were empty, spinning continuously but doing nothing. "I see," Jonathan said, and there was something soft in his voice.

"You do, don't you?" Izumi said. He glanced around the room. "I sit in here, and I feel like I'm solving things."

"Were there files?" Laurie asked. "I mean, there was more stuff you picked up in Las Vegas, right? Manuals and stuff?"

"I sold all that along with the books. The Archive, they took all of that."

Laurie and Jonathan exchanged looks. "What's the Archive?" Laurie asked.

"The Archive has all the books, all the files, so if you're wanting anything from the collection, you'll have to take your concerns to them. They hauled away all the libraries here, all the books and journals and papers, everything. I tried to take good care of the books, but I couldn't protect them. People stole them, burned them, destroyed them, because people like destroying things. So when the Archive came in their big, big trucks and carried away everything, I was in no position to argue. It was for the best." He shrugged. "They paid me. I needed the money. I'd spent so much in Vegas on my children, and they paid me. Enough to set up my laboratory, enough to keep Philip fed, enough for my treatment."

At the mention of treatment, Jonathan shot Izumi a quick glance, but said nothing.

"What's the Archive?" Laurie asked again.

"They're a bunch of hoodlums." Izumi grimaced. "And by that I mean genuine hoodlums. You want anything from the Archive, you can find them at the Coliseum."

Jonathan frowned. "They're storing books at the Coliseum? The one in Exposition Park?"

"No, the books aren't there. You can tell them what you want, and they'll take you to the books."

"And I suppose they charge for that privilege," Jonathan said.

"You've got it wrong. The Archive is like a library, and no one charges for a library. It's all free. Not just books, either. They have magazines and videos and records and cassette tapes, everything.

They're just overprotective, that's all, and if they think you're up to anything funny, or if you're with the government, they'll beat you up or run you off." Izumi shook his head. "As I said, hoodlums."

"Why? If they're running a library, that's not illegal," Jonathan said.

"No, but they think the government might come in and commandeer it, and then they wouldn't do a damn thing with it. They've done it before. They've done it here, at the campus. All the JPL stuff, jet propulsion, you know? Robots in space. Satellites. The lab used to be here, but the government took it all away."

"Okay. Thanks for the information," Jonathan said. He hesitated and looked at Izumi. "Hey, is there anything we can do for you?"

"Me? No. Thanks, but I'm good. I'm just here." Izumi gestured around the white room vaguely. "I mean, no, clearly I'm not good, but it's mostly okay. It's better when I can get treatment, but I can't always afford it."

He smiled. "Some days I live in a house with a pool in Palo Alto and I'm married to Miss Oregon. Or maybe that was another life."

Laurie frowned. Jonathan nodded. "When you don't get treatment, you live in Palo Alto with Miss Oregon?" His tone was gentle.

"We have two kids. Maybe they'll go to Stanford one day, they've got good grades. Lots of extracurriculars. It's much nicer there. And I've been spending more and more time there lately. One of these days, I'll go there and never leave." He nodded at Laurie. "You're on television there, you know. Everyone knows you. My wife wears your clothes."

Laurie blinked. "What do you mean?"

Jonathan touched his elbow. "Skip it, Laurie, it's okay," he said, still with that same strange gentleness. "Thanks for all your help," he said to Izumi.

"Sure, no problem. Stop by again, any time," he said. He nodded again, chin bobbing rhythmically, like he was unaware of what he was doing. Keeping track of some beat in his brain, maybe. "I should get back to my work now, though. My research."

They left him there, in the strangeness of his nonfunctional laboratory, in the center of a ruined campus. They walked across the courtyard and headed toward the street where they'd parked their jeep. "What was wrong with him?" Laurie asked. "He got weird there at the end."

"Not sure. Something that affects his mental processes. Brain cancer, maybe. Or maybe he's just spent too much time by himself," Jonathan said. "He was harmless, at a guess. Just sort of sad and a little bit crazy."

"What did he say about Palo Alto and me being on television?"

"Sounds like he has hallucinations. I wouldn't think too much about it."

"So are we going to go to the Archive next? You said you knew where this Coliseum is?"

Jonathan was quiet for a long, long time. When he turned to look at Laurie at last, his lovely face was grave. "You saw the tape drives on his computers, right? The big reels on top? They were empty."

"I know. The computers weren't working. Probably never did, and probably he's too... too *off* to notice or care."

"He went to Vegas to buy those computers, and he set up that whole new laboratory for them. That's a lot of work. There's something about that, the way he's expended so much energy on something so useless, that you might want to watch out for."

Laurie fell silent. "I don't know what else to do," he said at last. "I know we're not going to contact a satellite. I *know* that. I just need to feel like I'm doing something."

Jonathan nodded. "You want everyone to know about your mom," he said. "I get that. You want to broadcast it to the world."

116

"I've spent more than half my life being afraid someone would figure out who I really am, and being ashamed of myself for hiding. And now that I've been forced out into the open, I want to do something about it," Laurie said. "And I want to keep following this path until I figure out what that something is."

"Okay, Laurie," Jonathan said. "I get it. I'm in this with you. I just don't want you to expect too much from any of this."

"We'll check it out," Laurie said. "We'll try to find this Archive. If it's too weird or scary, we'll back away and leave it alone, but if it's something we can use, why not? What's this Coliseum, anyway? Do you mean like Rome?"

"Sort of. It's this old stadium. They held the Olympics there, right before the bombs fell," Jonathan said. "The neighborhood's rough, but as long as we're careful, we should be okay."

It felt right, somehow, this idea of an Archive, and so Laurie nodded and jumped into the passenger seat of the jeep, relieved to leave the barren weirdness of Caltech behind.

CHAPTER TWELVE

The Coliseum was in the southern part of the city, a couple of miles south of the downtown area, in a neighborhood that seemed similar to what Laurie had seen of Los Angeles thus far. Some homes, mostly stucco with rusty chain-link fences and yellow lawns, some parking lots, some food stands. Signs of life, but not thriving. The Coliseum itself was located in a gigantic park, and Laurie's spirits lifted a little at the sight of this. Wide and green, it looked well-tended despite the general unkempt nature of the city.

"This is nice," Laurie said. "I like parks."

"It's okay. It's a little rough here, like I said before, so don't get too complacent."

They crossed the park on foot. It was twilight now, a warm breeze in the air. The palm trees bobbed overhead in a placid welcome. The Coliseum featured a huge arched stone entryway topped with the Olympic rings. A chain-link fence surrounded the entire perimeter of the structure, but the entrance stood wide open, so they walked on through.

Dozens of rows of seats encircled the stadium, leading down to a cracked concrete field at the center. Some of the seats were occupied. Families, mostly black or Latino, several mothers with young children who played rambunctious chase games up and down the rows. A cluster of teen boys in brightly-colored t-shirts and print shorts lounged on the steps, spreading themselves out in a manner that was territorial but not menacing. Jonathan and Laurie had the palest faces in the group, and they drew a few stares as they climbed down the steps, but nobody seemed hostile.

"What do you suppose we do?" Laurie asked. "Who do we talk to?"

"I don't know. Take a seat. Our presence has been noted. Either someone will approach us or they won't."

"So we just wait for something to happen?" Laurie frowned and squinted up at the sun. It was low in the sky now, but the day was still warm. "There's no shade."

"Tough it out. We'll see what happens. It's possible Izumi was feeding us a line of garbage, you know. So we'll wait, and if anything seems funny, we'll leave."

Laurie hated waiting. He was tempted to go up to one of the young mothers or one of the teens and ask if they knew anything about the Archive, but Jonathan probably knew best. He sat on the steps, cranky and restless.

One of the teens ambled over to them. Fifteen or sixteen, tall and skinny, with a short burst of wild braids that framed his face in a haphazard halo. "Hey, man, got a quarter for the payphone?"

Jonathan dug around in his bag and produced a handful of leftover change from their lunch. He fished out a quarter and handed it to the kid.

"Thanks, man," the kid said.

"Do you know where we can find the Archive?" Laurie asked. Jonathan frowned at him.

The kid grinned. "Be cool, man, be cool," he said. He turned and headed up the steps toward the exit.

"What do you suppose that means?" Laurie asked.

"Don't know. Let's just play it by ear."

Laurie didn't feel like playing anything by ear. He felt like finding a hotel room, one with hot running water and clean sheets where he and Jonathan could crash for the night, and then, preferably after a good breakfast, they could formulate a new plan.

After a long while, long enough that the shadows had lengthened and the sun was almost touching the horizon, the kid returned. He shot a quick two-fingered salute at them, which Jonathan returned, then rejoined his friends on the lower steps.

"What's happening? Why are you two giving each other secret signals?" Laurie asked.

"I think he's telling us he contacted someone on our behalf. Just simmer down, okay? You're oozing nervous energy, and it's putting me on edge."

"Sorry. But it's getting dark out, if you hadn't noticed, and this Archive is probably already closed for the day."

"Hush." Jonathan nodded toward the front gates. "That might be for us."

A very tall man entered the Coliseum. He had a shaved head and chestnut-colored skin. He wore a white sleeveless shirt that showed off his muscular arms and black canvas pants. His shoulder holster, with the shiny chrome butt of a handgun sticking out of it, was plainly visible. He was beautiful, with a face dominated by aggressively sculpted cheekbones. He moved gracefully in their direction, hands thrust in his pockets, face composed. Laurie and Jonathan rose to face him.

"You want access to the Archive?" the man asked. Traces of a Caribbean accent.

"Yes, we do. Can you take us there?" Jonathan asked. At the sight of the gun, Jonathan had gone on high alert, his shoulder blades tense.

"You came here in a jeep with the logo of a security company," the man said, with no change in his calm expression.

"We're not affiliated with the company. We're just borrowing it," Jonathan said.

The man smiled. "Ah. Borrowing. I see," he said. "Why do you want to visit the Archive?"

"We're researching satellites," Laurie said. The man gave a little gesture with his hand, as though urging him to elaborate further, so he kept talking. "We want to find out how to contact a communications satellite, one currently in orbit already, so we can set up a cable television network, but we don't know how to do that. This guy Izumi at Caltech told us he sold his entire collection of books to the Archive, including some stuff we were looking for."

The man nodded. "And who are you?" he asked.

"I'm Jonathan, that's Laurie. That's probably as much as you need to know," Jonathan said. "Who are you?"

"Maybe I should be the one who decides how much I should know." His gaze flickered back to Jonathan, implacable and composed. "My name is Escobar."

He held out a long, slim hand to Laurie, who was so taken off guard by the sudden display of hospitality that it took him a moment to realize he should shake it. "Nice to meet you, Escobar. Jonathan's not trying to be unfriendly, we've just been through a lot lately. Are you in charge of the Archive?"

Escobar smiled at Laurie. "No. But my ties to it are deep. I'll show you." He gestured toward the gate. "Shall we? We can go on foot. It's not far."

Jonathan seemed unconvinced, and maybe a little irritated with Laurie for undercutting his authority, but he followed Escobar without protest. Right outside the Coliseum, Laurie spotted a payphone. It looked like it was in decent condition, clean and undamaged. Surprising. Didn't see many of those around these days.

"That kid in the Coliseum works for you, doesn't he?" Laurie said. "He called you and told you about us."

"Mmm. He said you two seemed harmless, but out of place, and he was concerned about your vehicle. The Archive asked me to check you out first, in case there was any trouble," Escobar said. "But there's no trouble, is there, Laurie?"

"God, no. Are you kidding me?" Laurie said. "I mean, it's not like we haven't had our share of trouble lately, but it's nothing that could affect you. We're not *dangerous*."

Jonathan was looking murderous now, probably at the way Laurie was making them sound naive and ineffectual, but this was the right approach, he felt sure of that. If Escobar had any misgivings about them, they wouldn't get to see the Archive, and at the very least, this seemed like it could be interesting.

"I wonder." Escobar smiled again. "Even the mildest people can be dangerous."

They trailed him over a road crisscrossed with long-disused train tracks, dry weeds sprouting up and around them, until they reached a sprawling complex of buildings several blocks long, surrounded by a low iron fence. Jonathan frowned. "What is this place?"

"Used to be a college campus. But many of the buildings collapsed or burned in the blast. It closed in 1984 and never re-opened."

He led them through an open gate. There was a small manned security booth to the side; Escobar raised a hand and waved at the uniformed woman seated inside. She glanced at Jonathan and Laurie, then nodded at him.

"What is it now?" Jonathan asked.

"An institution of higher learning, still. Only it's somewhat less formal these days," Escobar said. "I raised the funds to renovate what buildings were salvageable and brought in as many instructors as I could, because right now what we need—what the country needs, what the city needs, what this neighborhood needs—is education. Nobody knows shit these days, and it's *crippling* us, as much as the bombs did."

"You're running a university on your own?" Laurie said. The buildings were mostly unlit now, in the early evening, but they seemed well-maintained, especially when compared to the ruin of Caltech. No broken windows, no garbage.

"I have a great deal of help. People volunteer their time, anyone who is knowledgeable about a particular subject is encouraged to teach a course or two. And anyone who wants to learn may attend, kids, adults, whomever." He gave a modest shrug. "We've been operating in this manner for almost four years now. It's been rough, but we're growing. Free education, man. There's nothing more important than that."

"So what's the Archive?" Jonathan asked.

"What it sounds like. We collect books. Magazines, journals, what have you. Any school that closes, any library that closes, any bookstore that closes, hell, we send out big vans to collect it all and bring it back here. We search through garbage dumps all over the city looking for reading material that people have thrown away. My wife, this is her baby, she's a freak for knowledge, and as the economy kept getting worse and worse and more schools kept closing, she got it into her head that she needed to preserve all this knowledge before it got lost forever. So she's got computers and stuff, and she's trying to build up an electronic record of everything we have." He grinned, showing his teeth for the first time. It made him seem softer and younger and less glacially intimidating. "So if you're looking for satellites, well, she's the one you need to talk to. Here."

They'd reached a wide courtyard with a fountain in the center and meticulously cultivated hedges spaced at even intervals around the lawn. The water in the fountain ran clean. He gestured toward a marble building. Elegant and stately, three stories tall, flanked by slender palm trees. "This is the main collection. She's taken over a bunch of other buildings on campus with the overflow, and it keeps growing all the time, but right here is where she keeps the heart of it."

He led them up the stairs to a pair of tall double doors made of carved dark wood. He tugged on the iron ring-shaped handle of one of the doors. "After you," he said.

Laurie and Jonathan walked into a dark marble foyer. It was mausoleum-still and chilly. Escobar closed the door behind them with an echoing clang. He bounded up the stairs. "Nick? Hey, Nick, you around?"

This must've been the main campus library. Old and marble, with an engraved gilt ceiling and heavy brass chandeliers. It reminded Laurie of the east coast, of some of the government buildings he'd seen with his mother in Washington. The memory triggered a sudden pang of homesickness.

A woman emerged from a doorway behind the long wooden circulation desk. She was very tall, one of the tallest women Laurie had ever seen, with broad shoulders and a muscular build. She wore jeans and a shapeless black sweater with an unraveling hem and mismatched patches at the elbows. Her feet were bare, and there was a long smudge of dust across one cheek. Her hair was very thick and brown, hacked off indifferently at her shoulders. She came out from around the counter, wiped her dusty hands on her jeans, and faced the new arrivals. "I take it these are the ones Marco called you about?"

"Hey, Nick. The little one is Laurie, and the grumpy tall one is Jonathan." Escobar slipped an arm around her shoulders and leaned in to kiss her on her neck. "Boys, this is Nicola. Any research questions you might have, any topic under the sun, she's the one who can at least shove your asses in the right direction."

"Nice to meet you guys," she said. "Let's go behind the counter here, and we'll sit down and chat. You can tell me what you need." She nodded at Escobar. "I've got it from here. Meet you at home?"

"You sure?" Escobar said. "I can stay. Or send Marco to wait with you."

"It's fine. Thanks." She gave him a quick kiss. "Don't expect me any time soon, though. I want to blast through the rest of the *Omni* collection tonight. It'll probably be another all-nighter."

"Duty calls, I suppose." Escobar said. He grinned. "You're in good hands, boys."

He headed toward the front door. Nicola led Jonathan and Laurie behind the counter and through a door into what looked like a small lounge. "We can talk here," she said.

She pointed toward a chenille-covered sofa. The room also contained a pair of comfortable-looking armchairs and a low table covered with a messy stack of books. "Take a seat. Anyone want a cup of tea?"

"Please," Laurie said. He flopped down onto the sofa. Jonathan sat beside him, stiff and reluctant. Nicola poured hot water from an electric kettle into chipped porcelain mugs and dunked tea bags into them.

"Sugar?" she asked.

Jonathan shook his head. "As much as you've got, thanks," Laurie said cheerfully.

She handed him the mug and the sugar canister. "Better fix your own. You sounded like you meant that literally."

While Laurie happily doctored his tea, Nicola sat down on one of the armchairs and folded her long, long legs underneath her. "So...?"

"Satellites," Laurie said. After dumping an inch or so of sugar into his mug, he stirred it up with the spoon Nicola handed him. "What do you know about satellites?"

"Very little. Close to nothing. But I've got a pretty substantial science collection here, and I've indexed practically all of it, so I might be able to track down what you're looking for. What *are* you looking for, incidentally? What do you need to know about satellites?"

"How we could find one. How we could control one. How we could use one to set up a television network," Laurie said. "We were at this weird underground church in the desert, out in Nevada. It used to be a communications facility, and we think it used to control satellites, but we sort of ended up in trouble—which, I should point out, *totally* wasn't our fault—so we don't have access to it anymore. So we want to learn how to find another one."

"Laurie, maybe you should let me do the talking," Jonathan said. There was a note of warning in his voice. Laurie turned to him, startled.

"She's okay, Jonathan. We can trust her."

"How on earth would you know that, Laurie?" Nicola sounded amused. "I mean, I'm not saying you can't, but that's kind of a reckless assumption to make."

"Not really. I mean, you're nice, and you're obviously brainy, and you gave us tea. And you have really pretty hair, even if you don't know what to do with it," Laurie said. "So, yeah, I suppose there's a chance you're secretly an awful person, but you're not, are you?"

Nicola looked at Jonathan and raised her eyebrows. "He always like this?"

"Pretty much, yeah."

"It's probably a good thing he's got you to protect him," she said. It was light, even flippant, but even so, Jonathan frowned.

"Satellites, then," she said. "Can I ask why you need your own television network?"

On the sofa beside him, Laurie could feel Jonathan shifting, ready to jump in if he said the wrong thing. "I always wanted to be a television star. I could host my own talk show or something. People would probably like watching me."

"They probably would." Nicola smiled at him. "But there are easier ways of getting on TV than harnessing yourself to a satellite or whatever exactly is going through that very decorative head of yours, Laurie. This is Los Angeles. We've got networks here, and sure, they're filled with a whole lot of crap, but the good news about that is they're starved for programming. Why don't you take your idea for a show to one of them?"

Laurie and Jonathan exchanged looks. "There are networks now? I mean, I know some cities have channels that air old shows," Jonathan said.

"There's two networks that I know about. They're both at the fledgling stage, but they both broadcast to cities beyond Los Angeles." Nicola held her mug between both hands and inhaled the steam. "It's a place to start."

"Could I get my own show, though? How would I do that?" Laurie asked.

"Ask them," Nicola said. "I can put you in touch with some people. One of the networks, Atomic, they're in Hollywood, they've been trying to generate some original programming for months now, and they've got some funds behind them. One of their producers uses the Archive a lot. She might be a good person to talk to."

"That'd be great. Do you have a way to call her? Do you have a phone? Do you think you could call her now?" Laurie asked.

"Whoa, wait. It's nighttime, in case you haven't noticed," Nicola said. "Anyway, Escobar's got the only working phone on campus, in his office. Only other line in the area is the payphone at the Coliseum."

"Oh." Laurie sat back on the sofa, deflated. "So what do we do?"

Nicola considered. "I can write you a letter of introduction. Tomorrow, or whenever you want, you can visit Atomic and give it to my friend Donya. Whether or not she does anything with it, or with you, is entirely up to her. Sound good?"

"I guess," Laurie said.

"It's not like I owe you favors, kiddo. I'll help you if I can, but there's no reason I should knock myself out for you."

"I know. Thank you. I don't mean to sound ungrateful. It's just that it's really super important, that's all."

"I'm sure it seems that way to you. Bear in mind, though, it's not like being a television star is all that noble of a goal."

"It's not just that. You don't understand. I want to—"

Jonathan, who'd been mostly silent during the conversation, cleared his throat. "Laurie, stop," he said. There was a clear note of warning in his voice. He addressed Nicola. "Sorry. Laurie gets a little demanding when he sees something he wants."

"So I see. I'll write you that letter now." She rose to her feet. "You said you came from Nevada?"

"We just arrived here today."

"You've got someplace to sleep? Hotels in the neighborhood are brutally expensive, not to mention a little dodgy."

"We'll find something," Jonathan said. "Got any recommendations?"

"Like I told my husband, I'm going to be working all night. It's not luxurious, but you can crash right here if you want."

"You mean it?" Laurie asked.

"Why not? The couch is decent, I've slept on it myself plenty of times. I can rustle you up some blankets. And this campus might be one of the safest places in the city."

Jonathan frowned. It was Jonathan's nature to look at bursts of good fortune with suspicion. Probably a good survival trait, but Laurie felt a little sorry for him anyway. "We'd love to stay here. Thank you," Laurie said. Beside him, Jonathan said nothing.

"Great," Nicola said. "Bathroom's downstairs. There's a shower, but the hot water comes and goes, so don't expect miracles. I'll get you some bedding."

"You're being very nice," Jonathan said. It sounded like a criticism.

"Laurie seems like he could use a break. You, too, for that matter. You're both radiating stress." She nodded at them. "So relax for a bit. Whatever brought you here, whatever demons you're running from, you can take a breather from them for an evening. You're safe."

She left them alone. Jonathan got to his feet. He crossed to the door, peeked out, made sure she was gone, then began to pace. "She shouldn't be helping us this much. And she seems too interested in you."

"Many people take an interest in me. People tend to like me," Laurie said. "You're not really suspicious of her, are you? Because she seems awesome, and I say we take any help she can give us."

Jonathan exhaled. "She seems fine, I guess. It's been a long day, in which I've managed to destroy my career and become a fugitive, and I think I'm too exhausted to trust my own judgment."

"Then let's not think about it until morning," Laurie said. "Can I take the sofa? It's not big enough to share. The floor looks pretty comfortable," he added.

Another long exhale, this one punctuated with a snort of what sounded like amusement. "Knock yourself out, Laurie."

"Cool. Thanks." Laurie kicked off his sandals. He curled up on his side on the sofa, his face pressed against the soft chenille, and closed his eyes. Even before Nicola returned with the promised blankets, he was asleep.

CHAPTER THIRTEEN

Laurie woke in the middle of the night to a crypt-still library. The darkness was disorienting; it took him a few moments to work out where he was and what he was doing there. He sat up on the sofa. After he'd fallen asleep, either Jonathan or Nicola had tucked a blanket around him. He groped around the floor until he found his sandals and pulled them on.

He could hear quiet, regular breathing. Jonathan must be asleep nearby. He sat in the darkness for a while until his eyes adjusted enough to make out a heap of blankets and pillows on the floor, with Jonathan presumably slumbering somewhere within.

He heard muffled noises, music, a radio broadcast maybe. Probably Nicola was hard at work, doing whatever it was she did here. Curious, Laurie went exploring.

The circulation desk and the reference room beyond it were dark, but a faint light shone beneath the closed door at the back of the small lounge where they slept. Laurie eased it open noiselessly and found himself in the library stacks. Claustrophobic and cluttered, with preposterously low ceilings and rows and rows of cheap aluminum bookcases overloaded with books of all shapes and sizes. The shelves nearest to him held skinny boxes filled with old, ragged magazines, most of which had ceased publication years before Laurie was born.

Laurie wandered around the maze of bookcases, trying to find the source of the music. He stood still and listened.

The noise came from above him. Definitely a radio, probably located on the next higher level of the stacks. He couldn't find a staircase, but there was an elevator, flimsy and small, almost child-sized. He hopped inside and jabbed his finger at the worn button for the next floor up.

The door slid open to reveal a level very similar to the one he'd just left. Same low ceiling, same maze of cheap shelves. Low-dangling fluorescent lights bathed everything in a sickly glow. He followed the music until he found Nicola.

She was listening to an old cassette player, the sound muffled and scratchy. She sat on an overturned milk crate in front of a low desk, upon which were spread several yellowing newspapers. She paged through them methodically, lost in thought.

At his approach, she lifted her head and smiled. "Hi, Laurie. Couldn't sleep?"

"Just felt like exploring." He looked down at the newspapers. "What's that?"

"Back issues of the *Times*. These are all from 2001, just before they shut their offices down for good." She frowned. "Ideally, I should photograph these. Get them on microfilm, because we might have the last complete collection of back issues anywhere, and they're not going to last forever. But that's a project for another time."

She gestured for him to come closer. "I had a thought earlier that I wanted to check out. You might be interested in this."

Laurie stood at the other side of the table. Nicola rotated the newspaper around so he could see what she'd been reading.

He found himself staring at a photograph of his mom, taken before he was born. She wore a dark suit with a fabric bow at her throat. A circular plaque depicting the Senate seal hung on the wall behind her. She looked stern yet kindly and, to his eyes, beautiful.

He looked at the headline above the photo. "It didn't make the front page?"

"Maybe not, but it was still pretty big news. I remember her assassination was all anyone talked about that week." Nicola's eyes were bright. "You're her son, aren't you? Laurent Sparks?"

"How'd you know?"

"Kind of a wild guess. Laurie isn't that common of a nickname for boys, and you were about the right age. You look the same, too." She tapped on another section of the article. His class picture from boarding school, dressed in his uniform jacket and necktie, his hair messy, his chin raised, his expression imperious and unsmiling.

Nicola seemed sympathetic, almost wistful. "I wondered what had happened to you. The last anyone heard, you'd vanished from the hospital, and I think the assumption was…" She paused.

"That the Soviets killed me, too? Finishing the job?" A lump formed in his throat, and he had to look away. "No, I just walked out. I was still pretty injured. I guess it was just luck that I survived."

"And you stayed hidden all these years?"

"I was in a monastery." At her raised eyebrows, he gave her a half-smile. "I know, right? It was nice there, though. They treated me well, and it was safe."

"It wasn't the Soviets, was it? That never made sense, that they'd kill your mother like that. Do you know who it was?"

"I know who pulled the trigger. It was this security guard at the hotel we were staying at. I don't know who he was working for. Anyway, the guy, the guard, I ran into him in Nevada, and he recognized me. So Jonathan and I came here to get away from him."

"And this satellite business?"

"I want to tell everyone," he said. "Now that they know I'm alive, I want everyone to know what really happened to my mom. I don't know if it'll do any good, but I want the bad guys to get into really big trouble."

"Looking for a little payback?" Nicola smiled at him. "Can't fault you for that, I suppose. Something you need to keep in mind, though, is that it might make things a whole lot worse. Telling the world about your mom will be the most dangerous thing you'll ever do."

"Yeah." He exhaled. "But what are the options?"

"You could hide again," Nicola said. "If that's something you wanted to do, Escobar and I, we could help you with that. We've got resources."

Laurie stared at her. "You're really nice, you know."

"Some people would disagree with you about that," she said. "I liked your mom, Laurie. Not that I knew her personally, but she seemed like a cool lady, and she did this country a whole lot of good when we were in a whole lot of trouble. If she were still around, maybe things would be better. And I like you, Laurie. I figure you're the high-maintenance kid brother I've never had."

"Thanks." Laurie grinned at her. "And thanks for offering to hide me, too. I appreciate it, I do. I know I'm spoiled and I sometimes don't thank people enough, but I'm grateful to you, really. But I think I'm going to try to go on television anyway. I think that's what I need to do."

"I can understand that. Just be careful. And make sure Jonathan keeps a close eye on you."

"I don't know if he will. He won't stay with me forever. I think he's planning on hiding out in Mexico after I get settled."

"Ah. That surprises me. I thought you and Jonathan might be…"

Laurie shook his head. "No. Me, yes, but it's not mutual. He's just being nice to me, like you are."

"Ah." Nicola continued to stare at him. "Well. You should probably try to get some sleep. Sounds like you've had a long day."

"I guess." Laurie didn't feel like sleeping. He felt like staying here and talking to Nicola about his mom, about Jonathan, about his entire life, but sleep was probably a good idea, especially if he wanted to be fresh and alert for visiting the television network tomorrow. "Thanks for everything, Nicola."

She nodded at him. "'Night, Laurie."

He made his way back down to the lounge where Jonathan slept. When he opened the door, light from the stacks spilled onto Jonathan's sleeping face. He looked peaceful and lovely, his thick hair falling across his face in a disheveled tumble.

Laurie sat down on the sofa and drew the blanket around his shoulders. He sat upright in the darkness staring at Jonathan for a very long time.

CHAPTER FOURTEEN

Laurie's first view of Hollywood was a disappointment. Nothing but dirty sidewalks and run-down storefronts, everything struggling and decaying if not abandoned. The Atomic offices were located on Sunset Boulevard, and the movies of his childhood had primed Laurie to expect glamour. The reality was a small beige stucco office building surrounded by a grove of thick, squat palm trees. Even the palms looked diseased, their fronds a dull brown, their bark gnarled and spiky like reptile skin.

The lobby was bare and deserted, all plain white walls and nylon carpets, no chairs, no furniture save for the reception desk, which was unoccupied. But the door had been unlocked, with ATOMIC NETWORK painted in fresh gold letters on the front next to a cunning little logo of a mushroom cloud, and thus they were probably in the right place.

A young man in jeans and a turquoise polo shirt hurried through the lobby, a clipboard tucked under one arm, his brows drawn together. He paused in his stride at the sight of the visitors. "Oh," he said. "What do you want?"

"We're here to see Donya Kashani," Laurie said. Hopefully he wasn't butchering the pronunciation too badly. That was the name of Nicola's producer friend, the name on the letter of introduction she'd written for him.

The young man pulled his lips into a grimace. He was a kid, really, younger than Laurie, with spiky blond hair and wire-rimmed glasses, full of purpose and devoid of humor. "Why? Is she expecting you? I don't even know if she's here."

Without waiting for a reply, he shook his head and waved a hand at them. "Take a seat. I'll see if I can find her." He stalked off down the hallway.

"Take a seat where? On the carpet?" Jonathan asked.

Laurie didn't answer. The corridor was dull and white and lined with featureless doors. "I thought this would be more glamorous," he said. He couldn't hide the disappointment in his voice. "I mean, television. Hollywood. Wasn't this a really glamorous industry? I mean, way back, back when things were less crappy?"

"I don't know where you got that idea. I'm pretty sure TV has always been crap." Jonathan shifted in place. "What happens if she's not here?"

"I guess we'll come back later." At Jonathan's frown, Laurie corrected himself. "Or I can come back later by myself, if you're sick of all this. I don't mean to keep you tied to me if you want to get on with your life."

"It's not that. It's…" Jonathan shook his head. "Getting on television seems like such a long shot, and even if you do manage it, it might bring you more trouble."

"Well, sure, but there's always the chance it might do me some good, too. Anything that gets the truth out—"

Jonathan held a hand up to shush him. A slender woman with soft waves of black hair entered the lobby. She wore a tailored violet pantsuit over a crisp white blouse, paired with leopard-skin pumps with high, high heels. She had warm brown skin and enormous dark eyes, expertly lined to make them look even larger. A whiff of roses accompanied her. She stopped at the door. "Hi. I'm Donya. Carl said you asked to see me?"

"Hi, Donya. I'm Laurie. This is Jonathan. Nicola at the Archive said you'd be a good person to talk to?"

"That depends," Donya said. "What do you want to talk to me about?"

"First off, Nicola gave me this to give to you. I guess it's about me and about how you should help me, if you can." Laurie fished a small cream-colored envelope out of his back pocket and handed it to Donya. "I don't know what it says, but it's probably positive. I think Nicola likes me."

Donya slipped a slim pinky under the flap of the envelope and ripped it open. She slid out the letter, a single page written in scrawled penmanship, and read it. When she finished, she looked up and smiled.

"Okay, Laurie," she said. "You're right. Nicola does like you." She gestured for Laurie and Jonathan to follow her. "Let's find somewhere we can sit and talk, and you can tell me what you need from me."

They followed her down the corridor to a wide, low-ceilinged room divided into twenty or more cubicles. Only a few of the cubicles appeared to be occupied.

"How long has the network been operational?" Laurie asked.

"We've been on the air for just under two years. I'm still not sure you can call us 'operational'. That implies a level of functionality we've yet to attain. But we'll get there." She opened up a door and ushered them into a conference room. Small round table, four chairs, no windows. "We can talk here."

Laurie sat between Donya and Jonathan. "What kind of shows do you produce?" he asked. "I'd never heard of Atomic before yesterday. Nicola said you do a lot of research at the Archive?"

"Nicola is kind. For the most part, 'research' isn't quite accurate," Donya said. "We don't have the resources yet to do much in the way of original programming. Mostly what we do is little more than filling hours of airtime. I borrow tapes from the Archive, old shows or whatever that I can just slap on the air whenever we don't have anything of our own to show."

"But you do have some original stuff, right?" Laurie asked.

Donya nodded. "I anchor a news report twice a day, morning and afternoon. It's nowhere near as extensive as it should be—I'm good at my job, don't get me wrong, but I'm just one person, and we don't have the funds to support a full-blown news team. And we encourage any viewers with video cameras to create their own programming and send it to us. It's pretty unsophisticated. Mostly we get people filming their cats doing cute things."

"That could be good," Laurie said. "I like cats."

"It is all rather extraordinarily lame. But it's what we have." Donya crossed her legs at the knee, one leopard-print pump dangling off her slim foot. "The good news, though, is that we've got a big financial backer now. Husband and wife, they were rich before the bombs fell, and they've managed to hold on to their money since then. She was a big celebrity back in the early eighties, though you might not have heard of her. Gina Davenport?"

"Gina Davenport, sure. She was on some sitcom, right? *Togetherness*? She had gorgeous feathered hair. I didn't know she was still alive."

"She's still around, still looks good. Still interested in television, which is good news for us. She's just started her own talk show. It's called *L.A. Elite*," Donya said. "It's a little rough as of yet, but honestly? It's the closest thing we have to a hit right now."

"That's really cool. I mean, Gina Davenport. She's a big star. Or she was, I guess."

"You are very easily impressed, Laurie," Donya said.

"Probably. I've spent the last decade in a monastery. I was sort of under the impression that network television didn't exist anymore, so the existence of any programming at all dazzles me," Laurie said. "Can you give me some idea of your audience? How many people watch you?"

"I couldn't tell you. There used to be ways to measure ratings, but that was a long time ago. Theoretically, we can broadcast to any city in the country as long as we have an affiliate station there, but…" She shrugged. "We're in a few major markets. Los Angeles, San Francisco, Seattle, Houston, Salt Lake. That's pretty much it right now. Each affiliate gives us a monthly report, but that's nothing more than an estimate. There's no way to measure how many households even have televisions, much less what they're watching. If we're lucky, maybe a few thousand people know about us and watch us somewhat regularly."

"Oh," Laurie said. He frowned.

"Can you tell me what you need from me? Why don't we start there?"

"I have a news story for you. It's kind of a big one. I can't tell you what it is right now, but Nicola knows all about it."

"She does?" This came from Jonathan. "What the hell, Laurie? When did you tell her?"

Laurie waved a nonchalant hand. "You were asleep. It's no big deal. She guessed most of it anyway. I told you she was cool." He returned his attention to Donya. "So I have this big story, but I want it to go out to as many people as possible at once. And it might be pretty dangerous, too, both for me and for whoever reports on it. I guess the only good thing I can say is that it'll bring a lot of attention to your network."

"Okay, intriguing." Donya looked over at Jonathan. "You involved in this?"

Jonathan shook his head. "It's all his."

"But you can vouch for it?"

"He's got a good story. Knowing Laurie, he'll probably embellish the hell out of it, but at the core will be the truth."

Donya stared at them for a moment with her dark, dark eyes, then nodded. "Here's what I'm going to propose," she said. "We can arrange to have you as a guest on Gina's show, Laurie. She's our star attraction, and she and her husband can afford to do some special promotion for this, if your story is as good as you say. I'll set you up with Gina, give you a chance to talk to her, see if you're comfortable with each other. If that works out, she can interview you, and we'll put it on the air. Does that work?"

"That sounds great, thank you," Laurie said. Jonathan was looking a little unhappy, *quelle surprise*, but Laurie didn't care. The prospect of meeting Gina Davenport was too good to pass up.

"Let's see if she's in. Might be a little early for her. She keeps her own hours." Donya's tone was laden with dark meaning, as though her life was complicated by Gina's lack of adherence to a formal schedule, but Laurie understood. There was hardly any point to being rich and famous and beautiful if you had to show up to everything on time.

Donya led them up a flight of stairs. Laurie perked up at the sight of the second floor, which had all the glamour the ground level had been sadly lacking. Rose-colored walls and soft recessed lighting, a waiting area with plush velvet loveseats and leafy potted palms and copper-framed magazine advertisements from the early 1980s, when Gina had modeled fashions for some big designer. Caprini, that had been the label. She looked fresh-faced yet sultry, just a teenager but already possessing the beauty and sophistication that made her a star.

"Have a seat, guys, and I'll track her down." Donya gestured toward a loveseat and disappeared down the hall.

Jonathan's brow was creased. "You okay with this?" Laurie asked him.

"Mmnf." Jonathan shook his head. "It's probably fine. Just... be careful who you talk to and how much you say."

"Well, sure. Obviously. I think you're being too fussy, though. I have good instincts about people. I'm not going to trust anyone I shouldn't."

Jonathan didn't look convinced. The silence grew strained. It was a relief when Donya poked her head back into the waiting area. "She's here. Come on."

Laurie and Jonathan followed her into a large room that was equal parts office and boudoir. The walls were covered with what looked like patterned silk in a soft, shimmering gold. There was a dainty high desk made from pale wood with gilt edges, plus a burgundy satin chaise lounge piled high with gold-embroidered pillows. Reclining on the chaise, dressed in a gauzy blue peasant blouse and matching palazzo pants, was Gina Davenport.

"Gina, these are the guys I was telling you about. That's Laurie, and the tall one with the scowl is Jonathan. Guys, this is Gina Davenport."

"Well, aren't they adorable?" Gina asked. She fluttered long, languid lashes at them, and Laurie felt his heart go pitty-pat. "Have a seat, darlings, and tell me what you need from me."

Gina had to be fifty now, though she looked a dozen years younger. Her skin was smooth and creamy, her hair was dark and shiny, and her breasts, beneath the soft draping folds of her blouse, were high and improbably perky. She extended a slender hand toward a pair of cushiony chairs across from her, her manicured nails gleaming when they caught the light.

Laurie sank into a chair, which enveloped him like a humongous velvety marshmallow. "It's really cool meeting you. I mean, I wasn't even born when *Togetherness* was on the air, and yet I totally know who you are. You're so pretty."

Gina laughed. "Thank you for that lovely reminder of my looming mortality, Laurie. But I appreciate the sentiment nonetheless." She addressed Donya, who was still standing near the door. "You can go. I can talk to these lovely boys without a chaperone."

Donya looked irritated, but it passed. She smiled. "Sure thing. I'll be at my desk if you need me." She disappeared.

Gina turned back to Laurie. "So, my beautiful little friend, Donya hinted that you might have some terribly important secret you want to confess to me?" She batted her lashes again and uncoiled her body on the chaise.

"I do. Or I might," Laurie amended after a quick glance at Jonathan's disapproving face. "I don't know yet. It's kind of a big secret, you see, and it could be dangerous if I told it to the wrong person."

"And you think I'm the wrong person?" Gina said. Her full peach lips assumed a mock pout, which evolved into a sultry smile in the next instant. She winked at him. "You could tell me all your naughtiest secrets, darling boy. I'd love to hear them."

"This might be a bad idea." Jonathan's tone was mild. "Ms. Davenport, we don't want to waste your time here, but I'm not sure Laurie's ready to tell his story to anyone."

Gina's eyes narrowed just a little as she regarded Jonathan, before the smile returned to her lips. "You're the skeptical one, I see. How nice for you," she said to him. "But Laurie is capable of making up his own mind."

"No, Jonathan's right. I mean, I'm sure I can trust you, but it's just really important I do the right thing here. I don't want to make any mistakes. It's too dangerous," Laurie said.

"There's that word again. *Dangerous.*" Gina lolled back on the chaise. She drew her lower lip into her mouth and bit it, all while examining Laurie through that heavy fringe of eyelashes.

She straightened up, newly purposeful. "Here's what we'll do," she said. "You and your protective friend—Jonathan, was it?—will be my guests for lunch. We'll talk, we'll gossip, we'll have a few cocktails, and then maybe you'll feel close enough to me to spill all your secrets. If not..." She shrugged, a languid rolling of shoulders. "You'll go on your merry way, taking your unspilled secrets with you."

"That sounds awesome," Laurie said quickly, before Jonathan could mount an objection. "Perfect."

"I have a few errands to take care of this morning. Why don't you boys meet me at the marina later? I have an adorable little boat we can take out on the ocean."

Laurie frowned. "I'm not sure of my feelings on boats," he said.

"It's not so much a boat, really, as a yacht." Gina smiled. "Does that change your feelings? I have an excellent chef onboard. You'll dine like princes."

"Is there champagne involved in this somewhere?" Laurie said.

Gina laughed. "Laurie, my beautiful little one, I feel quite certain you and I are meant to be close friends." She rose to her feet. "If that's what it takes to lure you onboard, there will be champagne. Marina del Rey, sloop eighteen. It's the *Capri Queen*. Two o'clock?"

"Absolutely. We'll be there," Laurie said. He stood; Jonathan followed suit.

"Fantastic," Gina murmured. She extended her slim hand to Laurie, then leaned in and pressed her soft lips against his temple. She smelled like sandalwood and lilacs. "I can't wait."

Jonathan didn't say anything until they were outside the building, heading to the jeep. "We shouldn't go on the boat."

"Why not? Do you get seasick?"

"Boats are a terrible idea. If anything goes wrong, we'll be trapped."

"Yeah, but that assumes Gina would have a reason to trap us," Laurie said. "She doesn't know who I am, and there's no way she'll find out unless I tell her. And if there's anything suspicious, I won't tell her. Simple enough."

"She's creepy," Jonathan said.

"She's *famous*. And I thought she was nice. Kind of flirty, but that's not anything to hold against her. A lot of people flirt with me. Just because you don't doesn't mean it's something bad."

Jonathan jumped into the driver's seat and made a big production out of adjusting the rearview mirror. "You seemed weirdly into her," he said at last.

"Why 'weirdly'? I like being around pretty people and nice things. Surely you've figured that out."

"Yeah, but…" Jonathan shook his head. "Never mind."

"Do you know how to get to… where'd she say her yacht was? Marina del Rey?" Laurie asked.

"I know how to get to the ocean. We can find it from there," Jonathan said. "I can't talk you out of this?"

"Probably not, nope."

"Hell." Jonathan shook his head and backed out of the parking lot. "You're trouble, Laurie, you know that?"

"Yep. But admit it, you like me that way," Laurie said.

Jonathan rolled his eyes and didn't answer.

CHAPTER FIFTEEN

The *Capri Queen* was probably small by yacht standards, but to Laurie's eyes it was glorious, all white and shining in the sunlight, with brass railings and a deck of dark wood. Gina, now dressed in a ruffled crepe pantsuit the color of sea foam, stood on the deck and extended graceful tanned arms to help Laurie up the gangplank. "My darling boys, you made it!" She pulled Laurie into a quick closed-mouthed kiss, followed by a buss on each cheek. "Come with me. I'll fix you up with some bubbles, and then I want you to meet my husband."

They followed her across the deck to a standing bar, where a handsome young man in a bow tie and vest popped the cork on a fresh bottle of champagne and poured it out into flutes. Gina passed glasses to Jonathan and Laurie. "As promised, my dear," she said to Laurie. "Cheers."

"So these are your friends, Gina." At a voice from behind them, Laurie turned to see a darkly-tanned middle-aged man. He had a smoothly-shaved head and an unlined face. He was tall, and his upper body appeared muscular underneath his black collarless suit. "Hi, boys. I'm Kip. Gina's my wife."

"Nice to meet you. I'm Laurie." Laurie examined him. "You look familiar. You're famous, aren't you?"

Kip smiled. "I am, though I'm a little shocked that you recognized me, Laurie. My fame came long before your time." He accepted a flute from the bartender and took a sip. "In another life, I was a fashion designer. I suppose I was pretty well-known, back before the world changed."

Laurie was nodding before he even finished his sentence. "Kip Caprini, of course. I knew Gina modeled for you, but I didn't realize you two were married. That's really cool. My mom used to have one of your suits. It was emerald green, with a pencil skirt with a slit on the side, and the jacket had a mandarin collar. It was made in the eighties sometime, but she wore it long into the nineties."

"Your mother must've been a very stylish woman," Kip said. He smiled. "Are you the one with the big, bad secret?" His tone was a little mocking, but he didn't seem unfriendly.

"He certainly is. Only he doesn't know whether he's going to share that secret with me, so let's make sure to be extra-nice to him, okay, sweetheart?" Gina slid an arm around her husband's neck and leaned up to give him a lingering kiss. "Are we ready to cast off?"

"Let's do it." Kip disentangled himself from Gina and grinned at Jonathan and Laurie. "Ever been on a boat before, boys?"

"When I was a kid. Not for years, though," Laurie said. "Ah— we're not going to go very far out, are we?"

"Relax. It's a gorgeous day, and the seas are gentle. We're just going to have a nice lunch and a few drinks." Kip winked at him.

Lunch was steamed crab served with a cold lemony mayonnaise, with crusty bread and sweet butter and green grapes and more champagne than Laurie could drink. Even Jonathan relaxed and unbent a little under the force of so much good food. Laurie felt warm and expansive, like Gina and Kip were his oldest and most trusted friends in the world. Kip talked at length about his struggles to rekindle his once-burgeoning design career in a world that viewed fashion as a senseless waste of too-precious resources, a struggle Gina experienced as well with her attempts to recapture some of her former small-screen fame.

Goddamn, he loved champagne. He felt warmer and fuzzier and friendlier by the moment, and by the point in the conversation where Gina, herself gigglier and friendlier from the magical bubbles, got around to asking him about his secret, he was more than willing to spill. She was an attentive audience, her beautiful face displaying compassion and amazement at appropriate intervals as he spun out his tale. If she found any of it implausible, her face didn't betray her doubts.

"You poor darling," she said. She patted his forearm. "And you've been protecting him all this time?" she asked, turning to Jonathan.

"Well, yeah, but it's only been like a day and a half," Jonathan said. He seemed amenable enough now about Laurie sharing his secret. At least he hadn't tried to physically prevent him from speaking, which Laurie had half-expected. "It's not like protecting Laurie has been my life's work."

"What are your plans, Jonathan?" Kip asked. "I imagine going back to your old life isn't an option."

"I'll stick with Laurie for the time being, until I know he's safe," Jonathan said. "I don't have anything better to do, and I guess I sort of have an obligation to him now."

Laurie smiled at him, syrupy and oozing with warmth and love. "That's the nicest thing you've ever said to me."

"Oh, please." Jonathan looked embarrassed by the gushy sentiment but not, Laurie's bubble-fogged brain noted, displeased.

"Laurie, I'd love to interview you for my little show," Gina said. "*L.A. Elite*, did Donya tell you about it? Have you seen it? I think this is the very best way to get your story out to everyone in the whole wide world."

"That'd be wonderful," Laurie said. "You're so wonderful, Gina." When he reached for his champagne flute, his hand closed around air. Jonathan had picked it up and discreetly moved it just out of his reach. He opened his mouth to protest, then decided not to bother. It was lovely being here, surrounded by warm sun and cool ocean breezes, the sea blue and calm, the company delightful.

Gina and Kip exchanged a long, silent glance. "I'll tell the captain to take us to shore. We'll go to our beach house, I think, and continue this," Gina said.

"Sounds wonderful," Laurie said, and giggled. "Wonderful" was a perfect word, he'd never noticed how perfect, and it summed up exactly how he felt about everything right now.

Gina and Kip lived in Pacific Palisades. Laurie and Jonathan left the jeep parked at the marina and traveled up the coast in the back of Kip's luxury sedan. Nothing about the previous thirty years of economic devastation had hurt Kip and Gina much. Their house was huge and opulent, perched high on the side of a cliff with a panoramic view of the ocean. From outside, the house looked like it had been carelessly plopped on the hill by gigantic hands. It featured an entire wall of windows on the ocean-facing side. A glass staircase anchored to the windows on the inside led up to the second floor. Gigantic stark modern art paintings in vivid colors hung on the white walls. The living room was filled with white suede sofas and armchairs and a wide, low coffee table, gleaming and dense like a solid rectangular block of obsidian.

They were joined in the living room by a beautiful young man in a lightweight black turtleneck over tight black jeans. He was Asian and immaculate, with flawless skin and thick black hair worn slightly long. "Welcome back," he said to Gina and Kip. "I didn't expect you home this early."

"Galen, this is Laurie and Jonathan. They're going to be helping me with a very important story. Boys, this is Galen, my personal assistant," Gina said.

"Nice to meet you." Galen's smile was a little perfunctory, but his tone was gracious.

"Be a darling, Galen, and fix us something to drink, will you? Gin, I think. And some of those little cheese crackers, and perhaps some fruit or whatever."

Jonathan cleared his throat. "Nothing for me, thank you. I had plenty to drink on the boat. Laurie, too."

Gina shot them a dazzling smile. "Of course, darlings. Galen, we have some of that lime squash left over, don't we? The boys might enjoy that."

Galen frowned, a near-imperceptible creasing of his smooth upper lip, like something about the situation didn't sit well with him. Even Laurie's bubble-infused brain picked up on a certain new tension in the room. Galen met Laurie's stare, and Laurie felt a flicker of some new emotion. Fear, maybe.

Galen disappeared in the direction of what Laurie supposed was the kitchen. Gina glanced after him, then smiled at her guests. "I'll just give him a hand." She headed after him.

"Are you still designing?" Laurie asked Kip. "I mean, I don't know what kind of market there is these days for fashion—"

"There's none. No market at all." It was snappish, but Kip smiled to soften it. "Believe me, I wish there were. Women aren't interested in looking like women any more. Gina is a rare and beautiful flower in these parts. I know a lot of people have it rough, but still, you'd think they'd want a little glamour in their lives."

"I know I do," Laurie said. "I think what you do is so, so wonderful." He smiled, still loopy and dizzy from lunch.

"Have you given any thought to what will happen after Gina airs her story on you, Laurie?" Kip asked.

"I have no idea," Laurie said. "I think we're just sort of winging it, right, Jonathan?"

"We'll probably leave the country," Jonathan said. "We might have to."

"Mexico?" At Jonathan's nod, Kip settled back into the sofa. "Gina and I have a little place in Baja. Right on the water. We don't use it most of the year. You could move right in, look after the grounds. Doesn't cost much to live down there. You can dine like kings for pennies a day."

Jonathan frowned. "Why'd you be willing to help us like that? You hardly know us."

Kip flung his free arm around the back of the sofa and crossed his legs at the ankles. Expensive shoes. Crocodile, maybe. "We can afford it, and you seem like nice kids who need a break. It's a dangerous world out there. There are plenty of people who'd try to take advantage of you."

"That's right." Gina returned, bearing a tray of crystal glasses, with a somewhat disapproving Galen trailing her. She rested the tray on the table and distributed beverages to the group. Something with fresh limes and mint leaves and sparkling water, tart and sweet and delicious. Laurie was a little sad it wasn't more champagne, but Jonathan was probably right about having had enough already. Jonathan was always right. "What are we talking about?"

"I suggested the boys stay at our place in Mexico, at least until the heat from your story blows over a little."

"What a fantastic idea." Gina perched on the arm of the sofa next to her husband. She leaned into him, her body language slinky and seductive, as she examined Laurie and Jonathan. "Where are you staying now? Because we have plenty of room here. We could keep you safe and out of sight until the story airs."

"That's so nice of you," Laurie said. "We spent last night with our new friend Nicola, but I don't know if she's willing to put us up for more than that."

Gina froze. "Nicola? You don't mean Nicola from the Archive, do you?"

"Sure. That's who put us in touch with Donya. Do you know her?"

"Of course. Kip and I do a lot of business with the Archive. She's very useful, Nicola. Very... connected." Gina and Kip exchanged glances. Kip raised his eyebrows at his wife.

"Does Nicola know you're here?" Gina asked.

Jonathan shifted on the sofa. He frowned. "Does it matter?" he asked.

"This is no good, Gina," Kip said. "The bitch is trouble. If we get on her bad side for this..."

"She won't find out. I'll tell Donya the interview didn't pan out and the boys left on their own after lunch. She'll have no reason to suspect that's not the truth."

"Laurie, we're getting out of here." Jonathan was already on his feet. Laurie, who'd only half-listened to the exchange between Gina and Kip, was a little slower. He still wasn't at all sure what was going on, but some kind of adrenaline-fueled internal warning system surged into overdrive. He stood up, the glass of lime squash still in his hand. The room shifted. He felt unsteady on his feet, his fingers thick and numb around the glass.

The glass. Oh. "You drugged me," he said to Gina, or meant to say, but he wasn't sure whether he got the words out or not before everything swam and blurred and shifted, before the ground reached up to swallow him whole, before everything went dark.

CHAPTER SIXTEEN

Soft and warm and so very comfortable, swimming in a sea of fur and feathers... Laurie shifted his arms and felt nothing but softness against his bare limbs. He was lying on a bed, a gigantic bed, on top of a white fur comforter. So comfortable...

"Our sleeping beauty is waking up." A woman's voice, light and full of music. Gina.

"He'll be out of it for a while longer. Kid can't weigh much more than a hundred, hundred and ten. The drink hit him hard." Masculine and rough. That'd be Kip.

Ah. Yes. Kip and Gina had drugged him. That was right. That was something he should probably be very, very concerned about, but it was difficult to see the point. He was warm and comfortable, and it was nice just lying here. Perfectly safe...

"You sure you're not bringing a load of trouble down on us, my love?" Kip asked. "Let's think about it. If this twink's story is true, maybe your best option is to do the damn interview with him. Might bring you all that attention you've been missing so much lately."

His voice sounded mocking, even taunting. Alarm began to creep in around the edges of Laurie's fuzzy brain.

"Don't be silly, darling," Gina said. "That's not the kind of attention I want. I don't need to be on some government hit list. You either."

152

"You're not kidding." The bed jostled as Kip sat on the edge. "Maggie Sparks's kid, huh? I thought we'd heard the end of that Communist whore."

"I'd say pretty little Laurie is a totally different kind of whore." Gina giggled.

"We should get rid of the other one. He's sharper than this nitwit. He could cause trouble."

"Later. We can use him in case Laurie doesn't want to play along with us." Another giggle. "Can you wake him up? I want to have some fun with him."

"I'm awake," Laurie said. It came out a little slurred. He opened his eyes and struggled up to a sitting position.

This must be Kip and Gina's master bedroom. The bed was enormous and decadent, draped in soft fur blankets. The walls were papered in gold and cream. The ceiling was mirrored, which confused Laurie at first glance, and confused him even more when he realized he was naked.

"I'm awake," he said again, a little stronger this time, "and you two aren't nice at all."

"Aw, poor Laurie. Don't be like that." Gina sat on the bed beside him. "I think you'll find that I'm very nice indeed." She reached forward and pushed his hair out of his eyes. He twitched his head away from her. The room swam.

"Where's Jonathan?" he asked. "What did you do with him?"

"Hush. He's fine. He's just fine, and he'll stay fine, as long as you're a good pet," Gina said. She leaned forward. "Nobody's going to hurt you, Laurie. I just want to play a little."

Laurie stared at her for a moment. "This is really creepy," he said finally. "Where are my clothes?"

"We thought you could use new ones," Gina said. "Purely a charitable gesture on our part. Darling?"

Kip got to his feet and flung open the doors to a gigantic armoire that took up most of one wall. "Gina wants a well-dressed pet," he said. He tossed a handful of garments at Laurie, folds of dark blue satin and shimmering bronze. "Try those on. Inside out."

"Inside out?" Laurie asked, confused. Brain was still moving a little slowly. He picked up the clothes, swung his legs out of bed.

"I need to make alterations. Those are Gina's."

Gina giggled. "Later, I'll have Kip design an entire fancy wardrobe, just for you. Won't that be nice?"

With a wary glare at his captors, Laurie dutifully turned each garment inside-out and pulled them on. Narrow dark blue slacks, too long in the legs and too roomy in the hips, a button-down shirt made of shiny bronze jersey, a tiny tailored satin jacket that matched the pants. He stood in front of Kip. "Well?"

Kip frowned and pulled at the seams, tugged at the collar of the shirt, then stood back and scrutinized the effect. He picked up a pincushion shaped like a penguin off of the dresser and began pinning seams in place. "Hold still," he told Laurie.

"This is ridiculous," Laurie said. "Where's Jonathan?"

He pulled away from Kip and moved toward the door. Very casually, Kip slammed him back against the armoire and struck him hard across the face. "Knock it off and keep still, or I'll beat the crap out of you."

"Be gentle, darling," Gina said from the bed. She flopped down on her stomach on the pale fur and rested her chin in her hands. "Don't hurt him. Especially not that pretty face." To Laurie, she said, "Your boyfriend is fine, sweetie. If you behave yourself, we'll let you see him soon."

"And if you keep acting like a brat, we'll kill him," Kip said. He tugged at a seam experimentally, then nodded. "Okay, now take those off. I'll do some alterations."

"Give me something else to wear. I'm not thrilled with being naked around you two," Laurie said. He pulled off the clothes, careful not to prick himself on the needles.

Kip gestured with his head toward Gina, who rummaged in the armoire and produced a short gold satin robe with a collar made of violet feathers. Laurie yanked it on and belted it. "You two suck, you know that?" he said.

"Careful. We can get rid of you easily enough, if we decide you're too much of a pain in the ass. Your boyfriend too." Kip nodded at Gina. "This is her idea. Gina likes her fun."

"You're just such a little beauty, Laurie," Gina said. "I'll take good care of you. You'll like it here with me. We'll have a good time."

Laurie wanted to tell her he most certainly would not like it there, but he didn't feel like getting hit again. This was maddening, and embarrassing, and he couldn't help thinking he'd somehow blundered into this by falling too hard for Gina's glamour.

Gina leaned forward and stroked his cheek. Her touch was light. "Poor baby," she said, her voice throbbing with sympathy. "He shouldn't have bruised you. Come with me, and let's see if we can fix that."

She led him into the attached master bathroom. Under different circumstances, Laurie would be thrilled to pieces by this—it was huge and opulent, with a sapphire-blue bathtub and shiny copper fixtures—but right now he couldn't summon up anything more than frustration and worry. He obeyed without complaint when Gina ordered him, sweetly, to sit on a padded suede bench beside the tub.

She crouched in front of him and set to work on his face. Creamy foundation, bronze eyeliner, multiple glistening metallic shades of eye shadow, soft rose pencil on his lips, all of it applied with a light, expert touch. Treating him like her own living doll. He didn't resist any of this, even when she attacked his hair with a boar's-hair brush and a can of mousse. "You're just such a lovely thing, Laurie."

"Yep. I know. You said it before," he said. "Do you and Kip do this sort of thing often? Kidnapping, I mean, and nonconsensual makeovers?"

"Not as often as I'd like," Gina said. She giggled. "Don't fret so much. We're not going to hurt you. We're just going to have some fun for a while, and then we'll let you go, I promise."

Laurie wondered about that part. Earlier, Gina and Kip had sounded scared, actively scared, at the thought of Nicola finding out what they were up to, and while Laurie had a hard time imagining Nicola bringing much wrath and ruin down upon anyone, it occurred to him that Gina and Kip might take steps to ensure she never found out about this. It wasn't a pleasant thought. Still, he kept his concerns to himself and just let Gina paint his face and tug at his hair.

When she was done, and when Kip had finished his alterations, and when Laurie was fully dressed and painted and coiffed, he was forced to admit he approved of the result. They'd even given him a pair of Gina's shoes, black patent-leather lace-up booties with kitten heels, and he looked sort of fantastic, really, like a pop star from a bygone era. It compensated a little for being drugged and manhandled and held here against his will.

It was probably wrong to think he could get used to this kind of thing, particularly if it involved more champagne and the occasional bubble bath.

Gina squawked with delight when she saw him in all his borrowed splendor. "You're gorgeous, Laurie!" she said. She kissed him on the cheek. "Kip, what do you think?"

Kip yawned. "Kid cleans up nice, I suppose."

"Did you want to play with him first? I could watch you two," Gina said.

"Nah," Kip said. "You always nag me for playing too rough, and that sucks all the joy out of it. Have we thought about what we're doing for dinner?"

"Quail, I thought. I left instructions with Gwendolyn." Gina took Laurie by the hand. "Would you like more champagne, Laurie?"

"Probably, yes. But before anybody gets around to playing with me, I'd like to see Jonathan, okay?" Laurie said. "It's not too much to ask."

"You're not in any position to ask anything," Kip said.

"Darling, don't be so *brutish*," Gina said. She patted Laurie's hand. "I promise you, he's fine. But I have the distinct sense he'd want to ruin our fun, so it's best we keep him out of the way for the moment."

She led him downstairs, down the clear glass steps affixed to the wall, which gave the illusion of walking on air. Laurie, his stomach unsettled from all the various drugs and drinks and unusual foodstuffs he'd ingested recently, couldn't look down without feeling a wave of nausea. He could see straight through the steps into the living room below, and that made his legs quiver with vertigo. Gina slipped her arm around his waist and held onto him. As creepy and despicable as he found her now, he was grateful for the support.

Galen, elegant Galen, hovered near the front door, hands clasped behind his back. His anxious expression only worsened when he saw Laurie.

"Hey, Galen," Laurie said. "I think your bosses are planning on raping me. You okay with that?"

Gina giggled. "Hush, you," she told Laurie. To Galen, she said, "Darling, you're fretting about something. What is it?"

"Company," Galen said. After that first tense glance, he seemed to deliberately avoid looking at Laurie. "Lewis called from the gate. Nicola's here."

"Hell," Kip said. "What does she want? What did you tell Lewis?"

"I told him to stall her for a bit, say I was trying to find out if you were home."

"Hell," Kip said again. He turned to Laurie, his face dark with frustration. "Did you tell her you were meeting us?"

"Yeah. Yeah, I did. Of course I did. I told her Jonathan and I were going to see you. So it's no wonder she's checking up on us. She's taken a special interest in my well-being. She's going to be really mad when she finds out about this."

Kip glared at him through narrowed eyes. "You are *such* a pain in the ass," he said.

"I know. I really, really am. Always have been. Which is something you might have considered before you two decided to adopt me as your personal sex kitten or whatever," Laurie said. "So you should probably rustle up Jonathan from wherever you've stashed him and drag him out here before Nicola gets angry."

As if on cue, the doorbell rang once, a furious electronic screech, followed by a loud percussive series of thumps against the front door. Kip and Gina exchanged looks.

"We could kill her," Kip said. It sounded half-hearted.

"That would end poorly for us," Gina said. Her well-shaped eyebrows drew together prettily. She shook her head, then gestured with one dainty hand toward Galen. "Might as well answer that," she said.

Galen unbolted the door and threw it open. Sure enough, there stood Nicola. At her side was Escobar, who held his gun loosely by his side. Nicola looked furious; Escobar looked amused.

Without acknowledging Galen, Nicola strode into the living room. "You doing okay, kiddo?" she asked Laurie.

"Yep. Are you here to rescue me?" Laurie asked.

"That's the plan. Though looking at you, maybe you don't need it. I like the new image," she said. "Where's Jonathan?"

"Why should we tell you?" Gina asked. It sounded petulant. Nicola just fixed her with a look. Gina tried to match her glare, then gave up and huffed out a sigh. "We put him in the wine cellar. Galen?"

With a wary glance at Nicola and Escobar, Galen nodded once and headed toward the kitchen. Nicola watched after him, then turned to Kip and Gina. "Just couldn't help yourselves, could you?"

"We didn't know they were yours," Gina said. "Anyway, we weren't going to hurt them."

"Uh huh." Nicola stared at her, humorless and severe. "If I hear of you trying anything like this again, I'll revoke your borrowing privileges."

To Laurie, it sounded like an extraordinarily weak threat, but Gina's eyes widened a little. "You wouldn't dare," she said. "If I can't use the Archive, I can't do my show. If I pull funding, Atomic would collapse."

"I know. And right now the success of the network takes priority over punishing you—albeit very, very slight priority—which is why you're only getting a warning," Nicola said.

"Maybe you're not as all-powerful as you think, Strozyk," Kip said.

Nicola shifted her attention to him. Without taking her eyes off of Kip, she said, "Hey, Laurie? He the one that hit you?"

Laurie touched his cheek. He'd thought the makeup covered the bruises. Nicola had sharp eyes. "Uh-huh."

Nicola slapped Kip, hard, the noise like a gunshot. Kip raised a clenched hand and stepped toward her. At her side, Escobar shifted his shoulders. Just a tiny bit, but it was enough to make Kip freeze.

"You're dead, Strozyk," Kip said. "You both are. At some point, somehow, I'm going to see to that. I have *connections*, you know." He gestured to Laurie. "The little twink, too. I know who he is, and as soon as you leave here, I'm going to let everyone who's looking for him know exactly where to find him."

"Hush, darling," Gina said. To Nicola, she said, "Don't pay him any attention. He's just cranky because you ruined our plans."

Nicola didn't say anything. Kip fell silent, too, and just glared at her, his eyes narrowed into slits.

The silence was broken by the arrival of Galen and Jonathan. Jonathan looked disheveled and furious. Laurie perked up at the sight of him. "Hey, Jonathan," he said.

"Laurie. You okay?" Jonathan asked. He looked at Nicola and Escobar, at Kip and Gina. "They do anything to you?"

"Makeover," Laurie said.

"I can see that," Jonathan said. He looked bewildered. "Can we get out of here now?"

"I think so. Nicola is rescuing us," Laurie said.

"Well, good." Jonathan looked at Gina and Kip again, and his expression focused, darkened. "Glad to hear it."

"We'll be on our way," Escobar said. "Nick?"

Nicola nodded. "Right behind you," she said.

Galen held the door open for them, as composed and competent as before. As they started to leave, Kip called after them. "Don't get too cocky, Strozyk. Something happens to you, the void will produce someone to replace you."

Nicola didn't answer him. Once they were safely outside, once Galen had shut the door behind them, once they were walking down the long driveway toward a battered red sedan that seemed to belong to Nicola, Laurie turned to her. "Hey, thanks so much for that. That was cool," he said. "I mean, they didn't even try to argue with you or anything, they just let you take us and leave. How badass is that?"

"Glad you're impressed, kiddo," Nicola said. "Up until today, I would have said those two were annoying but harmless. I might have to revise that."

"How'd you know we were in trouble? How'd you even know we were here?"

Nicola shook her head. She shot a glance back at the house and didn't say anything until they were safely inside the car, Nicola behind the wheel, Jonathan and Laurie in back. The car was in pretty rough shape, but the interior was scrupulously clean. "You know Galen, Gina's assistant? He called the payphone at the Coliseum and left a message that you two might be in trouble. He owes me a few favors. Enough to rat out his bosses, lucky for you."

"Oh, good. I liked him. He seemed really nice," Laurie said.

Nicola just shook her head. She backed up the car, swung it around, headed down the twisting driveway. There was a wrought-iron gate at the bottom, and it was closed, which made Laurie a little nervous, but it swung open seamlessly as they approached. Escobar touched a hand to his forehead and gave the guard manning the security booth by the gate an informal salute.

"So I guess my interview with Gina is off, huh?" Laurie said. "Do you think Donya would interview me instead?"

Escobar turned around and leaned his elbow on the seatback to face Laurie. "Kid, I think you should stop thinking about getting interviewed and maybe think of ways to stay out of sight. Didn't you hear Caprini? He said he was going to tell the people after you where you are."

"Well, yeah, but I think that was an empty threat. He won't know who to tell." Laurie thought for a minute. "Hey, Escobar? Are you and Nicola going to be in any trouble for this? From what Kip was saying…"

"We'll be fine," Nicola said. Her eyes met his in the rearview mirror. "Don't waste energy worrying about us, okay? Escobar's right. We need to start thinking about how to lower your profile for a bit."

"Laurie and I will take it from here," Jonathan said. "You and Escobar have done a lot for us already."

Nicola's gaze shifted to Jonathan. "You're going to stick with him, right? You're not going to leave him alone, you're going to keep him out of trouble?"

"That's the plan," Jonathan said. Laurie felt a little quiver in his chest. Jonathan leaned forward to talk to Nicola. "Just drop us off by the marina. We parked in that area. That's where Caprini keeps his boat."

"It's a yacht," Laurie said. "It was great. As awful and gross as Gina and Kip turned out to be, at least they showed us a good time at lunch."

"You've got a very forgiving nature, Laurie," Escobar said dryly.

Nicola pulled to the side of the road next to the marina. Jonathan and Laurie clambered out of the backseat. She slid out as well and extended her hand to them. They shook it in turn.

"I'm always at the Archive. Call the payphone at the Coliseum if you run into trouble," she said.

"Thanks, Nicola," Laurie said. "You've been amazing."

She stared at him for a moment, then placed her hands on his shoulders, leaned down, and gave him a quick kiss on the forehead. Her lips were light and dry. "Take care of yourself, kiddo," she said.

Laurie stood in the parking lot and watched as Nicola and Escobar drove away. Jonathan nudged his arm. "You okay?"

"Yeah. I liked her. I just wish we could stay with them longer."

"We're better off on our own," Jonathan said. "Come on. Let's find the jeep."

Jonathan was probably right. At the moment, though, it felt like leaving Nicola was the worst idea in the world.

CHAPTER SEVENTEEN

It took them too long to realize the jeep had been stolen. They circled the marina parking lot on foot a few times before it finally sank in that it was gone, along with their best chance of getting out of the city.

"Probably for the best," Laurie said, taking a stab at optimism. "It was pretty identifiable, what with the big old Zephyr logo on the side. It made us an easy target."

"Maybe, but it means we're stuck here for the time being." Jonathan thrust his hands in his pants pockets and frowned. "You know what's weird, though, is I think Kip or Gina took the key."

"You sure? Why would they do that? Maybe you put it in your bag." Laurie's eyes widened as a thought occurred to him. "They didn't take your money, did they?"

Jonathan rifled through the contents of his canvas bag and extracted a roll of cash. Wasn't much of a roll, really. Laurie didn't know how much they had left, but it wouldn't last long. "Everything else is here. The key was in my pocket, and now it's gone."

"Kip and Gina wouldn't steal it, would they?" Laurie asked. "I mean, they seemed like the type of people who'd have lots of fancy cars. They wouldn't want a crappy old jeep."

"Maybe they wanted to make sure nobody could tie our disappearance to them. They knew we drove here." Jonathan scowled, his brows drawing together at dangerous angles. "That assistant, Galen.

He could've done it. I doubt he would have risked calling Nicola from the house anyway. Kip and Gina might have sent him to get rid of the jeep, and he called the Coliseum from a payphone while he was out of the house. As far as the jeep goes, all he'd have to do is toss the key into the front seat, and someone would come along and steal it. Which seems to be what happened."

Laurie frowned. "Hey, when Kip was talking to Nicola, didn't he sound kind of smug, like he knew he could cause us trouble?"

"What are you thinking?" Jonathan asked.

"Ferris. His ID was in the glove compartment, remember? If Galen found that, Kip would know that Ferris is the guy I told them about, the guy who's after me. He could contact him and tell him where we are."

Jonathan thought it over. "It's possible. But even if Kip and Gina know about Ferris, even if they told him we're in Los Angeles, it's still a big city. Apart from not having a car anymore, I don't know that this makes it all that much more dangerous for us."

"We could go back to the Archive and ask Nicola for help," Laurie said. "She could hide us."

"If Kip contacts Ferris, he'd tell him about Nicola, and that's the first place he'd look for you. We can't risk approaching her."

"So what's the plan?" Laurie asked.

Jonathan glanced up at the darkening sky. "Find someplace to sleep before nightfall. I can't speak for you, but I'm not really feeling the need for dinner after everything we ate and drank on the yacht."

"It was really good, wasn't it?" Laurie said. "I wish I could have champagne every day."

Jonathan stared at him. "Are you really that unaffected by what they tried to do to you?"

Laurie gave this more serious consideration than Jonathan was probably expecting. "I don't know. I'm kind of mad and embarrassed about it, and I don't like them much for doing that to me, but… it's over, right? Everything turned out okay. What's the use of obsessing about it?"

They walked north on a rough paved path that ran along the sandy beach. Just past Marina del Rey was Venice, a run-down, ramshackle beach neighborhood, not much more than cheaply-made shacks placed too close together, nothing like the poshness of Gina's house on the cliff.

"You know this city, right? Are there any good hotels in the area? Nice ones, with hot water and bathrobes and room service?"

"Hotels are a bad idea," Jonathan said. "We should keep a lower profile from here on out."

"From my experience, hotels are *never* a bad idea," Laurie said. Jonathan just threw him an exhausted look, so Laurie gave up and followed him in silence.

The beach was a wide expanse of pale sand, with nothing but the sea and the darkening sky beyond it. The sand was littered with dozens of makeshift tents, ratty structures made of canvas or cardboard or plastic tarps. Laurie wrinkled his nose.

"We're not sleeping on the beach, are we? We can't sleep on the beach. That's not right."

"Sure we can," Jonathan said. "It's a warm night, it's free, and it's anonymous."

"I'm not exactly dressed for sleeping outside, you know," Laurie said. It sounded sulky.

"No, you're dressed for engaging in nonconsensual kinky shenanigans with a couple of predatory assholes."

"I don't imagine they'd've been that kinky, actually," Laurie said. He trailed Jonathan across the sand in the direction of the tents. Sand trickled into the tops of his borrowed booties. "You suppose every beach in Los Angeles is like this? People sleeping out in the open, I mean?"

"Probably, yeah," Jonathan said. "Maybe there are some private ones where people like Gina and Kip go, but parks, beaches, any public space? You'll find people living there."

Laurie wrinkled his nose as an ocean breeze brought a wave of unwashed stink in their direction. "Smells like they've got some sanitation issues."

"Nobody's saying it's an easy life. I'm sure they'd rather have hotel rooms and champagne."

Laurie paused, long enough that Jonathan had to stop walking and face him. "Jonathan, do you think I'm shallow?"

"I think you're the definition of shallow, Laurie. I think you're the most astonishingly, bafflingly shallow person I've ever met."

"You don't mind, though?"

"It's growing on me. I'm starting to find it weirdly charming."

"Charming" was good. Laurie brightened at this. "How much do you mind this? Ruining your life for me, I mean. Getting stuck taking care of me."

By response, Jonathan placed both of his hands on Laurie's shoulders. Before Laurie could figure out what he was doing, Jonathan leaned down and kissed him.

A second of confusion, and then Laurie opened up. His hands slid up to cup Jonathan's face, his palms flat against those amazing cheekbones, and then he moved them around to the back of Jonathan's neck so he could pull him closer. Jonathan's tongue roamed around his mouth, his teeth nibbled lightly on Laurie's bottom lip, his stubble scratched against Laurie's painted cheek.

Jonathan pulled back first. His hands still on Laurie's shoulders, he grinned at him. "Like I said, it's growing on me."

Laurie had to swallow a couple of times before enough self-possession returned to formulate a coherent reply. "Good to know," he said.

"You're okay with this?" Jonathan asked. There was a trace of anxiety in his voice as he examined Laurie's expression.

"Oh, yeah. That was pretty much the best thing to happen in a really long time," Laurie said. It was nice standing here, warm in Jonathan's protective grasp. He was disappointed when Jonathan stepped away.

They continued walking along the beach. "So…" Jonathan said.

"So," Laurie said. "Are you *absolutely certain* you don't want to stay in a hotel?"

Jonathan laughed. "The beach is fine. It might be romantic, even. Come on."

They strolled down a paved pathway running along the edge of the sand, where a large outdoor street market was set up. Makeshift tables piled high with used clothing and supplies, stalls that sold roasted chickens and plastic bags of sliced mangos and paper cups of *horchata*. Jonathan walked up and down the length of the stretch, scoping out the contents of the stalls before making a few careful purchases. A large blanket, soft and worn, a length of lightweight plastic sheeting, a crude wire framework made from what seemed to be several dissected umbrellas. Supplies in hand, he led Laurie to a clear space on the beach, drove the framework into the sand, and set about draping and tucking the plastic around it until he'd created a small yet effective shelter.

"How'd you know how to do all this?" Laurie asked. He crawled into the shelter and spread the blanket across the sand. The interior of their tent was barely big enough for both of them, but that was okay. Cozy. Romantic.

"I told you I stayed out here for a while before going to Las Vegas. This is a cheap way to live." Jonathan slid onto the blanket beside him. Through the opening in their tent, they could see the ocean, dark and vast. "Public toilets are in that concrete bunker behind us. There's an outdoor shower, too."

"Sounds awful," Laurie said.

"It's pretty vile. You'll hate it. But you'll be surprised what you can get used to," Jonathan said. "This really is our safest option right now. You going to be okay with this?"

Laurie leaned against his shoulder and stared out at the water. "I'll make do," he said.

They stayed at the beach for two days. Jonathan was right, Laurie pretty much hated it, but he got used to it. Nobody bothered them. In fact, nobody showed the slightest interest in them. They lived cheaply, spending miniscule amounts of money on food and canned water.

They fell into a physical relationship with an ease that astounded Laurie. No awkwardness, no expectations, no angst, just an easy comfort in each other's company. Laurie thought he'd probably fallen in love with Jonathan at their first encounter, or at some point pretty soon after that. That his feelings were returned so simply and generously seemed wondrous, miraculous.

On the third day, while they were strolling through the outdoor market, Laurie saw a familiar face. Someone so unlikely, so far removed from the proper context, that it took him a while to put a name to the face.

Kirby. It was Kirby, the Zephyr guard from the underground church, out of his uniform, dressed in a plaid shirt and khaki pants. He wandered around the stalls, not looking at anything in particular, and Laurie gaped at him for far too long while his brain spun in useless circles.

Jonathan was deep in negotiations with a young woman selling pumpkin empanadas out of a pushcart. Laurie took his arm and pulled him away. "We need to go," he said in a low voice. He didn't dare look back at Kirby to see if he'd noticed them.

Jonathan glanced at him, nodded once, and strode down the path, Laurie still clutching his arm. They moved through the crowd, keeping their heads down. "What's going on?" Jonathan asked.

"Kirby. Kirby, that really creepy security guard from the church, I saw him back there."

Jonathan paused. Laurie tugged on his arm to keep him moving. "Are you sure?"

"Not at first, he looked weird without his uniform, but yeah, I'm pretty sure. He's here."

"But why would he be? He couldn't be looking for us, could he? It's just Ferris we have to worry about, not all of Zephyr. I mean, Ferris wouldn't want everyone to know he killed your mom."

"I know, it doesn't make sense, but it doesn't mean anything good that he's here, right?" For the first time since leaving Gina's house, Laurie felt a jolt of something resembling panic course through his body. "We can't stay here anymore, we have to hide somewhere."

Jonathan nodded. "Just keep walking."

They headed to the street and continued on the sidewalk, heads down, until they reached a beachside motel. It was dodgy and dismal, boards nailed over most of the windows, the neon sign unlit and broken, and yet, remarkably, it was open and operational. At Laurie's insistence, Jonathan rented them a room for the night. Tiny and grungy. Peeling wallpaper, stained carpet, a dingy white bedspread on the double bed. No television. It cost Jonathan far too much of his remaining cash, but Laurie felt a little more secure once they'd checked in. The door didn't look especially solid, but this had to be safer than staying on the beach, out in the open, while Kirby was out there.

Jonathan wasn't happy with this plan. He didn't say anything, but Laurie could sense his dissatisfaction in his brooding silence. He put the flimsy chain lock on the door and sat on the bed. "So," he said.

"So." Laurie swallowed. "Do you believe me, that I saw Kirby?"

Jonathan blinked at him in surprise. "Of course I do."

"Good," Laurie said. "I thought you might think I just wanted to stay in a hotel."

Jonathan almost smiled. "I know you wouldn't do that," he said. He gestured toward the bathroom. "But as long as we're here…"

"Yes. As long as we're here, I'm going to take a hot bath," Laurie said. "I mean, it'd be a shame to waste the opportunity, right?"

He was gravely disappointed. The bathroom had no tub. Just a small shower stall, the wall covered with black mildew and the tile floor bumpy with ancient calcium deposits. The water temperature never rose above tepid. No complimentary soap, no shampoo. Laurie cleaned himself off as well as he could and tried to savor the experience.

As soon as he shut the water off and wrapped the sole scratchy towel around his waist, he knew something was wrong. He heard a loud bang, like a slammed door, and then a shout. Jonathan.

He burst into the room. "Jonathan—"

The gunshot came almost simultaneously, and before Laurie could process what had happened, he saw Jonathan on the floor, both hands clutching his hip, blood spilling between his fingers and spreading into the gray carpet beneath him. Ferris, out of uniform, stood above him. He looked at Laurie, but kept his gun aimed at Jonathan.

He gestured with his head at Laurie. "Get dressed. Hurry. Or the next bullet goes into his brain."

Laurie froze, unable to move. Kirby was there, too, standing beside the door, which stood wide open, the wood splintered and the top hinges broken. Kirby winked at him. "Hey, princess," he said. "Thought you might've seen me at the beach."

"Jonathan?" It came out as scarcely more than a whisper. Jonathan's face was pressed against the floor, and he wasn't moving. He wasn't dead, Laurie didn't think he was dead, because his hands were still pressed to his side, but he didn't seem to realize Laurie was there, didn't seem aware of anything happening around him. "Jonathan, can you hear me?"

He started to crouch down, but Ferris grabbed his arm and yanked him up. "Get dressed. Now."

Laurie stumbled back into the bathroom. He pulled on his clothes, his borrowed finery from Gina, all of which was looking pretty shabby. His fingers trembled so much it was hard to button his shirt. As soon as he was finished, Kirby grabbed him by his arm and marched him out of the bathroom.

"You have to make sure he's okay," Laurie said. "You can't leave him, you have to tell someone, you have to make sure he's okay." His words tumbled on top of each other, a jumbled, incoherent mess.

"Shut up," Ferris said, quietly. "Another word, and he dies."

Laurie shut up. With one last look at Jonathan on the floor, he let Kirby drag him out of the dingy room and into the parking lot.

CHAPTER EIGHTEEN

An hour or so later, most of which was spent curled up in the backseat of a car, hands cuffed behind his back, out of his mind with worry over Jonathan, Laurie found himself hustled onto a small private plane and strapped into a large, comfortable leather chair. The plane seated eight, counting the pilot, and it was pretty posh. Wood paneling covering the walls, cognac-colored leather covering the seats, plush brown carpeting. There were two other passengers: Ferris sat up front beside the pilot, and Kirby sat in the back. Laurie stared out the window, unable to see much in the darkness as they lifted off from what was probably a private airstrip. He was still cuffed, but his hands were now manacled in front of him, which was more comfortable.

Didn't really matter. If they'd cut both his hands off at the wrists, it wouldn't really matter.

When they were safely airborne, Kirby slid out of his seat and plopped himself down across from Laurie. "You and Frisch, huh?" He shook his head. "Kind of a slut, aren't you, princess?"

Laurie didn't look at him. "Go away," he said.

Kirby chuckled. "I don't think you're in any position to be bossing me around," he said.

In his seat beside the pilot, Ferris turned around. "Leave him alone, Kirby," he said. He got up and walked over to them. "Move," he said.

Kirby sighed and returned to the back of the plane. Ferris sat. He examined Laurie in silence for a moment. "You need to use the can or anything?" he finally asked.

Laurie shook his head. He didn't trust himself to speak right now without shouting or sobbing, and neither option would improve his situation.

Ferris's expression wasn't exactly compassionate, but there was nothing hostile about it. "This isn't personal, you know. But you've been a loose end for too long, and it's time to wrap it up."

"You didn't need to shoot Jonathan," Laurie said.

"Be thankful I didn't kill him. He gets treatment in time, he could be fine."

Laurie looked over at Kirby, who was slouched in his chair, arms crossed over his chest, eyes closed. "What's he doing here?" he asked.

"He's been helping me look for you. After you and Frisch pulled your cute escape act, I headed to the church. Figured I might as well take care of a few problems at once, so I made everybody there happy by relieving him of his duties. When I filled him in on the situation, he seemed pretty game for the idea of hunting you down."

"How'd you find us?" Laurie asked. "Did Kip Caprini tell you we were here?"

"Well, you kids weren't all that careful, were you?" Ferris settled back in his chair and crossed his legs. "Yeah, it was Caprini. He called my office a couple days ago, mentioned you were near the beach, mentioned that you probably didn't have the resources to go very far. So I collected Kirby, and we drove out here to hunt for you. When you don't have money, there aren't all that many places to hide. If you were at the beach, you'd have stay close to a cheap supply of food. So we staked out the street markets, and sure enough, there you were."

"Why didn't you kill me back there?" Laurie asked. "Where are we going?"

"Got the order to bring you in, breathing and in one piece. Somebody wants to meet you."

"To make sure it gets done right?" Laurie asked.

"That'd be my guess. Proof. But who knows? Maybe you'll get out of this alive. Not saying that's likely, but maybe that can give you a little hope," Ferris said. "You hungry? I can bring you a sandwich."

Laurie shook his head. Ferris returned to his original seat. Laurie slumped against the side of the plane. He tilted his forehead against the window, the acrylic cold beneath his skin. They were traveling east, across land, in the direction of the rising sun, which was beginning to light up the sky around them. He looked down and saw fields, some of them still green even this late in the year. After years of living in the desert, after years of assuming the rest of the country looked as bleak and barren as Nevada, it was comforting to see signs of life.

It was a long plane ride, and Laurie figured he'd pretty much worked out where they were heading: Washington, where his mom once had an office, where he'd spent a great deal of his childhood. Maybe it'd be interesting to find out who was behind his mom's murder at last.

He didn't care. His mind kept flashing back to the image of Jonathan on the floor, bleeding out onto the carpet, and it was hard to care about anything beyond that.

Given that D.C. was so prevalent in his thoughts, he was surprised to see the island of Manhattan beneath him as the plane began its descent. The buildings were tall and blocky and nondescript, most of them built quickly and cheaply twenty or thirty years ago to replace the ones destroyed in the nuclear attack. Some of the ruined structures had never been demolished, and they stood out on the skyline, spectral dark shells, crumbling and spooky.

They landed somewhere on the outskirts of the city, some private airstrip in eastern Queens. They deplaned directly onto the tarmac, Ferris keeping a hold of Laurie's upper arm the whole time to make sure he wouldn't try to run. Probably wise. Now that they were back on solid ground, Laurie shook off some of the resigned despair that had settled over him on the plane. His brain started to mull over his options. If he could get away from his captors...

Ferris marched him over to a blocky sedan waiting on the tarmac. The driver, a gaunt, frightening man in a black suit, glanced over Laurie. He raised his eyebrows at Ferris. "This him?"

"Yeah." Ferris opened up the back door with his free hand and gave Laurie a shove. "Get in."

"He's smaller than I expected," the man said.

Ferris didn't answer. He climbed in after Laurie, still gripping his arm. Kirby slid in the other side, trapping Laurie between them. It was a gorgeous morning, clear skies, all the promise in the world spread out ahead of them.

Ferris leaned forward to talk to the driver. "Your boss at home?"

"He has an engagement this morning he couldn't reschedule. He'll return as soon as he reasonably can." The gaunt man's eyes met Laurie's in the rearview mirror. Cold and calculating. Laurie had to resist the urge to shudder.

They drove. A near-deserted expressway, only a few cars on the road. They crossed the Queensboro Bridge into Manhattan. He'd never lived here, but Laurie still felt a sense of homecoming. He was born on this coast, he'd visited the city many times with his mother, and this was familiar ground to him.

Heading uptown. Park Avenue to the Upper East Side, pulling into the subterranean parking garage of a tall building. Before they got out of the car, Ferris grabbed both of his arms and turned him to face him. "Make any kind of fuss, and you'll get hurt. Understand?"

In all likelihood, he was going to get hurt whether he made a fuss or not, so Ferris's point seemed moot, but Laurie nodded once.

No one was around. There'd been a guard stationed in a glass booth at the entrance to the parking level, but the elevator was unmanned. The gaunt man who'd driven the car inserted a key into a lock beside the button for the penthouse level and turned it. They zipped on up to the top.

The elevator doors opened into a private residence. Ferris gave Laurie a slight push, and he stepped out into what looked like an aggressively masculine parlor. Blood-colored walls, high-backed red leather chairs studded with brass nails, black lacquered end tables, rugs in geometric patterns in red and black, a gigantic mirror in a chrome frame high on the wall above a black marble fireplace.

"Where do we put him?" Ferris asked the gaunt man.

The gaunt man motioned for Ferris to follow him. "This way."

Ferris and Kirby half-led and half-dragged Laurie through the penthouse. The gaunt man directed them down a long corridor. He unlocked a door and flipped on the lights. "Put him in here."

Ferris glanced inside the room. "I don't suppose I should ask what he uses this for, huh?"

The gaunt man gave him a cold stare and said nothing. Ferris patted Laurie on the back. "In you go. Come on."

Laurie hesitated in the doorway. The room was small. Concrete walls, no windows. The only furniture was a low bench along one wall. There were iron bolts embedded in the floor with heavy chains attached to them.

Ferris gave him a shove. Seeing no alternative, Laurie stepped inside. Ferris unlocked and removed his handcuffs. "See you around, Laurie," he said. He closed the door, leaving Laurie alone in the room.

Inside, the door was reinforced with a thin layer of steel. The lock looked strong. Laurie tried the knob. It didn't budge.

A large surveillance camera was mounted high up in a corner. He considered giving a jaunty wave to the camera, just in case anyone was watching him right now, then decided against it. Nothing about him felt jaunty right now.

He sat down on the bench, rested his chin in his hands and his elbows on his knees, and tried not to think about his likely fate.

CHAPTER NINETEEN

He was left alone for most of the day, and in that time he managed to go bonkers. He'd never thought solitary confinement sounded too horrible—hey, everyone likes a little private time every now and then—but this was awful. He went beyond stir-crazy, whipped up into a frenzy of worry about his fate. His stomach hurt from fear.

He paced the limits of the small room. He did handstands against the wall, just because it felt good to move. He considered throwing a screaming fit, maybe pounding his fists against the door or smashing the security camera just to see if anyone would come, then decided not to bother. He tried very hard not to think about how Jonathan's lips had felt against his back on the beach, in those two glorious days before it all went to hell.

He tried very hard not to think about Jonathan, period.

Eventually, the scary gaunt man opened the door. No sign of Ferris. Laurie felt oddly dismayed by this. Ferris had murdered his mother and shot him when he was just a kid, and yet still he seemed more human than this guy.

The gaunt man didn't say anything, just gestured for Laurie to follow him. Laurie obeyed, trying to look cool and unruffled. They wouldn't kill him right away, surely. No way they'd drag him across the country just to kill him immediately. He still had time to find a way out of this, maybe.

This place was big. Whoever lived here, they had the whole floor. Laurie wasn't sure he'd be able to find his way back to the elevator. And even if he could find it, he wasn't sure he could summon the elevator without a key.

The gaunt man led him to a den. Same general décor as the rest of the penthouse, meaty and manly and wealthy, all bold, dark hues. Bookcases that rose to the ceiling were filled with shiny leather-bound volumes, the titles in gilt. They looked untouched by human hands.

One of the chairs was occupied.

A man. Middle-aged, trimmed white hair with vestigial traces of sandy blond. He was handsome and tanned and moneyed, clad in a cream-colored long-sleeved polo shirt, which was open at the throat to reveal a slim gold chain. He sat with his legs crossed at the ankles, loafer-clad feet outstretched. He looked at Laurie when they entered.

"Ah," he said. "Glen, that will be all."

The gaunt man—Glen—left without a word. The man gestured to the chair across from him. "Sit down," he said.

Laurie obeyed, feeling like a puppet. The man observed him, his stare hot on Laurie's skin.

"I'm having Scotch," the man said at last. He raised his glass. "Can I fix you a drink?"

"The last time someone offered me a drink, it turned out to be drugged," Laurie said. The man smiled.

"Then you should watch me very carefully to make sure I don't slip you anything nasty." He rose from his chair and moved to the sideboard. He poured about an inch of Scotch from a cut-glass decanter into a matching glass, added an equal amount of water, and handed it to Laurie. Laurie sniffed at the drink, then took a small sip. It seemed to scald his mouth, burn all the way down his esophagus.

They sipped in silence. "You don't look much like your mother," the man said at last.

Laurie frowned. "I don't know you, do I?"

One of his white eyebrows lifted. "Did you expect to?" the man asked.

"If you're the one who arranged to have my mother killed, yes. I thought I knew most of her enemies," Laurie said. "I'd made a list of the most likely culprits."

"Was Charles Sutton on your list?" the man asked.

Laurie nodded. "Senator. From… Massachusetts?"

"Connecticut. He passed away four years ago. Liver cancer." The man smiled. "I'm his son. You may call me Joel. I trust I can call you Laurie?"

"Then your father was responsible for my mom's murder?"

"He approved, but the decision was mine," Joel said. "It was vital to the strength of the economy that she be removed. She was well on the way to ruining the country."

"It's ruined already," Laurie said. "Nothing's being rebuilt, because there's no money and no manufacturing and nobody has a job, and too many of the schools have closed down, so nobody's learning anything, and the media's been pretty much dissolved, so nobody knows what's going on, so they can't figure out any way to help themselves. All of this is what my mother was working to prevent."

Joel just smiled at him, benign and tolerant, a kindly uncle putting up with a tantrum-prone nephew. "I can see you've been indoctrinated into her way of thinking, Laurie."

He spread his hands to indicate his study, the expensive furnishings, the wealth and taste on display. "Does this look like ruin? I own the top four floors of this building. I own an estate in Greenwich. What I have done, others could do as well. If they lack the wherewithal to help themselves, that's hardly my concern, nor should it be the concern of those in power."

Laurie shook his head. "What are you going to do with me?"

Joel pursed his lips and examined him for a moment. "You look like a doll," he said at last. "Not quite a boy, not quite a girl. Mr. Ferris tells me you're a deviant."

"Is that the way he put it?" Laurie asked.

"He said you were sexually involved with the young man who helped you escape." Joel considered him, his expression still benevolent. Laurie shifted, uncomfortable under his stare.

"I don't want to talk about this."

"We'll talk about what I want to talk about. We'll be two civilized, polite adults having a civil conversation." Another smile, thin and cold. "Tell me about your young man, Laurie. Tell me everything I want to know, in as much detail as you can give me, because the more you interest me, the longer you'll stay alive."

He could throw his drink in Joel's face. Head for the door, see how far he could get before scary Glen came along and dumped him back in that concrete room.

"There's not much to say," he said. "He could be dead now. Ferris shot him and left him to die back in Los Angeles."

"Sad. But the course of young love is never certain." Joel smiled at him again. "You might end up being very entertaining, Laurie. That's excellent news for you."

He rose, so abruptly that Laurie flinched back. "Why don't you freshen up, then join me for dinner? You can tell me all about your life in exile."

"Of course." Laurie set down his barely-touched drink on an end table. His hand shook, and his glass clattered against the smooth black surface. Joel smiled at that, the bastard.

"Glen will show you to the guest bathroom," Joel said. The words weren't even all the way out before Glen skulked into the room, grim and silent and creepy. Laurie inclined his chin, struggling to keep composed, and trailed Glen out of the room.

The guest bathroom was huge. The door didn't lock, which was a crying shame, because Laurie could use some private time to pull himself together. He started to shake all over, and his stomach felt like it was digesting itself, and maybe some of that was hunger but mostly it was because he was in a great deal of danger.

He stared at his reflection in the mirror. His hair was messy, his once-immaculate blue satin suit was rumpled and sad. He scrubbed his face, straightened his collar, finger-combed his hair into place, felt a little more secure.

He did a fast search of the bathroom. There was an assortment of toiletries and an old-fashioned razor stored in a silver shaving cup in the medicine chest. It wasn't a straight razor, just a single blade screwed into a heavy bronze base, but it was sharp. Laurie unscrewed it and held the blade in his palm, considering. If he got close enough, he could go for Joel's throat.

He'd probably be given a chance to get close enough. That wouldn't be the problem.

The bathroom door opened. Laurie closed his hand around the razor, careful not to clutch it too tightly. He expected to see Glen or Joel.

It was a woman. At first glance Laurie thought she was young, maybe a teenager, and then something about her appearance seemed to change and settle, and he realized she was well into middle-age. She had white-blonde hair, straw-dry and thin, her scalp visible in patches. Her skin looked translucent, almost a pale blue, stretched too tight across her high cheekbones. She was scary-thin and unwell, with bare arms like chicken legs, ropy and knobby under a sleeveless cashmere sweater with a draping cowl neck.

Her eyes met his in the mirror. She was beautiful, or had been beautiful in the not-distant past. Ill health radiated from her, waves of sickness and despair.

Glen appeared at her shoulder, staring first at Laurie and then at the woman. "Ma'am…" he said. There was deference in his tone.

"I want to meet him," she said. Her tone didn't leave any room for argument. "Leave us, Glen."

Glen hesitated. Laurie saw his hand hover momentarily at the lapel of his suit jacket, as though reaching for a weapon, and then he relaxed. He stepped back into the hallway.

The woman shut the door behind him. She nodded at Laurie's closed hand. "Is that for your wrists?"

Something about the shattering void in the woman's eyes made him tell her the truth. He opened his hand and showed her the blade. "It's for Joel," he said.

She almost smiled. She was too emaciated to smile; a tight grimace flickered on her face, pulling the skin around her mouth taut over her jaw, the mask of the dead, before she relaxed it. "Don't," she said. "You won't succeed, and it'll make things worse for you."

"You know who I am?" Laurie asked.

She nodded. "Oh, yes."

"Who are you?" he asked. "Are you Joel's wife?"

Another grimace. "I'm his sister. His twin. His other half, the other side of the coin. Joelle."

"You're sick, aren't you?" Laurie asked. "Is it cancer?"

"I'm dying," she said. "Started in the breasts, but now it's everywhere. Bones and brain."

"I'm sorry," Laurie said.

She shook her head. The fine hair rustled around her face, dry stalks of wheat in fall. "Don't be," she said. "It's the best thing to happen to me in a long time."

"Will you help me escape?" Laurie asked.

Another shake. "If you want to use the razor on your wrists, I won't stop you."

"I don't want to kill myself," Laurie said. He tried to keep his voice down, even though Joelle was speaking at a normal volume, because surely Glen was still waiting right outside the door. "And I don't want your brother to kill me, either."

She held out a hand. It looked old, withered and spotted with age. "Then give me the razor," she said.

He hesitated, then placed it in her palm. She screwed it back into the body of the razor and replaced it in the medicine cabinet. She touched three fingers of that frail hand against his wrist. "Come with me," she said.

She opened the bathroom door. Sure enough, there was Glen, leaning against the opposite wall. Glen moved forward; Joelle shook her head at him. She closed her hand around Laurie's wrist. "I'm taking him to my room," she said. "Joel can send you for him when he's ready."

Glen scowled, but didn't protest. He just nodded, his jaw set in annoyance.

Joelle guided Laurie down the hallway. She was unarmed and frail and sickly, and surely it'd be easy to break away from her. He *should* break away from her. He should run for the elevator and see if he could summon it before Glen reached him. He tensed, looking around.

Joelle patted his arm. "It's okay," she said. "It's okay."

They entered the kitchen, which was large and industrial. A sturdy woman in a white apron that reached almost down to the floor looked up from the sink where she was scrubbing pots. She paused in her work to stare at Joelle and Laurie, her expression filled with disinterest, then resumed her task.

Joelle didn't acknowledge her. She escorted Laurie through the room, all white-tiled floors and scrubbed steel counters and big, old, industrial ranges, to the door on the far side. She slid back the deadbolt and pulled the door open, her thin arms straining at the effort.

A staircase.

"Go down seven flights," she told Laurie. "The door to the twenty-second floor is usually left unlocked. If not, you'll have to smash out the window with the fire extinguisher. Go to your left, far left, and catch the freight elevator down to the parking garage. Don't take the main elevator, they'll catch you that way."

Laurie stared at her, his eyes wide. "Thank you," he said.

She shook her head. "Go."

He ran. Seven flights down, trying to remember what Joelle told him. The floors weren't numbered, so he counted in his head, trying not to get panicky or confused. A heavy steel door with a small window above the knob separated the stairwell from the twenty-second floor. He tried the knob—Joelle was right, it was unlocked—and flung the door open. Closed it behind him, flipped the deadbolt, ducked out of sight of the window in case anyone entered the stairwell after him.

The entire floor was dark and empty. No furniture, the floorboards bare, electrical wiring exposed on the ceiling. Joelle had said to go left, hadn't she? To the freight elevator? This was cause for confusion and alarm, because there wasn't an elevator, freight or otherwise, to the left. Panic settled in, his heart hammering in his chest as though it was going to burst free of his ribcage. He continued to the left and was relieved to see that, yes, there *was* an elevator in the far corner, hidden behind support pillars and a gigantic roll of old carpeting.

He pushed the button to summon it. He kept an eye toward the door, crouching behind the protection of the carpet roll while he waited for the elevator to arrive. His absence would be discovered almost immediately; Glen would keep him on a close leash, even with Joelle's orders to leave him alone, and he was far, far from safe here.

The freight elevator came. It was empty. Cavernous and unfinished, steel sheeting on the walls and floor. He pushed the lowest button, P for Parking, and prayed it wouldn't stop on any other level.

He couldn't get that lucky. It stopped on twelve, and two youngish men in gray jumpsuits and caps emblazoned with the logo of a courier service got on, pushing a metal cart loaded with yellow envelopes and brown paper packages between them. They glared at Laurie, irritated at finding him someplace he wasn't supposed to be, but said nothing.

They rode the elevator in silence down to the parking level. When the doors whooshed open, revealing concrete and darkness, Laurie resisted the temptation to sprint for the exit. He waited patiently, legs trembling with adrenaline, as the two men pushed their cart out. He strolled through the garage, hands thrust in his pockets, trying to look purposeful yet nonchalant. There was no pedestrian walkway, so he'd have to walk up the paved ramp toward the exit, which was blocked by a bar that raised and lowered after each vehicle. There was a guard booth beside the bar, and he could see a guard standing inside the booth, and that made this a little trickier.

The couriers loaded their cart into the back of a gray van and drove up the ramp. Laurie followed on foot after then. While the bar was still raised, he slipped beneath it and exited into daylight. He kept his hands shoved in his pockets and his face composed until he was up on the sidewalk, somewhere in Manhattan, out in the open and free.

CHAPTER TWENTY

Park Avenue. The buildings were tall and the street was wide. The air was crisp and a bit chilly, a far cry from the balmy temperatures of Los Angeles. Laurie balled his hands into fists in his pants pockets. From visiting here with his mother as a child, he had a rough idea of the layout of the city. If he headed south, he'd reach Grand Central Station, and from there maybe he could catch a train to… well, did it matter? He needed to go back to Los Angeles, ultimately and obviously, but right now, he had to get out of the city, far away from Ferris and Kirby and Glen and Joel.

He could catch a subway to Grand Central, that'd probably be fastest, but he didn't have the cash to buy a token. He could hail a cab and slip out without paying, but that'd bring attention and trouble and maybe police, and none of those things were desirable right now. He'd stay on the sidewalk, but he'd move fast, and he'd keep a low profile and stay alert, and maybe Joel wouldn't find him.

He walked. His borrowed booties hurt. They were cute as all hell, but they weren't the most practical footwear for urban prowling. South of 60th, the city took a nosedive. The Upper East Side had been nice, almost luxurious, with trees and well-maintained buildings and uniformed doormen. After he crossed into midtown, though, the ruin set in. The sidewalks were strewn with refuse; scaffolding, deteriorated and bonelike, surrounded abandoned buildings. Laurie felt safer here amongst these signs of decay. It seemed less possible that Joel, well-groomed and wealthy Joel, could reach out his tentacles and find him.

Grand Central Station, big and wide, loomed in front of him. He slipped through the bronze-and-glass doors into the enormous main hall, all marble floors and carved stone staircases and high ornate ceilings. Some of it was old and some was new; the walls had collapsed in the blast, but it'd been meticulously rebuilt, and now it was hard to tell what was original and what was part of the renovation.

They'd look for him here, of course. Anything he wanted to do here, he'd have to do it fast.

Maybe it'd be easy enough to slip onboard a train, maybe he could dodge the conductor until it had pulled out of the station. If he got caught, he could charm his way out of a sticky situation. He'd grope around in his pockets for a nonexistent ticket, bat his pretty eyes, maybe feign tears, and he'd get his way.

A train to Minneapolis was scheduled to leave in ten minutes. Minneapolis. Not ideal, but it'd do. Once there, he'd find another train that'd get him closer to the west coast. It'd work. He headed down to the lower level and entered the tunnel leading to the correct gate.

Crap. A uniformed transit agent stood outside the gate, checking tickets before letting anyone through. They'd changed the procedure since the last time he'd traveled, probably to prevent people from doing exactly what he'd intended. He couldn't slip past the agent, and he couldn't loiter here without bringing attention to himself. He climbed back up to the main level.

If he had a little money, he could buy a ticket. He could try his hand at pickpocketing. How hard could it be, really?

Not here, though. There were too many uniformed transit police milling around. Reluctantly, he went back outside.

He walked down the sidewalk, picking a side street almost at random, at a loss as to his next move. He was screwed. If only he had an ally…

Well, he had at least one ally, didn't he? Just not one in New York. He started searching for a payphone.

There was a bank of phones along the way to Times Square. The first four had their receivers missing, nothing but exposed wires, but the fifth one worked. The handle was sticky and smelled like vomit. Laurie tried to ignore that as he dialed for an operator.

"I need to make a collect call, but I don't know the number. It's in Los Angeles." He stood with his back to the payphone the whole time, the cord awkwardly draped over his shoulder, keeping an eye on the street in both directions. "There's a payphone by the Coliseum. It's in a park. Exposition Park. Could you connect me there, do you think?"

"Who's calling?" The operator, brusque and male.

"It's Laurie, calling for Nicola. Tell whoever answers that it's an emergency. Big emergency. Tell him Nicola will want to talk to me."

He heard silence on the other end of the line, for so long that he thought the operator had disconnected the call. He was about to replace the receiver on the hook in frustration when he heard the operator's voice again, tinny and distant: "I have a collect call for Nicholas from Laurie. Will you accept the charges?"

Laurie wanted to burst in that the operator had gotten the name wrong, then he heard a different voice, young and male. "Yeah, sure, whatever."

There was a click as the operator connected them, and then the young voice addressed Laurie: "What do you want with Nick?"

Laurie's brain froze for a moment, and then his thoughts began to organize themselves in a mostly coherent manner. "Can you get a message to her from me? Or tell Escobar, that'd work too."

There was silence on the other end of the line. Laurie paused, then dove in again. "This is Laurie Sparks, they know me, tell her it's Joel Sutton behind this. Nicola can look him up, he's the son of a former senator from Connecticut and he's the one who... well, he's the one who's responsible for my problems. She'll know what I mean," he said, with a quick look around. "I don't think there's anything she can do about it, but someone should know, he was holding me captive but I got away. Tell her they shot Jonathan, on the beach. Venice. We were in this motel near the beach, I don't know the name but I think the street was named Ocean, and it was the closest motel to the big street market. Could she... could she find out what happened to him?" He started to get a little choked up at that.

Another long silence on the end of the line. Maybe no one was there, maybe Laurie was babbling into the void. Finally, the guy spoke again. "You got a way Nick can reach you?"

Good question. "Not really. I can try to call again later, I guess. If she doesn't hear from me in a few days..." He swallowed hard. "If she doesn't hear from me, it probably means Joel Sutton found me. Just... let her know that, okay?"

"I'll tell her. Check back when you can, all right?" A click and a dial tone, and Laurie was left holding a dead receiver.

Well. Laurie felt better after that. If Nicola received the message, and if she could make sense of his jumbled words, she'd do her best to find out what happened to Jonathan. If Laurie dropped off the face of the earth, she'd find out what happened to him.

He'd done as much as he could on that end for the moment. Time to find some cash. Panhandle or pickpocket, those seemed like his best options. He drifted westward, keeping a covert eye out for a likely target. Maybe if he saw some businessman, someone who seemed like he could afford to lose his pocket money, someone who maybe wasn't paying too much attention to his wallet, maybe he'd risk it.

Times Square. Holy hell. He'd toured it before with his mother, years ago, and it had been sort of awful then, but now it was a monstrosity. This had been a blast point, skyscrapers reduced to charred metal skeletons in a flash. They'd done an okay job of rebuilding the area back when his mom had been in power—new buildings had gone up, putting flesh back on the skeletons—but it had slid back into decay since then.

Everything was falling apart. Buildings crumbling and collapsing, boarded-up storefronts everywhere. Some restaurants were open, but they looked scary. Cheap hotels, porno theaters, strip clubs, bars with black plastic sheeting stretched over the windows, either to block out the daylight or because the windows no longer existed.

Prostitutes. There were a lot of them here, dressed in skimpy outfits in the crisp fall air, tight sequined skirts and tube tops and teetering heels. Teased hair and lots of makeup, calling loud come-ons to passersby. They scared him a little, though he figured they wouldn't waste their time on him. Anyway, it was probably good they were here, because wherever there were hookers, businessmen with cash in their wallets probably weren't far behind.

He fell into step behind a portly man in a brown plaid suit. The back pocket of his poorly-tailored slacks bulged with the rectangular shape of what looked like a fat wallet. It'd be a bit of a trick to slip his hand into that pocket, grab the wallet, and run like the blazes without being caught, but he bet he could do it. He bet the guy couldn't run fast, he bet he could lose him in the crowd. His heart pounding, he closed the gap between them, just a little.

It was now or never. One step closer, mere inches behind him, one hand raised...

A black-gloved hand grabbed him by the shoulder and yanked him back. Laurie yelped in terror and spun around.

Not Joel, not Glen, not Ferris. Laurie found himself looking at a youngish woman with dark skin and a harried expression. She wore a police uniform, a blue wool jacket with shiny bronze buttons paired with a white-brimmed cap. She rolled her eyes at him.

"Kid, what the hell do you think you're doing?" she asked.

The man with the wallet turned at the commotion behind him, frowned once, and hurried along the sidewalk.

"What do you mean? I wasn't doing anything," Laurie said. He opened his eyes wide. "I was just walking."

"Not on this street, you weren't. You were hustling or pick-pocketing, and either seems like a poor fit for you."

"I was not!" he said. He added as much indignation to his tone as he could muster. "I wasn't doing any such thing. Like I said, I was just taking a walk." He glanced around. "Is this a bad neighbor-hood?"

The officer grunted. "Oh, kid, if you need me to tell you that, you're in worse trouble than I thought." Her expression hovered in strange indeterminate place between grumpy and amused. "Tell you what, I'm feeling benevolent toward lost nitwits today. If you're lucky, my largesse might extend to a hot beverage and a slice of pizza." She gestured with her head toward the drab exterior of a tiny café, a dinky hole of a place wedged into the street level of a condemned building, shoehorned in between a burned-out bodega and a shoe repair shop.

He probably should just go—nothing good could come from talking to the police—but he was famished. "Okay. That'd be nice. I mean, if you don't mind."

She shook her head, exasperated, like she'd been suckered into an unwanted afternoon of babysitting. "Come on." She pushed open the door. He was hit by a smell of hot grease and burnt coffee. Sickly yellow overhead lights, orange plastic booths and cracked Formica tables, dirty linoleum peeling up at the center. There was a tired-eyed heavyset woman in a red-and-white checkered apron standing behind a counter underneath a black plastic board with the menu spelled out in white letters: COFFE and COLA and something called a SASAGE DOG.

The police officer pointed at one of the vinyl booths. Laurie sat and waited while she placed her order, which she brought back to the table on a red plastic tray. A paper plate with a gigantic slice of cheese pizza sprawled across it like roadkill, orange grease pooling on the surface, and two paper cups of coffee. The officer took hers black; the one she passed to Laurie was the palest beige. "Figured you took yours white and extra-sugary."

"You bet. Thanks," Laurie said. He took a sip. The warmth slid down his throat and suffused his body. Sticky sweet comfort. Felt a little better already.

"Lucky guess." She sipped at her own coffee and scooted the tray in front of him. "Eat. You look ravenous."

He needed no further encouragement. The slice was sloppy and greasy and delicious. He managed to get sauce on his cheeks and chin with his first bite, which he mopped away with a wad of paper napkins. He swallowed a humungous wad of cheese. "Thanks so much. I needed that."

She just nodded, considering him. "Runaway?"

He shook his head and chomped down on another gigantic mouthful. "Nope. Too old for that. I'm small for my age," he said. "So it's great of you to look out for me like this, but I'm really okay."

"You were about to do a half-assed job of pickpocketing some poor jerk, so no, you're probably not really okay," she said. She took her cap off and rested it on the table. Her short, frizzy hair was pulled back into a tight bun. She looked young and pretty and competent as all hell. She had a bronze nametag on the breast pocket of her uniform coat. Officer Tally.

"You misinterpreted the situation entirely. I had no intention of stealing from him," Laurie said.

She just stared at him for a moment. "You know, 'protect and serve' is literally part of my job description, kid. Tell me what's going on, and then I can see about helping you."

"I can't," Laurie said. "I mean, there's nothing to tell. I'm fine."

"Live around here?"

"Just visiting. Got a little lost, that's all. I'll avoid Times Square in the future. Duly noted."

"Where are you staying?"

"Hotel."

"Which one?"

Laurie thought fast. He'd stayed in various hotels here with his mother. Just a matter of remembering the names. "The Plaza."

Tally nodded slowly. "The Plaza, sure. Up on Fifth, right on the park, where all the beautiful people hang out?"

"That's the one," Laurie said.

"The one that went bankrupt maybe five, seven years ago? That the one you mean?"

Laurie exhaled. "I may have gotten the name wrong."

She shook her head. "Okay, kid. Keep your secrets, if you want. But look, if you go around trying to pickpocket people, you're going to get arrested. And that's pretty much the best-case scenario."

He didn't say anything. His pizza slice was now a memory. He stared wistfully at the grease remnants soaking into the paper plate.

"I got to get back to my rounds," Tally said. "You want to take a walk with me?"

Without waiting for him to answer, she got to her feet. Crushed her empty cup, dumped the garbage on the tray into the trashcan beside their booth.

"Where are we going?" Laurie asked.

"Got a guy I want you to meet. You don't have a place to stay, he might be able to help."

Laurie trailed her out the door. "You mean like a homeless shelter?" he asked. "Or a church, some kind of religious thing?"

"Why? You got something against religion?" she asked.

"Not really. I used to be a monk," he said.

Tally scowled at that, as though she suspected him of making a joke she didn't understand, so he shut up and trailed her in silence.

CHAPTER TWENTY-ONE

Back through the heart of Times Square, which was a little easier to face with Tally at his side. She wasn't big, but she walked like a cop, all stride and swagger, and she had both a nightstick and a gun on her.

If Joel Sutton found him right now, would Tally defend him? Or would his money and power and obvious influence scare her off or persuade her to surrender Laurie to his clutches? She'd probably do her best to protect him, and her best would probably be pretty good, but Laurie couldn't be sure. He'd made some bad judgment calls recently—Gina and Kip sprang to mind—and he couldn't risk it again.

They walked along 42nd Street. Laurie knew this area, too. Bryant Park, the square of green behind the old library building. The library was long gone, nothing more than crumbling steps guarded by a single stone lion, and the park was now a sea of makeshift tents. Like the beach back in Los Angeles... Laurie didn't want to think about that.

The entire park was a homeless encampment. He shot a glance at Tally. Did she mean to leave him here?

She made her way through the maze of tents. The encampment seemed clean and well-regulated. A man with a huge red beard cooked hotdogs, pulling raw ones out of a clear plastic sack and rotating them over a small kerosene stove for a couple of minutes before topping them with grilled onions and wrapping them in paper and distributing them to the throng of people surrounding him. A teen girl with a half-shaved head sold used clothing along with what looked like t-shirts of her own design, splashed with dyes in bright shades to create mirrored Rorschach patterns. A gray-haired man sold necklaces made from drilled pieces of sea glass strung on knotted cords. Enterprise on a low level, all of it, but it was enterprise, and it seemed like a congenial, functional community.

It was too cold to sleep outside, but the tents seemed durable, made of sturdier materials than the ones back on the beach had been. A dozen or more small fires blazed away in metal trashcans, and maybe that helped keep everyone from freezing to death. Wouldn't be a pleasant life, or an easy one, but at least people were staying alive.

Tally led him to a card table covered with small flat canvases, upon which were drawn city scenes in vivid chalk pastels, stylized images of buildings and bridges. When Laurie was a child, his mother had drilled an appreciation for art into him, and he recognized the obvious skill in these, the strong sense of color and proportion. A man sat on a folding chair behind the table, a canvas rectangle propped on his knees, thick fingers gripping a stubby lavender piece of chalk. He drew a careful line and shaded it with his pinky to produce a smudgy, muted wash of color. He was brown-skinned and sturdy, with a wide, bumpy face. Upon spotting Tally, an enormous grin spread across his face, making his eyes and forehead crinkle.

"Officer! It is so wonderful to see you, beautiful Officer Tally." He had an accent that Laurie couldn't place, his words inflected with something melodic and strange.

"Sergio." Tally just nodded in response to his effusive greeting. She motioned toward the drawing in his lap. "Looking good. Saint Patrick's?"

"Of course." Sergio tilted the canvas so they could see it better. The bare bones of a cathedral, all Gothic architecture and towering spires, were in place. "The tourists, you see, they appreciate the classics."

"You do that all from memory?"

"Memory, yes. Because I must." Another flash of a smile. "And if I do not remember all the details, well, the tourists, they do not know the difference."

"Selling many of these?"

"Business, it is okay, but no more than okay. I do not do this to get rich, you know. Which is a very good thing, that." His eyes twinkled. He had unusually long lashes for a man, thick and lustrous.

"This is my new friend." Tally patted Laurie's shoulder. "You'll have to make your own introductions. I didn't bother asking his name, because I figured anything he'd tell me would be a lie, but he seems to be in some trouble. If you're feeling philanthropic tonight, I thought you might put him up. You've got the space."

Sergio smiled at Laurie, though he seemed a little cautious. He glanced at Tally. "He is not dangerous?"

"Can't imagine so. He might try to steal from you, but rest assured he'd do a real incompetent job of it. He seems like he's in over his head, and I don't know what else to do with him. I leave him on his own around here, he'll be robbed or raped or murdered in minutes."

"You have a hard view of the world for such a beautiful woman," Sergio said with a wink. "The people here, they are not so unkind. Some, yes, but far from all. The city takes care of those who need help."

Tally just grunted. Sergio turned to Laurie. "Do you wish to stay with me?"

"I wouldn't steal from you," Laurie said. "I promise. I wouldn't even try. I really could use a place to stay tonight." It was starting to grow darker, all long shadows and dusk, and the chill in the air was intensifying.

"Sergio's okay," Tally said. "He's one of the good ones." To Sergio, she said, "At a guess, I'd say the kid's okay, too. Harmless, at least. You game?"

"Of course." Sergio flashed his lovely grin at Laurie. "I am Sergio." He extended his hand.

Laurie shook it. It was warm and rough and calloused. "Hi, Sergio. I'm Laurie."

"It is very nice to meet you, Laurie." Sergio clasped his other hand over Laurie's, squeezed it, and released it.

Tally grunted. "Then that's settled. Anything going on here I should know about, Sergio?"

"No, no. All has been calm. On the up-and-up, as you would say." He bobbed his curly head at her. "Please have yourself a nice evening, beautiful Officer Tally."

"Thanks for the coffee and pizza. And... thank you," Laurie said to her.

She didn't say anything, just grunted again and moved on, a compact figure navigating her way through the maze of tents and stalls.

"Do you have one of these tents?" Laurie asked Sergio.

"No, no." Sergio shook his head. "My place, it is not far from here. My business is slow today, no one is purchasing my artwork, so I think we will go there now, yes? Perhaps you will help me pack up my chalks and my canvases?"

"Sure," Laurie said. At Sergio's direction, he scooped up pieces of thick, stubby chalk and packed them into an open wooden crate, then helped him collapse down the card table and chairs. "Thanks for this. Er... Officer Tally seems to think I'm a little shadier than I am. Not that you have any reason to believe me, but I really won't try to steal from you."

"You will, or you will not. It does not matter." Sergio gave him another huge grin. "Me, I hope you are honest, because I like honest people. But you have an angel face, and I have known many people who look like angels who have the souls of devils."

"I'm not sure I'm either. Somewhere in between, I guess."

"Then we will get along fine." Another grin. Sergio motioned to the west. "Here, we go this way, it is only a little distance."

"Where are you from?" Laurie asked. He had to hustle to keep up with Sergio, who seemed to glide along the sidewalk. Laurie was burdened with the crate filled with canvases and art supplies, but since Sergio was lugging the folding table and chair, he couldn't use that as an excuse. "I've never heard an accent like yours."

"Angola. You know where that is? Africa, you know Africa? But I have not been back there in many years, not since before the bombs fell." His smile was tinged with a wistful nostalgia that fell short of melancholy. "It is very hard to travel overseas now, you know, and I have no way to reach my family. I do not know if they survived. Thirty years, they may live, they may be dead. I only have hope."

"I'm sorry," Laurie said.

"There is no need for you to be. You are young, and it is old news now, and much less sad than it once was." Sergio tilted his head back and looked up at the buildings. Some intact, some ruined, some under construction. "Africa, you know, it was not hit so badly. This is what I have heard, that there are places, Africa and South America and Australia, where people thrive still, where they do not get sick as often, where the lands were not all burned and poisoned."

They reached the front of a building, a tall structure with old rickety scaffolding surrounding it. Laurie craned his neck back and couldn't see the top. "We are here," Sergio said.

He maneuvered the card table to the side and used his shoulder to push open the makeshift tin door. Laurie hung back. "It looks abandoned."

"It is my home." Sergio smiled at him. "People live here, you see. Myself, I have lived here two years now, and no one has come to say I must leave. I pay no rent, and it is better than the park."

Laurie followed him inside. A destroyed lobby, jagged gaps in the floorboards, a prevalent smell of garbage and human waste. There were people around, shadows in the corners that darted and whispered. Laurie moved a little closer to Sergio. "But... it's safe?" he asked.

"If you are with me, you are safe. I am known here, you see, and I have made many friends." He smiled down at Laurie. Too dark in here to see much of anything, but his teeth stood out, very white. "This part here, it is not pleasant, no, but upstairs, my home, it is comfortable. Please."

Gripping the crate tighter, Laurie kept as close to Sergio as he could as they crossed through the lobby. Empty elevator shafts, doors removed and cables dangling over a dark void. Sergio walked over to the adjacent stairwell. "Twelfth floor. It is a bit of a walk, this. I hope your legs are not too tired?"

"I can manage," Laurie said. Eleven flights of stairs. His feet still hurt in his booties.

The stairs smelled of urine and dead things, and it was too dark to see where he was going. Too dark to see if he was about to step in something nasty. His chest burned, his stomach churned, and his legs twitched with exhaustion, but he kept up with Sergio, all the way up to the twelfth floor. Sergio stood on the landing and smiled down at Laurie. "Here we are," he said.

The door was locked with two thick, chunky padlocks, one at the top and one at the bottom. Sergio unlocked both and flung the door open. Laurie entered cautiously.

One enormous space, no walls separating it, divided only by bare support pillars, three sides made up entirely of windows. No lights. He saw the Manhattan skyline spreading in all directions, all the skeletal buildings, most dark.

Sergio switched the padlocks from the outside to the interior and locked them inside. This meant Laurie couldn't leave if there was an emergency, if it turned out Sergio wasn't quite as trustworthy as Tally had assured him. It wasn't ideal, but he was safer inside here with the population of Manhattan, Joel included, padlocked outside, so he tried to relax.

"There is no power in the building, you see. I think sometimes I should find a generator, maybe convince my neighbors we should purchase one together, but it does not seem worth the expense," Sergio said. "I use kerosene for a little stove, and kerosene for a little heater, and I have candles and lamps, and it works very well for me. We have some water, there is a water tower on the roof, and all of us who live in the building, it is our responsibility to make sure it is full. So there is plumbing, but it is not good for drinking."

Laurie nodded, looking around. It wasn't warm in here, but it wasn't nearly as chilly as outside, and the windows and the walls protected him from the elements.

The vast space was mostly empty. Canvases were stacked in a pile in the corner next to buckets of supplies, paint and chalk and brushes. A ladder lay on its side against the windows; a large stack of blankets and pillows was piled on a mattress in the middle of the floor.

Sergio set down his card table and chair. "So you see, Laurie, there is little for you to steal if you were to rob me," he said. "Unless you wished to steal my drawings and my paintings, and if you were that passionate about them, I would be happy for you to have them."

Laurie stared at the skyline. He turned in all directions, seeing it through all the windows, the damaged panoply of Manhattan surrounding him. He stopped.

One wall had no windows. It was covered with a gigantic mural, ceiling to floorboards, and this took Laurie's breath away.

It was the Manhattan skyline. Sergio's artwork, clearly. Giant painted silhouettes of buildings, most of which no longer existed. Laurie saw the iconic tops of the Chrysler Building and the Empire State Building, along with dozens of tall structures that he couldn't identify, all framed against a night sky, glowing and sparkling in a way that outshone the real skyline outside. It took Laurie a while to realize it was painted in reverse, as though the wall were a gigantic mirror, reflecting the skyline as it had appeared thirty years ago before the bombs fell.

Only... no, it wasn't. It was a fanciful interpretation. He'd seen enough photographs of the way the city had looked back then to know this was wrong, that Sergio's painting featured far too many buildings, that this skyline was too bustling, too cluttered.

"This is beautiful," he said.

Sergio approached his shoulder. "It's how it should be. You see?" He gestured toward the windows, then toward his mural. "The buildings that are now gone, I have replaced them here. The buildings that should be, I have found their right place in the city."

"The buildings that should be?"

"The buildings that would be here. The bombs, they should not have fallen. It was terrible and it was wrong." Sergio observed his mural, his expression thoughtful. "If the bombs had not fallen in 1984, this is what Manhattan would be, here, now. Do you see?"

Laurie nodded. "I wish it looked like this really," he said. "I wish everything wasn't so scary and grim all the time."

"I wish for the same," Sergio said. "But this is the world we live in, Laurie of the angel face, and this world has many lovely things in it, too."

203

He moved toward a little camp stove, which had a rickety tin kettle perched over it on a framework of wires, and touched a long match to the can of kerosene beneath it. "I will make us tea now, and soup if you wish it, and perhaps you will trust me enough to tell me all that you did not tell Officer Tally, and then you will sleep, safe and warm. Okay?"

"Okay." Laurie sat cross-legged on the floor next to the burner, close enough to benefit from its small warmth, and watched as Sergio prepared bowls of dehydrated noodle soup and mugs of tea. He wrapped his hands around a proffered mug to warm them up. The tea tasted of dust and mint, and the soup tasted of nothing but salt, but the warmth was comforting.

They ate and drank in silence. Laurie mulled over what he should say. He inhaled the comforting steam from his mug. "I don't want to tell you who I am," he said at last. "I know I'm going to sound like I'm a liar, or that I'm trying to make myself important, but all I can tell you is it's dangerous to know too much. I'm in trouble, a great deal of trouble, and I don't know who can help."

Sergio nodded. "The police?" he asked. "Some police here, they are no good, they are corrupt and they do not help, but there are ones who are very good. Officer Tally, she has a kind heart and she is smart, and she would help you if you asked her."

Laurie shook his head. "No. No police," he said. Joel Sutton's opulent penthouse, his obvious prestige and privilege… If Laurie's name ended up on a police report, Joel would find him. "I need a whole lot of people to hear my story, all at once, or else I'm always going to be in danger. I was in Los Angeles before this, and I was trying to get on television, but that didn't work, and it ended up making things worse. So I don't know what to do."

"Ah." Sergio appeared to understand. Laurie hoped he hadn't given him too much information, hadn't been too chatty and reckless in his longing for a sympathetic ear.

"I will give the matter much thought. I have some ideas, some small ideas, but until I have thought on them, I do not want to say more." Sergio set down his empty bowl. "I will make up a bed for you, Laurie, and you will be safe tonight. Night is no time to make decisions. In the morning, you and I will be wise, and your path will be clearer.

Laurie stifled a yawn. "That sounds good. Thank you," he said. His brain was fuzzy and his body was sore. He'd slept some on the little plane from Los Angeles, a drifting, restless, anxious sleep that hadn't refreshed him, and now that there was a moment of respite from the terror of the day, exhaustion caught up to him. It was all he could do to finish up his tea, peel off his jacket and shoes, and crawl under the small mound of blankets Sergio prepared for him.

CHAPTER TWENTY-TWO

In the morning, Laurie felt sore but refreshed. Sergio was already awake and bustling about. Laurie smelled coffee brewing. Could be the finest smell in the universe.

He sat up as Sergio placed a mug beside his pile of blankets. "Good morning, angel Laurie," Sergio said, flashing his beautiful smile. "I hope you slept well?"

"I did. Thank you." Laurie rolled his neck from side to side to work out a crick. The air was chilly, so he kept a blanket wrapped around his shoulders as he sipped his coffee. Very strong and black, very bitter, but he doubted Sergio kept sugar or any kind of creamer on hand, so he drank it without complaint. "It was comfortable."

"I have rolls here for our breakfast, but they are old and not good," Sergio said. "I am not quite the Ritz, you see."

The rolls were little stones, small and brown and too hard to bite. Sergio dipped his in his mug to soften it up before eating, so Laurie followed suit.

"I have thought about your problem, Laurie," Sergio said between gnawed mouthfuls of coffee-soaked bread. "I have a friend, a journalist friend, and she and her lover, they have a newspaper. They do not have much money, but they have passion, and they are trying, you see. It is likely they will fail, as it is difficult to interest people in the news these days."

"Hard to blame people," Laurie said. "News is always bad, right?"

"That is not quite true. There is good news too, always, and if people do not know the bad, they cannot appreciate the good," Sergio said. "I think you should meet my friend and her lover, and you should tell your story to them. Maybe they will write about it and everyone will know your secret, and then you will be safe."

"That sounds okay, maybe," Laurie said. "I mean, I could definitely meet her, at least."

"Excellent." A flash of teeth. "I do not know how to reach her during the day, and I must earn my living now, so we will go see her tonight. I know where she works, she does not make money with her newspaper. I think you should stay here today. You will be safe," he said. "You may draw or paint, if you like, and there are rolls and soup to eat."

Laurie didn't want to be stuck here all day by himself, but neither did he want to kill time outside, hiding from Joel while waiting to meet Sergio's friend. "Okay. Thank you."

Sergio smiled again and sipped his coffee.

The day passed slowly. Laurie tried to sleep some more, but every noise in the building—the mysterious thumps from the floor above, the voices in the stairwell outside the locked door—made him certain he was about to be recaptured. Now that he finally had some time to himself, out of immediate danger, his thoughts returned to Jonathan. Alone in the huge, empty space, Laurie allowed himself the luxury of crying a little. Afterward, he felt better.

Night had fallen by the time Sergio returned home, bearing his table and chair and canvases under his arms. He pounded on the door until Laurie unlocked the padlocks and let him inside.

"Hello, Laurie. You are well? You will come with me to see my friend?"

"Sure," Laurie said.

"Very good. We will go now, I think she will be at work." He gave Laurie a sidelong glance as he ushered him out the door and into the stairwell. "The place we go, it is maybe not a nice place, and I do not know if you will like it, but I give you my word, you are safe with me. Okay?"

"Ah… okay." Laurie trailed Sergio down all those flights of stairs and out of the building. After a day cooped up inside, the outside air was a relief, even if the sense of anxiety and exposure, the fear of discovery and recapture, returned at once.

They walked south. Back through Times Square, cavern-like and deserted at night, then down Broadway to a tiny dark storefront dominated by a huge sign spelling out RIO in pink neon letters. A broad-shouldered bouncer in a purple double-breasted suit stood out front, right next to the pink velvet rope that was stretched across the doorway. Laurie blinked at the posters of lingerie-clad women pasted over the windows.

"This is a strip club. We're going to a strip club?"

The bouncer looked up. Heavy-set, clean-shaven, a tattoo of a lion over half of his face. "We prefer the term 'gentlemen's club', kid." He nodded at Sergio. "Hey, Sergio. The kid's with you?"

"Jagger. It is good to see you." Sergio and the bouncer shook hands. Sergio clapped him on the shoulder and gestured for Laurie to step forward. "This is my friend. He is here to see Cerise, she is working tonight?"

"Should be. It's her regular night." The bouncer shook his head at the folded bills in Sergio's hand. "No cover, man, it's cool." He unclipped the velvet rope and gestured with his thumb toward Laurie. "He don't look like he'll give the girls much hassle."

Sergio grinned and bobbed his head in thanks, then placed a hand on Laurie's back and gave him a small push forward. Laurie stepped into the club.

Disco lights, disco music, and a smell of fresh sweat. Too many bodies in too small of a space. Laurie flinched back, then forced himself to walk forward into the crowd. Sergio's hand was still on his back, resting between his shoulder blades. The customers were all male, older and bigger than Laurie, and he could get crushed in the crowd if he wasn't careful.

The club was one gigantic room with a platform stage at one end. There was an assortment of booths and tiny tables in the front and a bar at the back. On the stage, six nude women writhed and shimmied to the music. Topless waitresses in spandex shorts and knee-high boots ferried trays of drinks to the booths and tables.

Sergio nudged him. "To the right. We will wait there." They made their way through the crowd to an unoccupied booth against the far wall. Laurie slid onto the pink leather seat. His pants stuck to something sticky.

He must've made a face, because Sergio frowned at him. "You are okay with this place, this does not alarm you too much?"

"I wouldn't say *alarmed*, necessarily," Laurie said. "Do you go here often?"

"I do, sometimes, when I sell my drawings." He smiled. "My needs are few, you see. I do not buy fancy clothes, I do not buy fancy toys, I do not wish for a fancy place to live. But I do like beauty, and if I have money, I will buy drinks for beautiful women, so they will sit with me and talk with me. The women here, they are very kind, and they are very good to talk to."

"Uh-huh." Laurie squinted at the sextet of naked women on the stage, all of whom stared out at the crowd of men hooting at them, their faces humorless and blank. "You said your friend works here? Is she one of the women on stage?"

"Cerise, yes, she works here, but she does not dance. She serves drinks, and she talks to men, and that is how I find out she is a journalist, with her very own newspaper." Sergio scanned the crowd, then raised a hand to get someone's attention. "Here she is now, she will come over, and I will pay her to sit with us."

"Hey, Sergio." A woman stopped by their table. Skinny and leggy, topless, with small, pointy breasts. She had platinum hair that hung straight to her shoulders and a tattoo of a quill pen on her left bicep. "How're you doing? Who's your friend?"

"Cerise. It is very good to see you." Sergio gestured to Laurie. "Cerise, meet Laurie. Laurie, this is the beautiful Cerise Cherry." To Cerise he said, "Will you sit with us? I will buy us drinks, and I wish for you to talk to Laurie."

Cerise looked a little surprised, but amiable. "Sure thing. The usual?"

"Please." Sergio passed her a small bundle of bills, which she tucked into the waistband of her pink spandex shorts.

"Be right back." A wink to Laurie, and Cerise disappeared in the crowd.

Sergio turned to Laurie. "You will forgive me if I cause offense with this, but I think you may not have much use for beautiful women?"

"I like beautiful women a lot. I mean, no, I don't want to have sex with them, but I don't think they're icky. I don't mind being here, if that's what you're asking," Laurie said.

"Ah, I see," Sergio said. "It is a good attitude, that."

Cerise approached the table again. On her tray was a trio of tall stemmed glasses and, Laurie was overjoyed to note, a bottle of champagne.

"I like the way you choose to spend you money, Sergio," he said.

Sergio beamed. "It is good, is it not? My paintings, they do not make much money, but they make enough for bubbles and for the company of beautiful women, and that is all I can wish for in my life."

"Hear, hear," Cerise said. She popped the cork with a practiced air and poured out glasses, then slid into the booth next to Sergio. "Cheers, gentlemen."

"Cheers." They clinked glasses and drank. The champagne wasn't good, sticky-sweet and raisiny, but Laurie wasn't about to complain. He examined Cerise over the rim of his glass. She wasn't beautiful—even with heavy makeup, her features were nondescript—but there was something both smart and easygoing about her demeanor that he liked.

"Your name isn't really Cerise Cherry, is it?" Laurie asked.

"Sure is. On my birth certificate and everything. Not sure what my mother was thinking, unless she fully expected me to wind up serving drinks in a titty bar at some point." She smiled at him. Up close, she was older than he'd thought, with faint lines on her forehead and at the corners of her eyes.

"Sergio says you're a journalist? That you have your own newspaper?" Laurie asked.

She nodded. "That's why you wanted to meet me?"

"Laurie has a story for you," Sergio told her.

"Yeah? Let's hear it," Cerise said. She looked friendly, but not particularly interested. Laurie hesitated.

Sergio smiled. He leaned closer to Cerise and touched her hand, which was resting on the table, wrapped around the stem of her still-full glass. Apart from their toast, she hadn't touched her drink. Probably preferred to stay sober at work.

"Mind you, Laurie has not told me his story, so I cannot vouch for it. But he said it is something very big, and me, I believe him. He has been frightened by something, something bad, and maybe you will be able to help him."

"Could be, but I'd have to know his story first," Cerise said. "Want to talk to me, Laurie?"

Laurie shook his head. "Not with so many people around."

Cerise frowned. "After my shift, then. You can come back to my place and meet my partner, Mike. You can't get much more private than where we live. You can talk to us there. Cool?"

Laurie glanced at Sergio, who nodded at him. "Okay. That's fine with me."

"Cool." Cerise shot a discreet glance at the pink plastic digital watch strapped to her wrist. It was big and chunky, with a calculator built into the square face under the display. "I'm on the clock for another couple hours, so let's drink up and have ourselves a good time, okay? If management sees me here looking all businesslike, I'll hear about it tomorrow."

"Of course." Sergio threw her a big grin and segued into a lively monologue about his life, his paintings, his early career as a fashion designer, back in the days before the world changed. By the time Cerise's shift was over, Laurie was pleasantly toasty from his drink and felt much better about life in general.

He and Sergio waited for Cerise by the back door of the club. Cerise had changed into a short red tube dress with a black plastic rain slicker over it. She was accompanied by a thin young man in a flannel shirt and dirty jeans. He had glasses and a goatee, and he regarded Sergio and Laurie with some suspicion as Cerise made introductions.

"Guys, this is Mike, my partner. He usually meets me after work to escort me home." Cerise linked her fingers with Mike's and pulled him forward. "Mike, this is Sergio, I've mentioned him to you before, and this is Laurie. He's the one who maybe has a story for us."

"Hi, guys," Mike said. "Laurie, Cerise says she invited you back to our place to talk?"

"If that's okay," Laurie said.

"If Cerise says so." It was a little curt. "We don't like showing people where we live. Particularly not customers. No offense," he said, with a nod to Sergio. "But if she says you're cool, Laurie, then it's fine."

"He's okay. I mean, look at him," Cerise said, with a small laugh. "I don't think he could cause us much trouble if he wanted to."

"Probably not, no," Laurie said. "Sergio, you're coming too, aren't you?"

"If you wish for me to come, I will." Sergio's voice was gentle. "But I would rather go back to my own home now. You will be safe with Cerise."

Back at Sergio's place, he'd had somewhere to sleep behind a door that locked. Laurie felt a momentary panic at the idea of facing an uncertain future again. He forced it down.

"It's okay," he said. "You've already done a lot for me. Thank you for everything."

"It has been my pleasure." Sergio placed his hands on his shoulders and kissed Laurie once on each cheek, his stubble rough against Laurie's skin. "If trouble finds you, go to the park again. I am there every day." To Cerise he said, "Please keep him safe. He is special, this one."

With a nod at Mike, Sergio headed down the sidewalk in the direction of his building. Laurie watched him leave and tried not to feel bereft.

CHAPTER TWENTY-THREE

"Let's get moving. It's freezing out here." Mike led the way down the sidewalk, walking at a brisk stride. With her long legs, Cerise matched pace with Mike easily, her knee boots clicking on the sidewalk. Laurie had to hurry to keep up with them.

Cerise shot him a grin. "Still with us, Laurie? This will be fun." When they reached Times Square, she trotted down the debris-strewn steps of the subway entrance. Laurie picked his way down behind her, navigating around the smashed carcass of a rat, and followed Cerise and Mike to the turnstiles.

"We're doing this legally," Cerise said. Her face radiated with high spirits. "It's the last thing we're going to be doing that's legal down here, so it's best not to get stopped by the transit cops at this stage." She fished around in her shoulder bag and produced a crumpled gum wrapper, a quarter, and a few brass subway tokens. She passed one of the tokens to Laurie. "It's on me. Sergio was a good tipper tonight."

Laurie slipped the token into the slot beside the turnstile and pushed his way through. The turnstile looked like it hadn't been replaced since before the bombs fell; the metal bar was old and stiff and gummy, and it took a great deal of effort to get it to budge.

Cerise led the way along the platform to the furthest end. "We'll need to be in the very last car," she said. A little confused by all this, Laurie nodded.

It was a long wait, maybe an hour or more, and the platform was cold and a little scary. Not many people around, apart from a group of men in oil-stained jumpsuits who kept shooting veiled glances at Cerise, who seemed oblivious to their attentions. After far too long, a train arrived, a battered metal snake that rumbled and rattled and creaked its way along the platform. Doors opened with a hydraulic whoosh, and an unseen voice blurted out something unintelligible in a blast of muffled static over the intercom. Cerise and Mike strode through the doors without a pause; Laurie followed more tentatively. The doors whooshed shut behind him, sealing him in the snake's belly.

There were three other passengers in their car, two of whom were sprawled across multiple seats, their assortment of heavy garments making it impossible to determine age or gender. The third, a middle-aged black woman in a starched white nurse's uniform, shot Laurie a suspicious glare when she noticed him watching her, then returned her attention to the thick hardcover book in her hands.

"When we get off, stay close and do what we do. If we move fast, this is safe enough, but it's easy to die this way, too," Cerise said.

"Wait. What are we doing?" Laurie asked.

Cerise just giggled. She unzipped her long boots, wadded them up as best she could, and stuffed them in her shoulder bag. She squeezed her bare toes into a pair of lightweight slippers. She glanced at Laurie's feet, at the heeled booties from Gina. "You going to be able to run in those?"

"Not well. Is it necessary?"

"Just move as fast as you can. And remember, don't touch the third rail." The brakes screeched as the train pulled into the next stop. "This is us. Let's move."

"What?" Mike and Cerise were already jumping to the platform before the doors had opened all the way. Laurie hurried after them.

As soon as the train began to move away, Cerise hopped down onto the track right behind it.

"Jump. Now!" she hissed at Laurie.

Laurie jumped, making sure to stay far away from the covered third rail. He splashed in a puddle of an unidentified putrid liquid. Great. Mike landed right behind him. He grabbed Laurie's arm and shoved him toward the dark tunnel. "Move. We've got to hurry, kid. Run!"

Cerise was already booking it into the tunnel. She kept close to the wall to the side of the tracks. With Mike still gripping his arm, Laurie followed her. On the platform behind them, someone shouted something unintelligible after them. There was only about a foot of free space between the track and the tunnel wall, and if a train came by right now, they'd be smashed.

Twenty yards or so away from the platform, Cerise stopped. Laurie squinted in the darkness and saw the outline of a wooden door flush against the concrete wall. Cerise flung her shoulder against it, and it burst open with a satisfying pop. With adrenaline surging through him, Laurie almost knocked her down in his hurry to get through the door and out of the tunnel.

Darkness and a smell of garbage and stagnant water. As soon as Mike closed the door behind them, Laurie could see nothing. He heard Cerise panting for breath somewhere near him. "If you do it just like that, enter the tunnel as soon as the train pulls away, it's safe. They don't run the trains too close together, so there's plenty of time to get to the door. At least I'm pretty sure there is. Maybe someday I'll be proven wrong." Cerise groped down Laurie's arm until she reached his hand. She squeezed it in hers. "It's going to be dark, so just hang on to me and try not to trip. Mike and I have done this so many times by now, it's easier not to bother with flashlights."

She led him across a paved floor. Laurie's feet slid on what he thought were sodden newspapers. "When there are repairs on this line, the transit workers sometimes use this entrance, so we have to be careful. But we should be good right now," she said. She pulled him to the right. "We're turning a corner. Come on."

Disoriented and unhappy, Laurie followed her, trying not to stumble in the darkness. He'd never be able to find his way back to the tunnel on his own.

"Here we are. We're going to have to do a bit of climbing." Mike sounded far too cheerful about that. "Take a big step up, there's a concrete barrier here, it's about two feet off the ground, and it's pretty stable. It's not very wide, though, so try not to fall off." Mike placed an arm around Laurie's waist and gave him a boost up. "Now reach up, there's a platform right about at chest level, feel it? That's where we're going. Just take a little hop and haul yourself up there."

It took several attempts, and more than a little guided tugging from Cerise and Mike, but eventually Laurie struggled his way up onto what felt like a wide, cold concrete platform. He remained on his knees, unwilling to stand or move around until he knew more about his surroundings.

There was a hiss of a match being struck. Cerise touched the small flame to the wick of a makeshift oil lantern in a glass jar, which she positioned on a wooden crate. Flickering light filled the area. "Here we are," Cerise said. She gestured with her arms. "Home sweet home."

"You live here?" Laurie said. "Ah... wow."

The platform extended far back, so far that the end was beyond the scope of the light from the oil lamp. The ceiling was low; Laurie could stand upright, but Mike and Cerise, who were several inches taller than he was, had to duck to avoid grazing their heads. The platform held a mattress and blankets, plus a stack of canned goods and a few cardboard boxes filled with what looked like clothes and sundry possessions.

"It's kind of cool, isn't it? The newspaper sucks up all our re-sources these days, so we ditched our old place and crashed here so we could stay afloat." Cerise seemed chipper about this. "The first couple of months were a little grim, but I finally got a chemical toilet set up in the back, and that's made things a whole lot nicer." In the light from the lamp, her face looked bright and expectant.

"It's really... wow," Laurie said. "Unconventional."

"It is, isn't it?" Cerise plopped down on the mattress and pat-ted the space beside her. "So, come on. This is about as private as you can get in Manhattan. Let's hear what you have to say."

Laurie hesitated, then sat down. He began to tell his story. Mike lit a second lamp, then sat cross-legged on the floor and listened. Cerise seemed politely bored at first, and maybe a little skeptical, but as Laurie kept talking, her interest grew. Without interrupting him, she rummaged through her shoulder bag and produced a notebook and a pen, then began jotting down notes. He told her about everything—his mother, the monastery, the under-ground church, Ferris, Joel, Jonathan—and she remained silent until he was done.

"Wow," she said. "You're telling the truth, aren't you?"

Laurie didn't answer. Cerise chewed on the inside of her cheek, deep in thought. "I'm not going to lie to you, our newspaper is pretty dinky," she said. "Mike, he works at this old bookstore, and they've got this ancient printing press in the back, and his bosses let him use it for free. We put out one issue a week, or we try to. So we've got a staff of like eight people to do reporting and write articles. Some are pretty good, and some kind of stink, and nobody's getting paid for any of this. We haven't had much luck with advertisers, and we sell it on the streets, try to charge a little for it, but honestly, we usually end up giving away most of our copies for free."

"Ah," Laurie said. His grandiose plan of broadcasting his story to the nation seemed sillier than ever. "I don't know if you'd even want to print this. It could bring a lot of trouble for you, and it doesn't sound like you'd have any way to protect yourself."

"They'd have to find me first." Cerise grinned. "No, look, I'm definitely writing this story. This is enormous. And I don't know that I'm worried so much about anyone having me killed or whatever, but since I don't want to get my ass sued for character defamation, seeing how we're dealing with some pretty serious accusations about people with buckets of money, I'm going to need to corroborate your story."

"I don't know how you can. I mean, if there's still a working library around here, you can look up Joel Sutton, it seems like he's probably a big deal, and his dad was a senator, but I don't think that'd tell you anything about my mom's murder. It's not like you can interview him about this."

"The twin, though. What was her name? Joelle? She helped you escape, after all. Sounds like she might be willing to talk to me about her brother."

"I don't know if she would or not. And I don't know how you'd get to her. I had the sense she didn't leave the apartment much. She seemed really sick." He paused. "Ah... I don't want to seem like a coward, but... please be careful. He'll kill me if he finds me."

"Well, sure. I mean, it's my neck too, right? I ask too many questions, they'll go after me. Of course I'm going to be careful," Cerise said. "I'll have to think about the best way to get to Joelle. Do you want to crash here with us until the story comes out? That way it'll be easy for me to ask you questions as they come up, and besides, you probably want to keep a low profile, right?"

"Doesn't get much more low-profile than here." Mike, who'd been quiet during the conversation, nodded at Laurie. "Stay. It's not luxurious, but it's cozy."

"Ah... thank you," Laurie said. "That's very kind of you."

As Cerise and Mike bustled about redistributing blankets to prepare a bed for Laurie, as Laurie crawled beneath covers that smelled of mold, as the cold concrete permeated through the stack of loose cardboard he was using as a mattress, he allowed himself one more longing thought about the relative comfort of Sergio's place.

All total, Laurie spent five days with Cerise and Mike in their weird subterranean home. He felt anxious and antsy—he wished he could call the Coliseum again to see if Nicola had any news about Jonathan—but staying in one place seemed like the safest option. Maybe Joel would assume he'd escaped from New York by now. Maybe by the time Cerise's article came out, Laurie would be on his way back to Los Angeles, out of Joel's clutches.

Days fell into a routine. As Cerise worked nights, she spent her mornings with Laurie, asking him questions and typing up his replies on a battered black mechanical typewriter. The ink in the ribbon was on its last legs, and her transcribed notes looked diseased. Mike worked days at his bookstore, returning home in time to give Cerise a quick kiss and a grope before she headed off to the club.

Laurie dined on instant noodles and petrified granola bars and sticky, foul, cream-filled packaged snack cakes. The chemical toilet Cerise had set up on a dark corner of the platform behind a cardboard screen failed to thrill him. He did not, could not shower—as there was no running water, Mike and Cerise simply used the facilities at their respective workplaces—and he was starting to loathe the way he smelled.

On the second day, Cerise began what she termed her reconnaissance mission. She'd venture out in the early afternoon, leaving Laurie alone until she returned to change for work. She was keeping Joel's apartment building under discreet surveillance, she told Laurie, tracking the comings and goings of the residents, asking the doorman questions, and this made Laurie almost go out of his head with worry. No matter how much Cerise assured him she was taking all possible precautions, he fretted so much his stomach felt like it'd turned itself inside-out.

And then on the fifth day, Cerise didn't return. She was due at the club, and she hadn't made it back to grab her knee boots and spandex. Mike seemed nonchalant about this at first, but as the minutes dragged by with no sign of Cerise, he grew antsy.

"She could've gone directly to the club," he said. It sounded like he was trying to reassure himself. "I mean, one of the other girls could loan her a pair of shoes, right? If she was running late for some reason, she'd go straight to work."

Laurie didn't reply. If he spoke now, all his fears would pour out of him, drenching Mike with his barely-suppressed terror, and Mike didn't need that right now.

"I'll check it out," Mike said. He cleared his throat. "You know, it's fine, and she doesn't need me fussing about her, but I'd like to make sure she's okay."

"Do you want me to go with you?" Laurie asked. He didn't want to venture out into the dark, cold, dangerous night, but if Cerise was in trouble, it was his fault.

"Stay here in case she comes back. I'm going to run over to the club and see if she made it there. I shouldn't be gone long."

Laurie waited for Mike to return. There was no chance of ignoring the growing cloud of dread in his soul, so he let it embrace him. Alone in the damp darkness, he mulled over all the horrible things that could have happened to Cerise.

It was probably only an hour or so before Mike returned, though it was hard to tell for certain. Laurie didn't have a watch, and time moved strangely and slowly underground.

"No good," Mike said before Laurie could ask. His voice sounded tense. He grabbed the edge of the platform and climbed onto it with a practiced air. "She didn't show up, and she didn't leave a message with any of the girls. Manager's pretty pissed at her." He sat on the concrete for a moment, catching his breath. "Damn it. I hate cooling my heels waiting for her. What's the address of that guy she's investigating? You said he was on Park?"

"Park and 77th. But—" Laurie stopped. The only light came from the oil lantern propped up on the wooden crate, and it flickered and bobbed and cast weird shadows that made Laurie jumpy, but he could almost swear a new shadow had moved along the far edge of its light, right in the darkness behind Mike.

A wide, sweeping arc of motion emerged from the shadows, and then Laurie saw a hand bringing something, maybe a length of pipe, down on Mike's head.

A sickening thump. Something warm and wet splashed over Laurie, and even in the darkness, he knew that was blood.

He scrambled back along the concrete. He grabbed for the oil lamp with some wild thought of using it as a weapon, but before he could reach it, the hand snaked out from the shadows and grabbed his ankle. Laurie tried to lash out with his free leg and kick his unseen assailant away, but a second hand closed around his other ankle and yanked him back.

The hands dragged him across the concrete. While Laurie flailed around and tried to grab something to anchor himself in place, the hands released his ankles, seized him by his hips, and pulled him off the platform. He fell to the ground several feet below.

He landed on the low concrete barrier he'd climbed on to boost himself up to the platform when he'd first arrived here. It bruised his tailbone and sent a shock of pain down his spine.

A hand grabbed him by his collar. He found himself pulled back against a strong figure. "Laurie Sparks," a male voice said, laced with satisfaction. Ferris.

"You killed Mike," Laurie said, his voice little more than a choked gasp.

Ferris patted Laurie on his shoulder. "Come on, kid. You've gotten me into enough trouble already. Let's not drag this out."

Laurie wanted to tell him he had every intention of dragging this out, but he never got the chance. Ferris shifted his grasp, holding him around the chest with one strong arm, and pressed a damp cloth over his mouth and nose. Laurie tried to turn his face away, but a sickly chemical odor permeated into his sinus cavities and seared his lungs. Within seconds, darkness swallowed him.

CHAPTER TWENTY-FOUR

Backseat of a moving car, hands bound in front of him with a knotted plastic cord, slumped against someone's shoulder. Laurie blinked and sat up straighter. Ferris sat beside him, with Kirby behind the wheel. They drove down a wide highway, which was bordered on each side by high concrete barriers that obscured the scenery. It was still dark outside. "Where are we?" Laurie asked.

Ferris grunted. "Connecticut."

"Where are we going?" His head hurt. Hard to think about what had happened. The attack in the darkness, Mike's blood splashing on him... A wave of nausea surged over him, and he had to shut his eyes to fight it down.

"Not far."

Laurie opened his eyes and stared out the window at the scenery. In the darkness, he could see the tops of trees and power lines above the barriers. "Did you kill Cerise?" he asked. "Is that how you found me?"

"Doorman told Sutton she'd been asking questions about him, Sutton got suspicious and called us. We tried to get her to tell us where she'd stashed you, but she wouldn't budge. Lucky for us she had a timecard in her bag for that sleazy club she worked at. Staked it out, waited until the boyfriend came calling, followed him into the subway. And there you were." He shook his head. "Kid, all in all, you've been a whole lot of trouble."

"Well, that's not exactly my fault, is it?" Laurie said. "You could have just pretended you didn't recognize me. Back in the desert, I mean. Everyone would have gone on assuming I was long dead, and you wouldn't have had to go to all this bother hunting me down."

"That's occurred to me, yeah. It would've been easier. But there's a little something called professional pride, kid. I don't like loose ends," Ferris said. "And I'm picking up a healthy wad of cash for this, too. Nice perks. Got to travel in that fancy little plane and everything. That's probably more important than the professional pride, come to think of it."

Kirby exited off the interstate and headed into a town. Greenwich, the exit sign proclaimed. Looked like a nice place. Big houses set far back from the road, wide green lawns behind tall iron fences, plenty of working street lights, no visible signs of economic decline.

Ferris nudged him in the ribs. "So, hey. Indulge my professional curiosity. Did Sutton tell you why he wanted your mom dead in the first place? What'd she ever to do him?"

"Red spy." That was Kirby, chiming in from the front seat. "His mom was a Commie trying to sabotage the economy. Isn't that a good enough reason?"

Ferris ignored him. He kept his attention on Laurie. "Any idea?"

Laurie let out an exhausted snort. "Taxes, I guess. She kept pushing to raise the tax rates on the wealthy to fund the redevelopment efforts. He didn't like that much."

"Fair enough. Money's as good a reason to kill somebody as any. Better than most," Ferris said.

Laurie was quiet for a moment. "Don't take me to him," he said. "He doesn't just want to kill me."

Kirby glanced into the backseat. "Sutton tried to get into your pants, huh, princess?" he said. "Take heart. You look like crap right now. He probably won't want to touch you."

"Shut up, Kirby," Ferris said without heat. To Laurie, he said, "That true?"

Laurie didn't answer. Ferris continued. "Look, this is just a business transaction. I hand you over to him, I pick up some cash, and my part in this is done."

There didn't seem to be any point to saying anything further, so Laurie kept quiet. Kirby turned down a shady, tree-lined street and pulled up in front of a wrought-iron gate. Beyond it, situated on the top of a small hill, was a mansion. It was pale blue with a wide white porch and a matching pair of white-topped turrets that rose above the roof. There was an intercom affixed to the stone fence on the side of the gate; Kirby rolled down his window and jammed a button with his thumb to activate it. After a long moment, a voice came over the speaker, thick with static: "What?"

"We got him," Kirby said.

There was no reply. They sat in the car and waited. Laurie swallowed hard, staring at the house. A warm yellow porch light blazed, friendly and welcoming, like nothing awful could ever happen there.

Ferris touched his arm. "You get close enough to Sutton, bite his jugular. Hard as you can. Do it right and it'll kill him. It'd take balls, but you're tougher than you seem. You might be able to pull it off."

Laurie stared at him in surprise, then nodded.

Someone walked down the long drive from the house to the gate, a tall, gaunt man in a dark suit. Glen. Laurie felt his stomach tighten. Ferris reached over him and opened the car door, then gave him a small shove. "Move it," he said.

Laurie climbed out of the car, fighting to keep his balance with his hands bound in front of him. Ferris took hold of the back of his neck and walked him to the gate.

From the other side, Glen observed Laurie impassively. He slid the gate open a couple of feet and gestured with his hand for Ferris to send Laurie through.

"Payment first," Ferris said.

Glen reached inside his suit coat and withdrew an long yellow envelope. He handed it to Ferris. Ferris opened it up and thumbed through a thin sheaf of bills.

"He's all yours," Ferris said. He pushed Laurie forward and released him.

Seeing no alternative, Laurie crossed through the small gap in the gate. Glen pulled it shut behind him.

"You want us to stick around?" Ferris asked. "He might give you the slip again."

"He won't," Glen said, his tone curt and cold.

Ferris hovered on the other side of the gate, looking like he wanted to say something else. Then he shook his head and slid into the passenger seat. Kirby backed the car up and flipped a U-turn. Laurie watched until the car had disappeared from sight, heading back toward the interstate.

Glen took hold of Laurie's upper arm. Without a word, he steered him up the driveway toward the house. Helpless, Laurie followed him up the porch steps and through the heavy maple door and into an exquisitely furnished living room. Queen Anne chairs with graceful curving legs and backs, seats upholstered in richly patterned fabrics, oil paintings featuring bucolic landscapes hanging high on the blue-and-ivory striped wallpaper.

And of course Joel was there as well, in all his middle-aged preppie glory, polo shirt and khaki pants and tasseled loafers. He sat in a leather armchair, his Scotch resting on the end table at his elbow, a lit cigar dangling between his thumb and forefinger. He looked up as Glen and Laurie entered. "Ah," he said. He gestured to Glen. "Untie him."

Glen produced a pocketknife from the inside of his coat, something with a long sliding blade on a bone handle, and sliced through the cords around Laurie's wrists. All the while, Joel observed Laurie in silence, taking the occasional puff on his cigar, his expression neutral.

"You're filthy," Joel said at last. "And stubble doesn't suit you."

Laurie didn't answer. Joel gestured to Laurie's shirt. "Is that your blood?"

Laurie noticed, with a sense of dull surprise, that a long splatter of Mike's blood had dried to brown across his shirt. He shook his head.

"Well, then." Joel settled back in his chair. "Shall we finish what we'd started before all this foolishness?" A smile tugged at the corner of his mouth. "Get yourself cleaned up. Shave. Then we'll sit down for a civilized dinner. You can get me caught up on your recent adventures."

Laurie had nothing to say. Wordlessly, he let Glen lead him down a hallway. Glossy parquet floors patterned with alternating strips of light and dark woods, dainty wood end tables with slim, elegant legs, china vases filled with fresh flowers, everything clean and pretty.

Glen ushered him into a bathroom. "No tricks," he said.

Too dispirited to answer, Laurie just shook his head.

Glen left him alone while he showered. The rush of hot water cleared his head a little. Once clean and freshly shaved, he felt more up to the challenge of getting himself out of this situation, alive and intact.

The razor... He held it in his hand, considering. Ferris had suggested biting, but this would be more effective, if he had the nerve to go through with it. With a sense of déjà vu, he unscrewed the blade, then replaced the disassembled razor in the medicine chest.

228

Glen provided him with a fresh change of clothes, a snow-white shirt with a white feathered collar and mother-of-pearl buttons at the long cuffs, paired with dove-gray suede pants. Not Joel's clothes, surely. Must be from the sister's wardrobe, the twin. Joelle.

The pants had no pockets, but the razor fit in his palm, hidden from view. He held it loosely, keeping his hand relaxed, praying he wouldn't drop it.

He followed Glen back down the hallway to the formal dining room. A long cherry wood table with matching chairs was set with delicate blue-and-white china plates and heavy silver cutlery. Dinner had already been plated. Steaks, red and rare, accompanied by small piles of scalloped potatoes and creamed spinach. There were three place settings; Joel sat at the head of the table, with Joelle across from him.

Joelle stared at Laurie. She looked more unwell than ever. Purple shadows like dark gashes beneath her eyes, gray-blue skin pulled tight over her face. "He's wearing my clothes," she said, her voice flat and uninflected.

"I didn't think you'd mind. You won't have use for them for much longer." Joel glanced at Glen. "Any trouble?"

"He's hiding something in his left hand," Glen said.

"Ah." To Laurie, Joel said, "Hand it over."

Laurie hesitated. Joel nodded at Glen. Glen took his wrist and pried his fingers open. The razor blade dropped to the table. Glen picked it up and slipped it into his coat pocket.

"Break his wrist," Joel said.

Before Laurie had time to react, Glen pushed his thumb against the outside of Laurie's left wrist while pressing his other fingers against the opposite side. Laurie felt bones shift, then heard the loud snap before he felt the white-hot agony, like an electrical jolt along all the nerves in his arm. He yelled in pain.

Glen pulled out the chair opposite the final place setting and steered him into it. Laurie clutched his broken wrist to his chest, bending over while the currents of pain coursed through him.

"Thank you, Glen. That will be all," Joel said. Glen nodded once and left the room.

Joel picked up a wine bottle from the table and filled the balloon goblet at Laurie's place setting. Dark red, darker than blood. Joel raised his glass. "Drink, Laurie," he said. "It might help you unwind."

Afraid to refuse, Laurie picked up his glass with his undamaged hand and took a sip. Strong and smooth, a small burn in his throat when he swallowed. Liquid courage. The fiery pain in his wrist ebbed away into dull, throbbing waves.

"Eat your steak," Joel said. "I imagine you haven't had too many regular meals lately." There was nothing but mild kindness in his words and demeanor, and even still, Laurie had to fight to keep himself from shuddering.

With his broken wrist, Laurie couldn't use his knife to cut his steak. He took a bite of the potatoes, and his throat constricted so much it was difficult to swallow. He drew patterns in his spinach with the tines of his fork. Heavy silverware, monogrammed with curling engraved letters: CJS. Joel's father, probably, the senator.

Joel sawed away at his steak. "My sister's clothes suit you, Laurie," he said. "Don't you think so, Joelle?"

Joelle didn't reply. She wasn't eating much, either. Joel reached out and touched the soft white feathers at Laurie's collar. Laurie flinched.

"That's one of her designs," Joel said. "Years ago, back before the bombs fell, she was quite the little seamstress. Worked for all kinds of famous designers, even took a stab at her own collection. It never amounted to much, but she seemed to have something of a knack for sewing."

"It's very nice," Laurie said to Joelle tentatively.

Joelle gave him a small, tight smile in response. "Thank you."

"He looks like you, don't you think?" Joel said to Joelle. "The way you looked when we were his age, I mean, so small and delicate and lovely. That was my very first thought upon seeing him."

Joelle stared at her brother. "You mean for him to replace me," she said. "After I'm gone."

Laurie set down his fork. Joel took a sip of his wine. "You have to admit, it's an elegant solution." He pursed his lips, considering. "He's a deviant, of course, but it's not as though you haven't had some leanings in that area yourself, sister of mine."

For a moment, fleeting traces of some strong emotion, anger or anguish or both, registered on Joelle's face, before the impassive blankness returned. She raised her chin. "I'm not dead yet, brother of mine."

"Of course not. But there's no sense denying the inevitable, is there? It's prudent to make plans for the future now."

"While we're on the subject of my health…" A new note entered Joelle's tone, something brisk and purposeful. "I received an interesting package from the oncologist at the penthouse yesterday."

Joel frowned. "The courier delivered your pills, didn't he? I saw the package."

"Mmm. But there was something unexpected in the delivery this time. I took it with me, just in case I'd need it here."

"I don't see—"

"Let me show you." Joelle rose from the table. Joel looked wary. She crossed over to the china cabinet, inside which gilt-edged porcelain plates were displayed behind glass doors. "I think I might have a guardian angel. Or I suppose it's more likely our young friend Laurie does."

She opened the doors, removed the lid of an ornate tureen, and picked up something from inside it. When she turned around, Laurie saw she held a handgun.

Joel got to his feet. "Where did that come from, Joelle?"

"As I told you, it came with my pills." Joelle smiled, the impression of her skull standing out beneath her too-tight skin, the grimace of the dead. "It must be a gift from the gun fairy."

"The gun fairy..." Joel's eyes narrowed. "That stripper whore who was poking around the building, did she give you that?"

"It could be, I suppose," Joelle said. "But I prefer to think it was magic."

She raised and fired. The shot was loud and incongruous in the demure setting. Joel's head snapped back, a perfect red hole appearing in the center of his forehead.

He collapsed backward, toppling his chair as he fell. It clattered against the parquet floor. Glen entered the room within seconds of the shot. While his hand was still reaching inside his suit coat, Joelle adjusted her position and fired again.

Her first shot went wide and slammed into the wall. The next one caught Glen in the neck, a hair below his chin. Glen grabbed for the doorway to support himself, then slumped to the floor.

Laurie froze, unable to process the scenario that had just played out in front of him. Joelle placed the gun on the table, then sat down again. She lifted her wine glass. Her hand was steady as she raised it to her mouth and drank.

She smiled at Laurie, pale lips now stained with red. "Eat your steak, Laurie," she said.

Laurie stared at her.

CHAPTER TWENTY-FIVE

After Joelle had finished her meal, but well before Laurie had recovered from the shock of the sudden burst of violence, she led him into the kitchen, dumped some ice into a clean white dishtowel, and handed it to him. "Hold this against your wrist. It'll keep the swelling down until you can visit a doctor." She smiled. "I have some marvelously effective painkillers, if you wish. It's one of the few advantages of being a terminal cancer patient."

"No. Thank you. It's okay." The ice increased the pain in his broken wrist, but he held the towel in place until the whole area grew numb.

"Let's sit in the living room, shall we?" Joelle said. "I could use a drink."

She led him back through the dining room, stepping lightly over Glen's corpse on the way to the front of the house. Laurie couldn't look at Joel, dead and stiff, his sticky red blood pooling and drying on that beautiful floor.

Joelle guided him to the sofa. "Scotch?" she asked.

Laurie shook his head. Joelle fixed herself a drink at the sideboard, then fixed him one despite his refusal and placed it on a porcelain coaster on an end table by his elbow. She settled herself in an armchair. Thin wisps of hair hung in her eyes, limp silk from a plucked and dying dandelion. She wore a pale cream sleeveless cardigan that hung off her emaciated frame, her hands bunched in the pockets, her upper arms like bundles of twigs.

She watched him in silence. "Go ahead and cry, if you like," she said. "It might help."

"Someone will hear the gunshots, won't they?" he asked. "Will you be in trouble?"

Joelle shook her head. "Over the years, the neighbors have heard much worse coming from this house, I'm sure," she said, and something in her tone sent a chill down Laurie's spine. "Though that gives me a thought."

She rose to her feet. A small gray metal box hung on the wall beside the front door; she slid open a front panel and pressed a series of buttons. She opened the front door wide, revealing the darkness beyond the porch, then returned to her seat. She curled her legs up beneath her and sipped at her drink. "I disconnected the burglar alarm and opened the front gate," she said. "It'll make it easier."

"Easier for what?"

"Easier for you to leave, once you're ready. Easier for someone to find me, once Joel's absence is noted." She smiled at Laurie. "I met your mother. It would have been while she was in the Senate, before you were born. I don't remember much—I wasn't really myself back then, even less of a whole person than I am now—but I know she was kind to me."

"She was a kind person." Laurie took a tentative sip of his drink. He still wasn't sure he cared for the taste, but the warmth that infused his chest at the first swallow seemed to do him some good, so he took another drink. "She was amazing." Tears sprang to his eyes.

"My father hated her, hated her so, so much. So did Joel." She thought for a moment. "Far beyond her policies, far beyond anything she'd ever done to them. It was personal. The men of the

Sutton family, they've always had a few little problems with women."

Laurie swallowed. "He... Joel called you a deviant?"

"I like girls." She smiled. "And you like boys. And Joel... Joel liked me." She shook her head.

It didn't seem like she was talking to him anymore. "I had girl-friends when I was younger. Lovers, and he murdered them. Everyone who loved me, he'd destroy them as soon as he found out about them."

"Thank you for saving me," Laurie said.

"It needed to be done." Her eyes were large and serious. "I think you might be a remarkable young man, Laurie. I think you should live and go on to do remarkable things."

She raised her glass to drink again, then froze, the glass hovering inches from her mouth, her eyes fixed on the front door. Laurie turned around.

Someone stood in the open doorway, someone very tall, dressed in a tattered black sweater and jeans. Someone very familiar and very dear.

"Sorry to interrupt," Nicola said softly. "Laurie, I take it everything's all right now?"

Escobar came up behind her and stood at her shoulder. Nicola appeared to be unarmed; Laurie couldn't see Escobar's hands, but he was willing to bet he wasn't.

It took Laurie a moment before he could speak. "Why are you here?" he asked.

"That's not much of a welcome." Nicola smiled. "You left a message for me. Sounded like you could use some help. So Escobar and I, we took a road trip."

She walked into the house. She paused at the entrance to the dining room and looked down at Glen's corpse in the doorway, at Joel's corpse beside the table. "The gun came in handy, I see."

Joelle's eyes were bright with curiosity. "You must be my gun fairy."

"I suppose I am," Nicola said. She nodded toward Joel's corpse. "I did plenty of research on Joel Sutton back in Los Angeles before we left. Found his addresses in old public records and hoped they'd still be good. We staked out the Park Avenue place before coming here, but we didn't see any sign of you, Laurie."

"But you knew about me?" Joelle asked.

"I knew Joel had a twin. From the groundskeeper at the building, I knew about your illness. He was pretty convinced you were Joel's wife, though. Would've sworn to it. That, combined with some nonspecific but nasty rumors about his past, was enough to suggest there might be something unsavory going on."

"Nick saw the courier drop off the shipment from your doctor for you," Escobar said, with a nod at Joelle. "It gave her ideas."

"Under the circumstances, I thought adding a gun to an already volatile situation might not be the worst idea in the world," Nicola said. "It seems to have come in handy."

Joelle inclined her chin. "Laurie and I are having drinks," she said. "Would you care to join us?"

"Thank you very much," Nicola said. "But we've got a long drive back to California, and I think Laurie might be anxious to see someone."

Laurie's heart gave a little hiccup in his chest. "Jonathan? Jonathan's okay?"

"Bullet nicked his hipbone and he lost a lot of blood, but he'll be fine. He managed to crawl into the motel parking lot before losing consciousness. Manager dropped him off at the state hospital, they checked him in as a John Doe. We tracked him down and transferred him to a better place. I've been calling home along the way for updates, and they say he's out of danger. Awake and everything."

Laurie barely processed anything she said after her first few words. He shook his head. "I'm pretty sure I'm going to start crying," he said.

"Go right ahead. Nothing's stopping you." Nicola walked over to him and leaned down. With an awkwardness that suggested this was unfamiliar territory for her, she wrapped her arms around his shoulders and gathered him against her. "Glad you're okay, kiddo."

Laurie pressed his forehead into her neck. The sobs came at once, loud and inexorable. Nicola clutched him to her and rocked him like a baby, until he was all cried out, exhausted and embarrassed. He pulled back and wiped at his face with his hands.

She patted him on the back. "Is there anything we can do for you?" she asked Joelle.

Joelle shook her head. "I'm going to sit here and drink, I believe," she said. "Do you need money? I have a great deal. There's Joel's car, if you want it. Anything you want, you may take. I won't need any of it."

"Thank you, but we're fine," Nicola said gently. She extended a hand to Joelle. Joelle took it in her own frail, withered one.

"Thank you for protecting Laurie," Nicola said.

"You, too," Joelle said.

Laurie, tear-stained and spent, watched them in silence. It seemed like something passed between them, something strange and remarkable and beyond his comprehension, and then Nicola turned to him.

"Come on," she said. "Let's go see Jonathan."

CHAPTER TWENTY-SIX

Two solid days of driving to Los Angeles, with almost no stops, Escobar and Nicola trading shifts behind the wheel, Laurie dozing in the backseat, states and scenery flying by in an undistinguished blur. Ordinarily he'd find this interesting, towns and cities and wide stretches of barren land, but right now he wanted to get back to Los Angeles, back to Jonathan, as soon as possible.

The hospital was more like a nursing home, in a restored Victorian mansion south of downtown, not far from the Coliseum and the Archive. Jonathan had his own room on the third floor, clean and cozy, windows open, the tops of palm trees bobbing on the horizon outside. He smiled when Laurie entered the room.

"Hey," he said. His hair was tangled and greasy, and his skin was too pale, but he looked beautiful and alive.

Laurie was tongue-tied, filled with too much to say and no way to say any of it, and he thought he'd probably start crying again if he opened his mouth. He'd done an awful lot of that lately.

Jonathan smiled at his silence. "I know. Me, too," he said.

Laurie sank into a floral-patterned armchair at the side of his bed. "I thought you might have died," he said at last.

"Yeah, well, if we've learned nothing else from all this, it's that Ferris is a crap shot, right?"

Laurie burst out laughing. It sounded a little unhinged, an asylum cackle, too loud for the room, and it degenerated into sniffles and tears within seconds. Jonathan reached out a hand. Laurie took it in his own, and it felt gloriously warm and alive.

Donya passed him a cup of coffee, then sat down in her chair behind her desk. She wore an impeccably tailored cream-colored suit that looked amazing with her dark hair and skin. She stared at him for a moment, then leaned back in her chair and took a swig of her own coffee. She shook her head.

"I'm surprised you'd trust this network again. And I'm flat-out shocked and more than a little horrified that you'd trust Gina, after what she tried to pull."

"I don't trust Gina. But she *does* host the highest-rated program in Los Angeles," Laurie said. "Even though she's a creep, appearing on her show will still give me the most exposure. And she really owes me one. I mean, *really* owes me."

"There's probably something to that. Anyway, from what Nicola tells me, it sounds like Gina is going to be on her very best behavior around you," she said. "I just want to be sure you know what you're doing."

"I'm sure," he said. "It's a story that needs to be told."

"And you're the person to tell it." She smiled at him. "I've got a feeling the camera is going to love you, Laurie. Maybe if this works out, we should see about getting you your own show."

"Do you know, I was thinking much along those very lines?" Laurie said.

Out the window behind Donya, the sky was clear and pale blue and limitless. When he was done here, Nicola would pick him up and drive him back to the hospital to see Jonathan, and he'd stay there until the nurses kicked him out, and then he'd spend the night with Nicola and Escobar in their rambling old house near the campus. The world rolled out in front of him, bursting with possibilities.

And all was well.

Interested in reading more about Laurie Sparks? Check out his alternate-timeline adventures in Morgan Richter's award-winning novel *Bias Cut*, available from Luft Books. Here's a sample:

CHAPTER ONE

WHEN NASH CALLED to ask for a favor, it took Nicola a moment to consider the request. Nash was a good friend, dating all the way back to their undergrad days at Berkeley, and she was a pretty decent person, and perhaps most apropos to Nicola's present situation, she ran her own business and thus might be a possible source of future employment. Everything considered, it wouldn't be a bad thing to have Nash owe her one.

Still, the forced cheer in Nash's tone made her wary.

"Maybe. I don't know. What's up?"

"I've got an interview set for noon today, but this other thing just came up. I've already rescheduled once, and I don't want to seem like a flake by postponing it again, so . . . Could you do it? It'll be fun, I promise."

"Let me think. Who are you interviewing?"

"Laurie Sparks? From *NYC Elite*? It's on MTV, I don't know if you've seen it."

NYC Elite. A reality show, Nicola knew, though she hadn't watched anything on MTV in years. Decades, maybe. She'd seen glossy advertisements plastered on subway walls and adorning the tops of cabs, some nonsense about a gaggle of nubile young creative types making their way in the big city. Actors, or artists, or an assortment of both.

It looked annoying as all hell. The title alone set her teeth on edge. "Never heard of her."

On the other end of the line, Nash giggled. "Him. Laurie Sparks. He's a boy. LSD."

"Huh?" Somewhere along the line, Nicola had lost track of the conversation. She picked up a slim gold pencil and scrawled "Laurie Sparks" onto a tablet by the phone. The tablet had gold-bordered pink sheets patterned with fancy hats and stiletto-heeled shoes, drawn in a spindly Gorey-esque style that made them look like squashed spiders. Spiders would be an improvement.

The tablet was Donya's, the pencil was Donya's, the glass-topped slim-legged console table it rested upon was Donya's as well. Everything in the apartment, the rose-colored throw rugs and the plush amethyst sofa and the pink crystal chandelier, it all belonged to Donya. The bulk of Nicola's worldly goods, twelve boxes filled with pots and pans and paperbacks, were stacked in a storage locker on the west end of Pico back in Los Angeles. Until she found a job, it didn't seem right to clutter up this dainty jewel box of an apartment with her unfussy, utilitarian things.

Alex had kept all the furniture, back in L.A. He'd offered to divide it up, but she hadn't had much use for it.

"LSD. Laurie Sparks Designs. Adorable little shop on Prince. Those coats with the hoods attached with loops that all the skinny hipster chicks are wearing, you've seen those, right? They were huge last year. Those are his, he designed those. He's kind of a big deal."

Nicola glanced at the clock. Almost eleven. "Look, I'd love to help, but I can't interview someone I've never heard of before. It'd be a disaster. I wouldn't know what to ask him."

"No sweat, I threw together a bunch of questions already. I'm emailing them to you right now. Please? This month has been crazy.

Normally I've got Heather to help with the site, but she's visiting her folks in Buffalo, and I'm *slammed*."

"What's your conflict? A better interview?"

"No. Well, yeah. Paula Abdul." Nash giggled. "She's holding a group interview with a bunch of bloggers this afternoon, I just now wrangled myself an invite, and . . . I mean, I can't pass it up. It's *Paula*."

"Laurie Sparks will be crushed to hear he rates lower than Paula Abdul."

"Does that mean you'll do it?"

Nicola closed her eyes and overrode her knee-jerk impulse to refuse. "What do I have to do?"

"Thanks, Nick." A rush of gratitude flooded through the phone, an almost tangible warmth, and Nicola immediately felt better about the decision. "I'll let his people know about the change. You're going to meet him at noon in the tearoom at the Shire-Kinsey. On Eighth, near . . . 46th or something, I don't know. Midtown. You'll have to tape it, obviously. Do I need to loan you a recorder?"

"I can borrow one from Donya."

"Great. Pick up the tab for whatever he orders; I can reimburse you tonight, if you want to meet for drinks later. Just ask him my questions, try to engage him in conversation, flatter his ego. Don't make me look bad."

"Don't mention Paula, in other words?"

"That, yeah. But bluff your way through it the best you can. Maybe you shouldn't mention that you don't know anything about him."

"Why not? Does he have an ego problem I should know about?"

"No, nothing like that. I haven't met him, but he's adorable on his show. You'll love him. He's this huge drama queen. Totally over the top," Nash said. "Hey, I've got to run. Check your email. And thanks again."

"Give my best to Paula," Nicola said, but Nash had already clicked off, before she could point out that "huge drama queen" didn't sound like much fun at all.

She pulled on her gray suit, the one she kept pressed and ready for interviews. Black loafers without heels, good for navigating the subway. No jewelry. A quick dash of lipstick, just to be fancy. Then she plopped down in a chair (tiny, dainty, gold-painted) in front of Donya's laptop (sleek and high-tech, with a lavender protective cover featuring a silk-screened print of swallows in flight) and prepared to do some lickety-split research on Laurie Sparks.

A rustle of keys at the front door. Nicola looked up as Donya entered. "Hi. I thought you were going to Arizona?"

"Change of plans." Donya dropped her oversized satchel with a thud. "The Cold War retrospective got scrapped. So, no Titan Missile Museum." She slipped out of her shoes, four-inch crocodile pumps. "Ouch. These have been destroying my feet all morning."

She padded across the living room, bare feet on the gleaming wood floors, then flopped into an overstuffed armchair and tucked her legs beneath her. She looked like an urban Scheherazade, all face-framing wings of black hair and large dark eyes.

"Sorry about that," Nicola said, most of her attention still on the laptop screen. Laurie Sparks. The first search result was his company site, LSD. Women's clothes, young and flashy. Dark wool coats and short satin dresses. Wasn't too helpful, so she moved on to his Wikipedia page.

"No biggie. We're going in another direction. Less newsy, more breezy. More gossip and entertainment pieces, in other words. The Cold War didn't cut it." Donya was a correspondent for a prospective reboot of *PM Magazine*. It was set to launch next month, though the focus seemed to shift daily. "They're sending me to L.A. tonight, so I have to repack. Need to bring my glamorous

Hollywood clothes instead of my I'm-a-serious-journalist wardrobe. I'm doing a new segment. *The Facts of Life: Where Are They Now?*"

"High concept," Nicola said. She scanned the Wikipedia article. Laurie—Laurent, actually—Sparks was all of twenty-two. His clothing line had shown a profit of close to fifty million dollars the previous year. Egad.

"Totally." Donya smiled. "You want me to bring anything back from L.A. for you?"

"My self-respect, if you should happen to find it. I think I left it somewhere on the Sony lot."

"Will do." Donya looked at Nicola as if seeing her for the first time. "Hey, you're wearing your interview outfit."

"I am indeed."

"Is this a good thing? Do you, in fact, have an interview?"

"Yeah, but I'm on the wrong side of it." Nicola printed out the Wikipedia page and checked her email. Yes, there was a message from Nash already, containing a short list of questions and directions to the Shire-Kinsey Hotel. She printed that as well. "You know my friend Nash?"

"The *HyperReality* girl? Sure."

"I'm interviewing some reality star for her site this afternoon. Is it okay if I borrow a recorder?"

"Knock yourself out. That's cool. Which reality star?"

"Laurie Sparks? *NYC Elite*?"

Donya snorted. "Oh, boy. Nash hates you."

Nicola turned to look at her. "She assured me I'll love him."

"She lied. He's a mouthy little fameball. Mind you, I only watched that damn show once, so I might not be the best judge, and honestly, he's probably no worse than anyone else on there, but . . ." Donya rolled her eyes. "At a guess, he's going to drive you crazy. Oil and water."

Nicola looked at the tiny snapshot on Laurie Sparks's Wikipedia page. It was cropped from some larger photo; the caption indicated it was taken at a press conference for the launch of *NYC Elite*. A puff of bleached hair, dark smudgy eyes. Could be Laurie Sparks, could be Debbie Harry, or Madonna circa *Who's That Girl?* She skimmed the article. "Hey, his mom is Maggie Sparks."

"Who?"

"Former Senator from Pennsylvania. She was a big deal in the eighties. Sort of a bad-ass. She pushed for unilateral nuclear disarmament, not that it went over very well at that time."

"Huh. Too bad the Cold War got scrapped. I could've interviewed Laurie's mom," Donya said. "Is Nash paying you for this?"

"I'm getting a free lunch out of it, I think. Maybe post-interview drinks, too. This is just a favor for a friend. No big deal."

"Sure." Donya smoothed the hem of her skirt over her bare knees. "You going to be able to cover your share of rent next month?" Casual, so casual.

"Yeah, no worries." She could cover it, probably. "I'm good."

"Great." Donya glanced at her and frowned. "Do you want to borrow something to wear?"

Nicola looked down at her outfit. "Is this okay?"

"Sure. But he's a designer, you know, and that jacket is, what, Gap?"

"Old Navy, I believe. For me, Gap is aspirational." Nicola retrieved Nash's questions and the Wikipedia article from the printer tray. She'd take a crash course in Laurie Sparks on the train. "He's a designer, I'm not. If he doesn't like what I'm wearing, then screw him."

"You're interviewing him, Nicola. You're trying to establish rapport. It should be *friendly*." Donya looked at her. "You're going to be nice to him, right?"

"I'm always nice."

"You're a pussycat. But you've got to admit, you've been a little raw since moving here."

Nicola felt a quick stab of irritation. "Not without reason," she said.

"No, but there's no sense taking it out on little Laurie Sparks. Don't bite his head off, okay?"

"Good advice. I'll take it under consideration." Nicola picked up her messenger bag.

"Let me get you that recorder." Donya disappeared into her bedroom. She was gone a suspiciously long time. Nicola heard the jangling of coat hangers and winced.

Donya came back with the recorder, plus a handful of colorful silk, an ornately patterned square of blue and gold and black and violet. "Here. It's vintage Hermès." She draped the scarf around Nicola's neck, tucked it beneath the lapel of her jacket, and tied it into a loose knot. She stepped back and scrutinized her handiwork. "Check it out. See the difference?"

Nicola glanced in the mirror that rested atop the brick mantel. The scarf made the gray of her suit look richer, brought out a hint of blue in her muddy eyes. She looked wealthy and glamorous. She felt silly and affected. "I can't borrow this. I don't want to lose it."

"I don't want you to lose it, either." Donya smiled. "You're meeting Laurie on his own terms, see? You're putting him at ease by showing him you're a stylish woman who can work an Hermès scarf, right?"

"If you say so." She glanced in the mirror again. Damn it, the scarf really was an improvement. "Thanks, Donya. It looks great."

"Good." Donya gave her a quick hug and an airless kiss on each cheek. She smelled like jasmine tea and tuberose. "Have a blast. You can tell me all about it when I get back in town."

And Nicola was off, striding toward the subway entrance. It was a sticky late summer morning, the last gasp of heat before the cooler days of September, and it was much too warm for her jacket. She'd be sweaty and gross by the time she arrived at the hotel.

As soon as she was a safe distance from their apartment, Nicola whipped off the scarf. She folded it into a tiny triangle and stuffed it into a zippered pocket in her messenger bag.

ABOUT THE AUTHOR

Born and raised in Spokane, Washington, Morgan Richter graduated with a BFA in Filmic Writing from the University of Southern California's film school. She has worked in production on several TV shows, including *Talk Soup* and *America's Funniest Home Videos*, and has contributed pop culture reviews and essays to websites such as TVgasm and Forces of Geek, as well as to her own site, Preppies of the Apocalypse. She is the owner of Luft Books, an independent publishing company, and the author of *Bias Cut*, *Charlotte Dent*, and *Wrong City*. *Bias Cut* won a silver medal at the 2013 Independent Publishers Book Awards and was a 2012 semi-finalist for the Amazon Breakthrough Novel Award (ABNA). *Charlotte Dent* was a 2008 ABNA semi-finalist. She currently lives in New York City.